Holding Her Heart

MELISSA TEREZE

GPC
PUBLISHING

First Edition June 2021
Published by GPC Publishing
Copyright © 2021 Melissa Tereze
ISBN: 9798505229095

Cover Design: May Dawney
Editor: Charlie Knight

Find out more at: www.melissatereezeauthor.com
Follow me on Twitter: @MelissaTereze
Follow me on Instagram: @melissatereze_author

All rights reserved. This book is for your personal enjoyment only. This book or any portion thereof may not be reproduced or used in any manner without the express permission of the author.

This is a work of fiction. All characters & happenings in this publication are fictitious and any resemblance to real persons (living or dead), locales or events is purely coincidental.

ALSO BY MELISSA TEREZE

ANOTHER LOVE SERIES
THE ARRANGEMENT (BOOK ONE)

THE CALL (BOOK TWO)

THE ASHFORTH SERIES
PLAYING FOR HER HEART (BOOK ONE)

OTHER NOVELS
MRS MIDDLETON

BREAKING ROUTINE

IN HER ARMS

BEFORE YOU GO

FOREVER YOURS

THE HEAT OF SUMMER

FORGET ME NOT

MORE THAN A FEELING

WHERE WE BELONG: LOVE RETURNS

NAKED

TITLES UNDER L.M CROFT (EROTICA)
PIECES OF ME

Aileen Clare Glover

1960 - 2021

1

The leg of Aster's jeans rode up slightly, and she caught a glimpse of the invisible socks she was wearing. *Huh. Not so invisible when I can clearly see I have bloody odd ones on.* She frowned, staring down at her feet; had she always had one that looked slightly bigger than the other? Perhaps it was the shoes she was wearing. She'd never noticed before.

She unbuttoned the top of her shirt, puffing out her cheeks as she ran her hands down her thighs. What if the images she'd brought over today were terrible? That would mean she'd ruined someone's wedding day.

Okay, she was thinking about complete rubbish now. This always happened when she was nervous, especially when she was meeting with the woman who was technically her boss until she handed over her work. Two weeks ago, someone by the name of Eden Kline had contacted her via an assistant requesting her skills for a wedding. Aster had been initially panicked, she always felt as though she didn't perform well when someone called her with a last-minute offer, but she had to admit…she'd excelled and then some this time around. It helped that the couple getting married were ridiculously photogenic, but she still had to receive final approval from Eden before she released the images to the client. It was then down to them to select the pictures they wanted to use for their wedding album.

Aster owed her best friend. If it hadn't been for Grace's recommendation, she wouldn't be sitting here now, potentially with a chance of getting in at *The Garden of Eden*, the leading event planning business in the north of England. If this meeting went well, they may consider calling her back for more work in the future.

Aster had done her homework the night she'd returned home from the wedding, and the reviews on all of the relevant sites spoke for themselves. Eden Kline was known to have a great rapport with her clients. But deep down, Aster knew Eden was likely putting on a show for any potential business. She'd worked with these event planning companies before, usually freelance, and she was yet to come across a boss who didn't love the sound of their own voice.

The click of a door startled Aster. Her stomach rolled as the receptionist got to her feet and the phone started to ring. She spoke into the receiver, replacing it only moments later. "Eden is ready for you now."

Aster nodded, gripping her camera bag before slinging it over her shoulder. "Thank you."

She'd dressed in a simple pair of black skinny jeans with a grey tailored blazer covering her white fitted shirt. Aster had chosen to wear her hair down this morning; Grace always told her she looked more comfortable with her locks flowing, though Aster had no idea what she meant.

As she stopped in front of Eden's office door, Aster took a calming breath and placed her hand on the polished chrome handle. Shoulders pulled back, she entered the room, her smile bright but not too enthusiastic.

"Oh, hi." The woman who stood from the desk in the window

beamed a million-dollar smile, smoothing her pencil skirt before she rounded the desk. "Aster, right?"

Aster relaxed immediately. Eden didn't have a demanding or icy presence. "That's right. Nice to meet you."

They exchanged a handshake, nothing overly dominating on Eden's part. "Interesting name."

"Blame my mother. She was a keen gardener." She was yet to meet someone who didn't insist on knowing the origin of her name. These days, it was easier to get it out of the way during the first meeting. "I'd say she chose it simply because she liked it, but I have two sisters called Lily and Rose, birth name Primrose, so..."

Eden motioned towards a couch against the bright white office wall. "Mm. Very Alan Titchmarsh. But I like it. Can I get you something to drink before you show me your work?"

Aster eyed an area containing a kettle, several sizes of cups, and a coffee machine. Clean and tidy. Just how she liked it. "I'd love a coffee if it's not too much trouble."

"None whatsoever." Eden busied herself at the coffee machine, standing heavier on one leg as her hip jutted. She was very well put together, her pencil skirt finishing high up on her waist and a cream blouse tucked in. She wore black heels—at least six inches, her legs naturally tanned, not orange like some of the women around here. Elegant, but not overbearing. That was the vibe Aster got from her potential boss.

As the beans ground, the scent of fresh coffee wafting towards her, Aster relaxed further. Eden didn't appear imposing, humming along to a tune in her head as she prepared their drinks. Aster was...pleasantly surprised.

"I have to admit, I did hire you for the wedding two weeks ago on a whim. But Grace spoke very highly of you."

Grace. Aster smiled. "How do you know Grace?"

"She plays football with my best friends' fiancée," Eden said, turning and crossing the room, placing two cups down on the small coffee table in front of Aster. "And Dom wouldn't tell me to hire someone for the sake of it."

"Oh, you know Dom?"

"Dom is engaged to Blair. We've been best friends since school. I was lucky Dom was there when I called Blair in a panic. I was away in Paris and my usual photographer let me down."

"Oh, that's not cool."

"No, it's not. But Dom called Grace and asked if she thought you would be keen. Thankfully, you were."

Aster blew out a deep breath. "Well, then I hope I don't disappoint."

Eden smiled, her deep chocolate eyes gentle. "I asked for your handle on social media. I *have* seen what you're capable of. It's why I called Grace immediately and asked for your number. I'm sorry I didn't call you myself, but Maxine was taking care of things while I was away."

"Oh, don't worry." Aster released her grip on her camera bag, unaware she was latching onto it for dear life. "Everything came together so it's fine."

"So…" Eden paused, her smile spreading across her face. "Can I see the magic you created?"

Magic? Bold of her to assume. But Aster did appreciate the faith Eden appeared to be putting into her. Aster knew she was good with the camera, knew she was one of the best when she put her mind to it, but Eden and her assumptions were making Aster more anxious than she already was. "Of course, yeah."

"My computer is on. You get everything set up for me, and then give me a shout when you're ready." Eden crossed her long legs, placing her hands on her knee as she sunk back into the couch. "I've been wanting five minutes to myself all day. Now is the perfect excuse."

Aster gulped her coffee down, almost burning her throat as she did so. Eden and the thigh she was showing wasn't what she'd expected this morning. The mental image she'd had in her mind was one of a stuck-up, middle-aged woman, but no...*this* was entirely different. "Right. Yeah. I can do that."

She approached Eden's Mac, her white, high gloss desk tidied to perfection. *Does she actually do any work here?* The first thing Aster noticed was the small cactus plant beside the computer; she had one in her own home office. The second observation was the framed photograph of Eden with Blair. Eden's eyes were bright, her smile taking over the entire frame. It was clear they were close.

"Are you freelance?" Eden's sudden question sent Aster's head upright.

"I am, yes."

"And do you prefer freelance?" Eden fisted her hand under chin, her elbow resting on the arm of the couch. "The freedom to do what you want, when you want?"

"That's a tough one. Guaranteed work is my dream, I expect that applies to most people, but I do like the freedom. Except sometimes, there's too much. You know?"

"Freedom?" Eden asked, her eyes pinning Aster to the chair.

Lord, that is an intense stare. Aster nodded as she returned to the screen. She plugged her hard drive into the Mac, blowing out a breath as the icon appeared on the desktop. "Okay, it's ready."

"I can hardly wait."

Eden shot to her feet, her long, dark, beach wave bouncing as her heels hit the floor. Aster admired the slight blonde highlights woven through Eden's glorious head of hair, not too much volume at the root.

She was happy to be here this morning. Ecstatic, to be fair.

"Okay, so...if there's anything that concerns you, give me a shout. I'll wait over on the couch."

Aster rose from the chair only to be gently pushed back down by Eden's hand. "Stay there. View them with me."

"O-okay." Aster swallowed, watching the hand still resting on her shoulder from the corner of her eye. It was gentle but demanding. And if Aster concentrated, she could feel the warmth of Eden's hand penetrating her blazer. When Eden removed it, Aster untensed. But then Eden bent at the hip, her free hand resting beside Aster's as her other took control of the mouse. "I can make any changes you think are needed before they go to the client."

"T-these are..." Eden paused, her smile warm as she scrolled through the images slowly. She leaned in, narrowing her eyes. "Wow. You certainly know how to capture beauty."

"Thank you." *Not the outcome I expected today.* Second-guessing herself never did Aster any favours. She knew exactly what she was capable of, but her inner critic always had different ideas. Aster wrung her hands in her lap, diverting her gaze as Eden offered the gentlest smile while she focused intently on the screen.

And then Eden turned her head towards Aster. All she could do in return was meet Eden's eyes. Wow, this woman was stunning. *And please, stop looking at me with those eyes.*

"Can I ask how old you are?"

"Thirty-two. Why?" Did Aster's age have some kind of relevance in all of this? It wasn't what she thought about while she sat outside in the waiting room.

"I'm very impressed." Eden offered a single nod. "Can I keep a copy? I'd like to look through them this evening with a glass of wine."

"Sure, yeah. These are only copies anyway." Aster took a blank USB from the side of her bag, copying the images over to it for Eden. "All done. They're all watermarked, but not because I don't trust you. I just didn't expect you to want them."

"Do you have a business card?"

"Um, yeah." Aster frowned, reaching once again into her bag. She removed a holder, slipping a card from it. "Here you go."

"Thank you." Eden's fingers brushed Aster's, a thrill jolting up her arm. *Oh, no. That's not supposed to happen.* "I'm going to enjoy looking at these in depth this evening, but I think the client is going to be very happy with them."

"I hope so."

"And I was wondering if we could meet at the end of the week?" Eden powered off her computer, backing away from Aster and giving her some space. "I'd like to discuss some things with you."

Aster could make herself available. It was no issue. Especially if it meant she was able to see Eden again. She was *very* easy on the eye. *In your dreams, Bennett.* "Sure. Let me know where and when."

"I will." Eden held out her hand. "And thank you for stepping in when I was desperate."

Aster offered a slight shrug of her shoulders as she shook Eden's hand. *God, she has the softest skin.* "That's okay. It was a quiet weekend."

"Don't expect that to be the case for much longer, okay?" With a perfectly quirked eyebrow, Eden turned and walked to the door. "It's been lovely meeting you, Aster. I'll see you at the end of the week."

"Thanks. See you."

2

Eden blew out a frustrated breath as she stopped in the middle of the walkway. She didn't have time for this. Her usual photographer, Jay, was once again crying off from a gig she'd sent to him, and now she had to find *another* replacement. It wasn't the end of the world, he'd given her more time to find someone else than he had last time, but it still didn't make Eden's life any easier. And this afternoon was supposed to be her own time. Time to spend with her *supposedly* neglected best friend.

That is his final chance.

She'd said that before today, but he was too unreliable. This was the final straw.

"I swear if you turn around and leave, I'm going to chase you and tackle you to the ground!"

Eden smiled, looking up from her phone to find her best friend standing with a hand on her hip. "I'm not leaving. But I do need a minute or two."

"What does a best friend have to do to get your attention? I haven't seen you for *weeks*."

Eden frowned. "That's not my fault. You're living the life in lesbian land. *You* forgot about *me*."

Blair huffed, shaking her head. "I could never forget about you. Come on, we'll figure out your dilemma over a bottle of wine and some good food."

Eden could get on board with that. Blair had a knack for fixing everything. "You're right. I'll sort this out once we're sitting down." Eden stepped towards her, linking their arms together. "Come on. I'm starving."

"Me too. Busy morning."

"Oh." Eden's eyebrow rose.

"With work. Not with Dom." Blair had met her fiancée eighteen months ago, falling head over heels for the footballer unexpectedly. Eden wouldn't have said they were suited to one another on first inspection, but they were. Plus, Dom was besotted with Blair. She worshipped the ground Eden's best friend walked on. "I didn't realise I'd be so busy when I got a job."

"Jobs will do that to you, friend. That's why it's called work."

"I know. But I've barely seen Dom this week, and tomorrow, she's leaving early for a game with the team, so it's another day without her."

"Woman, you're obsessed. Is the sex *really* so amazing that you can't manage a day by yourself anymore?"

"It's not about the sex," Blair said, her long blonde hair falling over her shoulder. "Dom…gets me."

"And that's why you're marrying her." Eden hip-checked Blair. "But, speaking of marriage, one of my photographers has let me down for Saturday's all day, all night event."

"Ouch. I wondered why you had a face like a smacked arse when I met you."

"It's just…I don't need this today. I've been looking forward to meeting you since last week when we arranged. And I wanted no interruptions. We have neglected each other for too long lately."

"Don't worry about me. I'm fine."

"Still. I miss you. And I know Dom is there and you're living your life, but I'm starting to feel a bit left out."

Blair stopped, turning to face Eden. "You know you're welcome at ours anytime you want. Dom is always asking if we have plans. Come around, have dinner, stay over for a few days."

"I'd love to, but I'm up the wall at the minute."

"Then we'll arrange something," Blair said, leaning in and kissing Eden's cheek. "Today, while we catch up."

Eden nodded, following Blair into the bar and grill along the main road. It was the place they always met, and it was the place where they'd spent many a drunk afternoon, reverting back to their teenage years without a care in the world.

Eden stepped up behind Blair, smiling at the waiter. "And I can't get drunk today."

"When do we ever get drunk?" Blair grinned, glancing over her shoulder. "You're a lightweight."

"I'm serious. I have to oversee everything on Saturday. I have to be at the hotel for 8 a.m. The last thing I need is a hangover tomorrow."

"Don't worry. This is a catch up. No alcohol will be consumed."

"Oh, no. I need a *glass* of wine. But I don't want a bottle." Eden shoved Blair towards their table, laughing as they slid into their booth. "Now, tell me how my beautiful Harold is doing…"

"He'd kill you if he heard you calling him Harold."

Eden knew he would. But she still called Blair's son by his birth name when Harry wasn't around. "How's he getting on?"

"Really well. He's rehearsing for some major production they're putting on. He's settled this year. It's lovely knowing he's okay. And he has Jack, of course."

"Have you thought that maybe he doesn't worry about you anymore?"

Blair lowered her eyes to the menu. "I wish he'd never had to worry about me. But he's my son, and he loves me. I guess I would be worried if he didn't show some concern."

"But he loves Dom now. And I know he had a bit of a wobble about it, but he wanted what was best for you, Blair. You can't complain about that."

"No, I know. He was on FaceTime with Dom this morning. I was in the shower. I don't know what the hell they were talking about, but I came into the bedroom to find Dom rolling around the bed, laughing."

"I love how much they get on," Eden said, glancing at her phone to the side of her. "And I want to continue this, but I need to sort out Saturday. Would you give me five minutes?"

"Who are you going to bring in instead?" Blair eyed the handset cradled by Eden's fingers.

Eden smiled. "Aster. Hopefully."

"So, it worked out well when you asked her to step in the other week?"

"It did. She's so good, Blair. I don't know why Dom didn't mention her sooner. She was at the office on Monday, and it was lovely meeting her."

"I don't suppose Dom thought you were looking for more staff."

"I'm meeting with her tomorrow. I didn't say what it was about, but she's freelance, and I was considering asking her to join my team. Full time."

"Oh?" Blair quirked an eyebrow.

Eden focused on her phone, smiling when she brought Aster's contact details up. They'd spoken briefly on the phone on Tuesday evening, and Aster seemed willing to jump on board this weekend for a wedding Eden had booked in. Eden loved the enthusiasm Aster appeared to have. It was refreshing to hear. "She opted for the afternoon when I put this one to her, so I stuck Jay on the morning. Should have known he'd let me down; he usually does."

"Well, if Jay doesn't know a good job when he sees it, maybe it's time he looks for something else. You don't have the time to piss around with no-shows, Ede's. You have enough to contend with without all of this."

"I know. And Aster is *very* talented."

Eden looked up at Blair. Why was her best friend wearing a strange look on her face?

"I'll send her a quick message and then I'm all yours."

E: Hi. Do you have plans Saturday morning?

As much as Eden wanted Aster on board for the entire day, she wouldn't disrupt any plans Aster had. After all, it wasn't her fault Jay had disappeared again.

A: Hi. No plans. What's up?

E: Are you sure?

A: I'm sure. I don't make plans when I have to work the same day. Did you need something?

E: Could I interest you in some extra work? Same wedding but all day?

A: Absolutely.

Eden breathed a sigh of relief, relaxing back into her seat as her crisis was averted.

E: Fab. I have the day off, but I'll be home in the next few hours if you wanted to drop by and pick up the schedule. Or I can just email it over to you.

A: I can come by if you want me to. I'm not busy. Send over the address and I'll be there.

E: Great. I'll see you this evening.

With Aster saving the day for the second time this month, Eden slipped her phone into her bag and gave her full attention to Blair. "All sorted." She picked up the menu. "Remind me to thank Dom for contacting Grace. It's helped me out a lot."

"You know Dom. She'd do anything for anyone."

Eden lifted her gaze. "I know. It's why she's perfect for you."

3

Aster blew out a deep breath, stepping off the lift and into a corridor. Eden had texted her the address over an hour ago, so here she was, ready to do whatever was needed. As she rounded the corner, it became apparent that Eden Kline was a woman who had a high-class style. *Thank God I dressed up a bit.* She wasn't sure Eden would appreciate her showing up in her lounge clothes. Aster didn't usually think too much about her appearance, she was a take it or leave it kinda girl, but Eden had a way of making her sit up straight. When she pinned her with her eyes, Aster was all ears, everything else falling away around her. Though Eden was wonderful, she commanded attention.

Uh-huh. She can have my attention. Aster stopped suddenly, her eyes wide as she took a second to think about the thought which had just floated through her mind. Yes, Eden was gorgeous, but she was also potentially Aster's new boss. Throw in the fact she was also probably straight, and it would be a waste of time thinking about her. But Aster could admire her silently, couldn't she? Or was that inappropriate? *It is wholly inappropriate.* "No. Don't do that," Aster spoke low in the corridor. "Be cool and do your job."

She curled her hand, knocking gently on Eden's front door. The click of heels on wood caught her attention, her heart rate slightly elevated as it often was lately.

When the door opened, Aster waited with her best smile. "Hey."

"Come in. You may need to prevent me from downing the bottle of wine I picked up on the way home from meeting Blair."

When Eden opened the door wider, Aster's eyes took in the layout. Open plan, bright and airy, but cosy too. She'd expected to see something from a home interior magazine, but Eden's place *looked* lived in. So, that was something.

"Doesn't sound good." Aster followed Eden into the open space, closing the door behind her. The scent of jasmine wafted through the air, and the curtains were pulled back, exposing the huge windows in the living room area. Wow. This place was pretty. "I'm assuming your photographer is a no show again..."

"I think it's time I brought him into the office. I need someone reliable. And I know he has stuff going on, but I still have a business to run. I can't contact you every time he cries off."

"I don't mind." If it meant she got to spend time with Eden, Aster would always make herself available. "I need all the gigs I can get."

"I suppose it doesn't matter anyway," Eden paused, kicking off her heels as she shrugged her jacket from her shoulders. Aster could only stare. "I love your work most."

"Well, thanks." Aster fought back a blush, her eyes wandering down Eden's legs. She wore a pencil skirt again, a white blouse contrasting beautifully against her tanned skin. *Damn.* "What time do you need me Saturday?"

"The makeup artist is arriving at 9:30. I'll be there from 8 onwards."

"Perfect. And it's the usual? Makeup, preparations, yada yada..."

Eden turned, smiling at Aster. "I'm glad you find these things as interesting as I do."

Aster blanched. "Sorry, that sounded unprofessional."

"When you spend your life dedicating time to brides, it's hard to always be chirpy about it. I probably wouldn't be so miserable if I knew I'd have my own happy ending. Now, sit down so I can have five minutes of normality and then we will sort out arrangements for Saturday."

Eden's phone buzzed on the expensive glass coffee table.

When Aster watched Eden hesitate to answer, she furrowed her brow.

"Sorry, just a minute." Eden held up her hand. "Liam, hi."

Liam? That had put a dampener on Aster's ideas. Okay, she didn't *have* any ideas per se, but knowing Eden was likely involved made her life easier.

"No, not really. I have a lot on. I'm working day and night Saturday, so it'll be an early night for tomorrow." Eden moved her phone from her ear, rolling her eyes as Liam spoke down the phone. "Mm. Yeah. No, I know."

Aster looked around. Did she pass as someone who wasn't eavesdropping?

"Right, well I'm sorry you feel that way, but it doesn't change the fact I'm not available to join you tonight *or* tomorrow at a club."

She's far too pretty and dedicated for clubs around here.

"Okay, I'm going now. Bye." Eden hung up, throwing her phone to the couch. "Why don't men understand the word 'no'?"

"You're asking the wrong person." Aster picked at a spot of lint on her jeans, offering a slight smile. "The husband?"

"God, no!"

"Sorry. I didn't mean to assume." Aster made a mental note to have a word with herself once she left this apartment. It was none of her business.

"Liam is my 'boyfriend,'" Eden said, rolling her eyes as she air quoted. "We've been together for six months. Paul and Beth are going out tonight—his best friend and wife. He seems to think I want to be in with his crowd, and I don't. I have far too much to concentrate on without clubbing. I'm 42 for the love of God!"

"And how old is he?" Aster asked, clearing her throat. She hoped it wasn't too personal.

"Thirty-five."

Aster nodded. "Maybe he hasn't matured yet."

"He's going to get the shock of his life when he discovers I'm planning on joining Ashforth for their holiday."

"Gran Canaria?" Aster's eyebrow rose. She may not know anything about Eden, but she was fairly certain it wouldn't be her scene. "You're actually going?"

"Mmhmm. Blair is dragging me along with Dom."

"Well, I'm sure you'll have a great time."

Eden frowned. "You're not going?"

Aster had considered it. Her best friend, Grace, was the goalkeeper for Ashforth FC. But it didn't appeal to Aster. Not when she would be the only single one there. And as much as she loved the idea of a holiday romance with someone she likely wouldn't see again back in the UK, Aster couldn't bring herself to accept Grace's invitation. It would mean paying for a room on her own since Grace would be staying with Mia, another player on the team *and* Grace's girlfriend. "No, I won't be going."

"Why?"

"I think maybe if Grace and Mia weren't together, I probably would, but I'll only be third-wheeling with everyone."

"Great. That's going to be my job, isn't it?"

"Which?"

"Third-wheeling." Eden snorted. "Maybe I should tell them I can't commit to it. I mean, I'm not even gay, so I don't know why I'm going to a Pride event with a team full of lesbians."

"Don't get me wrong, it's a great trip. Really great."

"But?"

Aster chewed her lip. "You have to keep your wits about you. Or you'll wake up in bed with a load of women and no idea how it happened."

Eden barked a laugh. "Wow. You're certainly selling this to me."

"Just…don't want you to get caught out."

And then Eden's eyes brightened. She'd clearly had some kind of lightbulb moment.

"So, why don't you come with me?" Eden suggested. "We can share a room, you won't have to third-wheel, and we both get a holiday out of it before wedding season truly begins."

"Um, I don't have a wedding season to get ready for. I'm usually only booked for maybe five weddings at the height of it. It doesn't require me to need a break before *or* after."

"Ah, but that's where I'm hoping you're going to be wrong," Eden paused. "You know we were supposed to meet tomorrow at the office?"

"I do. I have it in my diary and everything…"

Eden shifted, clasping her hands in her lap. "Well, I was wondering if you'd consider joining my team. Full time."

"Y-you mean…" Aster's eyebrows rose as she pointed a finger at her own chest. "You want *me* to work with *you*?"

"You sound surprised, Aster."

"I am. You're the number one event planner in most of the UK. What could I possibly bring to your team?"

Eden cocked her head, offering Aster a gentle smile. But Aster found herself focusing on Eden's exposed neck, how her shirt showed the slightest hint of collar bone. *Sweet Jesus.* "I've been running my business for almost fifteen years. And in those years, you're the best I've come across."

Aster lowered her eyes, her cheeks reddening. "I'm sure that's not true but thank you."

"And I want to give you a chance. You stepped up for me a few weeks ago, and I didn't expect such quality in your work if you were available at the drop of a hat."

"I...I don't put myself out there like I know I should. Yes, I know I'm good, but it's the confidence of standing in front of people and *telling* them that which I struggle with."

"So, come and be on my team. You'll receive a steady income, plus commission on every event you work."

"I...can I think about it?"

Eden nodded. "Absolutely."

"And the Pride thing. Can I think about that, too?"

In her heart, she would love to know she was going on holiday, but in this moment, Aster wondered if she would be doing it for the wrong reasons. To share a room with a woman she felt a growing attraction to? No, it would never work. Aster would never torture herself like that.

"Think about it all."

Aster scratched at her forearm. She did so when she was nervous. But did she need to feel that way? Eden was completely unavailable in every sense of the word, so why not enjoy a holiday…and get a full-time job too?

"Just let me know. The team don't know this yet, and I trust you to keep it quiet, but Blair has booked us into a fancier hotel. The team are staying somewhere…well, undesirable."

"Oh, I know exactly where the team will be staying. And if I did go, I wouldn't be joining them."

"You could stay with us at the five-star boutique off the strip…"

Aster was tempted. She hadn't been abroad for two years. But her reasons played on repeat at the back of her mind. Eden watched her expectantly, a perfectly defined eyebrow arched. "I'll…definitely think about it."

"Save your new boss from complete humiliation and come along. You know you want to," Eden said, winking. But it only made things worse. When Eden winked at you, it was only natural to melt into a puddle. "Cocktails. Bikinis. Tapas."

Please stop. Aster thought. "Like I said, I'll think about it. All of it."

Eden sighed dramatically. "Fine. But if someone comes along with a better offer, I want the chance to up my own offer first, okay?"

Aster smiled. Nobody had ever been so excited by her work before. "I don't think you have anything to worry about. Nobody is going to come along and sweep me up. Now, let's get back to the schedule for Saturday. Then I can get home and prep."

"You have a decent work ethic, Aster Bennett. But me? I want to lie on the couch and drink wine all night."

"Oh, please. You have *everything* memorised for Saturday. I'm sure you don't need to frantically rush around like I do. I'll walk through my door and panic mode will set in."

Eden got to her feet, her hands landing on the zip at the back of her pencil skirt. As she walked across the room, lowering the zip ever so slightly, Aster's mouth hung open. "I'll be right back. Let me change, and then we'll discuss the plans."

"Holy fuck!" Aster murmured. "Why am I doing this to myself?"

4

Eden felt her phone buzzing in the back of her skirt; she kept it jammed into the waistband when she was rushing around at events. She knew who it would be, it was *always* Liam during the weekends, but she wasn't available right now. And he knew it, too. The vibrating stopped, giving Eden a moment to think about what she should do. She could take five minutes outside—a business call, if you will—or she could ignore Liam's calls and do her job.

If I don't answer the phone, he'll keep calling.

She sighed, spying an exit to the left of her.

Aster was leaning against the wall close to the door, focused fully on her equipment as she changed lenses. *She's so good.* Eden watched her for a moment, taken aback by Aster's confident stance. But as she did so, she also recognised what Aster was saying on Thursday night when she explained to Eden how she didn't put herself out there. *She should. She's amazing.* When Aster was behind the camera, she was an entirely different person.

Eden paused in her thoughts. She'd spent most of the day watching Aster, getting to know her quirks and her mannerisms. At one point, she'd almost lost her footing as she followed Aster across the dancefloor, her eyes fixed on her long blonde hair and how it shone as the spotlights caught it. *Why are you staring at your photographer?* Okay, it was weird. At least, Aster would think so if she looked up to find Eden glaring.

And then Aster did exactly that.

Her brown eyes narrowed as she focused on Eden, a warm smile playing on her lips.

But then Eden was interrupted by the buzz of her phone again. *For the love of God!* She rushed towards Aster, holding up her ringing phone. "I need to take this call, okay?"

"Sure."

Eden pushed through the door, hitting accept as soon as the music inside the venue died down a little. "Liam, I'm working. You know I am."

"I know, babe. I was wondering how much longer you're going to be. I've told a few friends we'd meet them this evening."

Eden frowned. "Why the hell would you? You know I can't."

"You can. You must be nearly finished now." Liam laughed, sending Eden's anger through the roof. "Come on, Eden. You're *always* working. Live a little."

"I'm *always* working because I have a business to run. You may live off mummy and daddy's money, but I don't." She pinched the bridge of her nose. Eden would usually apologise for saying something like that, but it was all truth. Liam drove around in his sports car, meeting friends and playing golf, barely a day worked in his life. But Eden, if she wanted to be successful, had to work for it. She wasn't jealous—far from it, actually—but it did infuriate her when Liam said the things he did. "I'm working. And then I'm going home."

"Well, should I call over once I've been out to dinner with them?"

"No. Don't bother." Eden ended the call, leaning back against the brick wall outside the hotel. Liam was fun to a point, but he didn't fulfil her in any way at all. "You need to cut him loose. He's doing nothing for you whatsoever." She wedged her phone into the back of her skirt, tugging on the door handle.

Aster moved around the room with ease, stopping to chat with the bridal party between shots. The bride had already complimented Eden on her choice of photographer. Aster knew how to give off an air of ease and comfort; it was important when she was spending an entire wedding day with the happy couple. Eden didn't want someone to share their private moments if they couldn't be inconspicuous and discreet. No, she wanted someone exactly like Aster.

Aster threw her head back laughing as the bride leaned in to speak to her. Eden's belly swirled as the light caught her exposed jawline, sending a wave of something unfamiliar through her. "Wow. What was that?" She backed up, resting against the wall and giving herself a moment. Was it…attraction? No, it couldn't be.

As Eden placed her palms flat against the wall, she lowered her head, taking a deep breath. For some reason, one which was unknown, Eden found herself gravitating towards Aster at any given opportunity. Perhaps it was because she was so approachable. Or maybe Eden was looking for a friend. God knows she needed one lately. With Blair off living a blissful, engaged life, Eden felt as though she went home every night and sat alone. Yes, she continuously turned Liam down at every turn, but he wasn't the man she needed. She just needed…something. Someone who could occupy her time. Someone she could be satisfied with instead of spending Sunday alone, week after week. Someone who made her think, made her laugh. Someone she enjoyed being at home with.

Love, in an ideal world.

"Earth to Eden…"

Eden frowned. Aster was waving a hand in front of her. "Sorry?"

"Is everything okay? You've been in a world of your own for the few minutes I've been standing here."

"Yes, of course." Eden smoothed the front of her blouse, shaking her head. "Tired. It's been a long day."

"Well, I'm just about finished. I've spoken with the bride, and I believe we have everything she wanted."

Eden smiled and offered a single nod of the head. "You're free to go then. I'll look forward to seeing what you've got."

Aster chewed her lip, lowering her camera. "I was wondering…what time do you finish?"

"Oh, I finished about an hour ago." Yes, she hung around. Mainly because the idea of going home alone after such a beautiful day was a miserable thought. "I like to stick around."

"You don't want to get home to Liam?" Aster asked, toying with the camera strap on her wrist. "It's Saturday night."

"No. Liam is…busy." *And we do NOT live together. Ever!*

Aster shrugged. "Well, I was planning to head up to the rooftop bar. You're more than welcome to join me if you'd like to?"

I'd love to. Eden relaxed her shoulders, glancing behind Aster. Everything appeared to be perfectly fine here. Eden wasn't needed. "I could probably come with you for one."

"Brilliant."

Eden almost gasped when Aster beamed a huge smile. One so huge it almost knocked her through the wall.

"Let me get my stuff together. My equipment. I can meet you up there if it's easier for you?"

"Y-yes." Eden swallowed. Why had the air suddenly dried up in here?

"Perfect. I'll see you in a few. No rush, though."

Eden watched Aster turn and move through the crowd on the dance floor. Why had she so readily agreed to a drink with Aster? And why did her heart pick up every time Aster smiled at her? *You need a friend and some fresh scenery. This can only be a good thing.*

And Eden would make sure it was a change for her. She was tired of Liam or nothing.

Aster sat at a table close to the edge of the rooftop. Her face felt heated, and her hands were clammy. She'd just…invited Eden up here. It seemed like a good idea at the time, but now, as she sat alone swirling her whiskey, Aster believed she'd made a mistake.

You've spent half of the day staring at her.

And she really had. She was also certain that she had images of Eden on her camera. Nice pictures, of course, but it was crossing the line, and Aster knew it. Grace would know what to do, and Aster had considered calling her, but as she lifted her glass from the table, the lift doors opened, and Eden walked out of them. *Okay, smile and act cool.*

This was ridiculous.

"Hi. Sorry I took a while. I got talking to the bride," Eden said, pulling out a chair. "She's singing your praises."

"Oh, I'm sure she's not."

"Mmhmm. She is."

Aster sipped her whiskey. "She hasn't even seen the pictures yet. She could hate them."

"We both know that's not going to happen." Eden looked pointedly at Aster, one corner of her mouth upturned. Okay, Aster was a sucker for a woman with a sexy smirk…and Eden *definitely* had one.

Instead of focusing on the drop-dead gorgeous woman next to her, Aster continued with their conversation. "She could, though. She could hate them, and then you'd be disappointed."

The frown lines across Eden's forehead deepened. "Where has that confident woman I saw earlier gone?"

"I-I don't—"

"When you have that camera in your hand, you go off into a

world of your own. I saw it with my own eyes. You knew exactly what you were doing, where to be, and I'm certain that if I'd asked you to climb up a fifty-foot ladder to get the perfect shot, you would have."

Aster was surprised by everything Eden had said. In all honesty, she wasn't sure her boss had even noticed she was in the room today, so to hear that Eden had effectively 'studied' her, piqued Aster's interest. "Nothing else matters when I have the camera in front of me."

"Let me get a drink and then we can get comfortable up here." Eden stood, but the barman came towards her. She ordered a whiskey for herself and another for Aster.

"So, I was thinking," Aster started. She'd done a lot of thinking last night, and she knew what she wanted deep down. Something guaranteed. "Is the offer to join the team still on the table?"

Eden's eyes shone. "One hundred percent."

"Then I'd like to accept."

Aster held out her hand, but Eden turned and threw her arms around her instead. Shocked was her first reaction…aroused, her second. "That's brilliant. I'm so happy you agreed." Eden pulled back, holding Aster at arm's length. "*So* happy."

"M-me too." Aster ignored the shiver that ran through her body. Eden was pretty…that's all this was.

Eden jumped back. "Sorry. That was completely inappropriate."

"It's fine. It's nice to see someone who is excited to have me around."

Okay, that sounded as though Aster was looking for sympathy, but it wasn't like that. She was content with her own company; she always had been. While Grace was pining after Mia, Aster went home each night and relaxed. She didn't have anyone to answer to, nobody demanding anything of her, and it worked.

"I see very good things with you around." Eden returned to

her seat, smiling as the bartender brought their drinks. "Thank you."

Aster had to change the subject. When Eden told her things like that, it only made that attraction grow. Completely unrealistic and unfounded attraction. "Why event planning?"

"I'd like to say I had this big epiphany when I was younger, how I'd always seen myself doing this, but that would be a lie. I saw a market for it, took a chance with numerous loans, and it paid off for me. Thankfully, I love what I do. Especially nights like this when I see the smile my clients are wearing."

Aster focused on the smile Eden was wearing. And then her eyes dipped to Eden's full lips, her light makeup, her neckline... "N-nice."

"People will always want to celebrate something. Birthdays, weddings, christenings. You name it, there's a celebration for it. And over the last ten years or so, it's only gotten more lucrative. You wouldn't believe the price people will pay for a baby shower or a christening."

"I can imagine. I've seen the pictures on social media."

"But it's weddings that I thrive on. I love them." Aster noted the way Eden's eyes lit up. It only made them all the more enticing. "You know, seeing the love two people have for one another. That happily ever after. Isn't it what we all want?"

"I...guess so," Aster told Eden what she assumed she wanted to hear. "Are those plans on the horizon for you and Liam?"

Eden cast her gaze on the table, offering a wry smile. "Not likely."

"No?" Aster asked, aware that she could be overstepping. "Tell me to mind my own business..."

"Actually, it's nice to sit here and talk like normal people do. If I'm not working, I'm with him. If I'm not with him or working, I'm at home pottering about."

Eden didn't appear to be too happy with that.

"Liam is...different. Sort of. I don't know." Eden ran a hand through her hair. Aster was mesmerised as it fell back into place. "I mean, he's nice. But he demands so much. He called me tonight while I was working to ask how long I'd be. Said he'd made plans for us."

"He didn't know you were working?"

"Oh, he knew. He has my schedule. But he likes to try to take things out of my hands and then seems to be offended and pissed off when I can't make it."

Aster snorted. "This is why I'm single."

"I did wonder…"

"If I was single?" Aster didn't recall that having any bearing on her potential position at *The Garden of Eden*.

"Yes. This job can be demanding, especially when wedding season arrives. I wanted you to be prepared for that."

"Oh, it's fine. Even if I did meet someone, they'd probably leave me within a week."

"You have a very bad habit of putting yourself down."

"Self-deprecation. I'm aware that I do it." Aster smiled, finishing her second whiskey. "So, what's going on for the rest of the night with you?"

"Nothing whatsoever." Eden sunk back in her seat, crossing her legs. "You?"

"Not much. It's been a while since I sat in a bar with someone else. It's nice."

Eden turned her watch towards herself, glancing back up at Aster as she quirked an eyebrow. "Fancy one or two more? I have nowhere to be in the morning."

Aster grinned. "I…would."

"You're sure I'm not keeping you from anything?"

"Nothing."

"Then I'm getting a bottle of champagne for us. We should celebrate you joining the team."

Aster blushed. "You don't have to do that. It's no big deal."

"Are you joking? It's a big deal for me." Eden stood, placing a hand on her hip. "I've just added a superstar to my team; it's a *huge* deal."

Aster was looking for some kind of comment to make, but she genuinely had nothing to throw back at her new boss. Eden was…a joy to be around. And the constant ego boost was beginning to grow on her. "Okay. Let's do this."

5

Eden lowered her sunglasses over her eyes, slowly climbing from her Mercedes. She'd managed to grab a parking spot at the field, unheard of on game day for Ashforth FC. This wasn't something she'd always done—caught the latest women's football game—but Blair had started dragging her along when Dom was playing. Something about sisters sticking together when the weather was rubbish. And today…it was.

She lifted her handbag from the passenger seat, resting it in the crook of her elbow as she looked around to locate Blair. When she finally spotted her, Blair was waving frantically in Eden's direction. Yes, she was late. No, she didn't care.

For the last three weeks, Eden had met with Aster for drinks on a Saturday night. If they were working, they hung back at the bar. If not, they got ready and made an effort to keep one another company. They just got on, and if Eden were being honest, she preferred Aster's company to anyone else.

Last night had gone on longer than either of them had anticipated, but she'd had a wonderful night. Sitting with Aster and talking about anything that sprang to mind had been refreshing;

Eden hoped they could keep doing it. Aster was a breath of fresh air in her life.

"Come on! Move yourself!" Blair yelled, and it wasn't at the players on the pitch. No, she was yelling directly at Eden. "Sometime today would be great!"

"Alright. I'm coming." Eden winced as she yelled back, her head throbbing...slightly. "Give me a sec. This field is like sludge."

"Welcome to my world." Blair crossed the distance, meeting Eden in the middle of the field and linking their arms. "One thing you never are...is late."

"Mm. Late night, sorry." *A very late night.*

Blair smirked, squeezing Eden's arm against her. "With the one and only Liam, huh?"

There was more chance of hell freezing over lately. "God, no."

"Why do I feel like we need to have a serious conversation?"

Eden didn't know why Blair thought that. They hadn't had a serious conversation since Blair met Dom. And that was eighteen months ago. Eden wouldn't make a big deal out of it, but Blair hadn't wanted to know about Eden's life much since Dom arrived on the scene. But it was fine. Life moves on.

"Eden?"

"I'm fine. I didn't spend the night with Liam. I was with Aster." Blair wasn't aware of their newfound friendship. Perhaps it was time to tell her.

Blair stopped, gripping her best friend's arm. "Aster?"

"Yeah. We hang out on Saturdays."

"Oh, well...that's nice."

Eden had to agree. It was nice. Too nice, actually. "Yeah. She's lovely."

"Mm. You keep saying."

"And I don't know, I think I just got carried away last night. In the end, she had to call me a cab." She didn't make it a habit to have many blow-outs, but once a year was okay. Last night had been that opportunity, and Eden had foolishly grabbed it with both hands.

Blair narrowed her eyes. "And did Aster, like, take you home?"

"She did. Which was sweet. But it's not a very good impression I made, is it? Taking your drunk boss home from work."

"I'm sure she didn't mind. But maybe don't do it again. You know, you want to keep it professional."

"I do. Or I *did*. We get along so well, we decided to make it a regular thing. If she's available."

"Oh."

Eden didn't miss the frown Blair wore, but what she wanted to know was the reason *for* that frown. Surely, Blair didn't have something against Aster. She was a sweetheart.

"What?"

"Nothing." Blair's voice pitched a little higher. "It's just, you're her boss, and you don't know one another."

"We know one another. We have lunch together most days." Lunch had become Eden's favourite time of day recently.

"I mean, sure. Yeah. If that's what you want to do."

Eden sighed, waving at Dom as she sprinted down the sideline. "Look, I know you probably think it's all a bit odd since I don't usually bother with anything unless it's work related, but you're okay, Blair. You have Dom now. And I love that, I do, but I feel lost. I feel like I'm merely existing some days when I sit home alone."

Blair opened her mouth to speak but fell short of creating any words.

"I wanted so much happiness for you," Eden said, stopping and turning to face her best friend. "And you have that. Let me find my happiness now. And if it comes in the form of a friendship with Aster, so what?"

"I thought you had happiness. Liam, your business, us."

"Liam *is not* my happy ending. Please understand that."

"And that's okay." Blair shrugged. "If you want to hang out

with Aster, go for your life. But you do know that she's a lesbian, don't you?"

"I'm not sure what relevance that has. I've been best friends with you for almost 40 years."

But Eden knew exactly what Blair was hinting at. It was probably a good idea to avoid saying how she was feeling about Aster. It was already a muddled mess in her head.

"You know what I mean."

"Actually, I don't." Eden frowned. She never wanted to lie to Blair, but she wouldn't understand.

"Have you thought that maybe she's being very friendly for *other* reasons?"

Eden took a step back. Blair had no right to say that. Of course Eden knew Aster was a lesbian. It hadn't gone unnoticed. But now, hearing Blair accuse Aster made things harder for Eden. One, because it meant Blair would be keeping an eye on their every move. And two, because Eden didn't feel like she could confide in Blair about the unexpected attraction she felt towards her photographer. And Blair was *always* the person Eden confided in. From childhood, right up to current day, they'd been so close. But now that didn't feel like a possibility…and Eden had nobody else to talk to.

"I…I think I'll go and say hi to the team." Eden made a beeline for the substitute players further down the sideline. "Well, that was a kick in the stomach," she muttered to herself. "But it's fine. Everything is fine."

It wasn't fine. It hadn't been fine since the moment she met Aster. But she couldn't do anything about that now. It was too late to stop looking at her in a way she'd never looked at any other woman before.

I can't be attracted to her. I'm straight!

Aster rushed across the field, stopping dead as Dom scored, the ball thrashing the back of the net. She cheered and whooped, clapping as she continued her sprint towards the team. Grace was in goal, but Mia was on the sideline, substituted for what looked like Fi. They had a love-hate relationship, but most people did when Fi was involved.

"Hey! Sorry I'm late."

Mia placed a hand on her hip. "What time do you call this, Miss Bennett?"

"I call it reasonable for a Sunday morning." Aster yawned. She wasn't hungover, but she was tired. Eden had kept her out last night until after 2 a.m., a time Aster hadn't seen in a few years. "How's it going?"

"4-1 to us now that Dom's just scored that screamer."

"Looks like a semi-final trip then, right?" Aster rubbed her hands together, grinning. "I love away days."

Mia nodded. "Still got thirty minutes to go, but I don't see them coming back. And Grace has been amazing in goal."

"As always."

Aster watched Mia as she swooned over Grace. She loved that her best friend had found the love of her life; it was unmistakable every time she watched Grace and Mia together. Really, it was beautiful. *I want that, too.*

"Hey, do you two have plans later? I was wondering if I could pick your brains about something." After a month of Saturday's with Eden, it was time to open up. Aster needed the advice.

"Usual Sunday night out with the team, but sure. Come over and get ready with us, and we'll talk."

"You're sure?" Aster wrinkled her nose. "I don't want to get in the way if you have plans beforehand."

"We don't."

"Okay, well—" Aster cut herself off when she spotted someone who looked like Eden standing alone. Blair was here, she was talking with a supporter Aster didn't recognise, but Eden looked…distracted. "I'll be back in a few, okay?"

Mia nodded, turning back to the other players who were soaked to the bone beside her. The rain hadn't lessened today.

As Aster cleared her throat and glanced down her body, checking she looked presentable, she sidled up beside Eden, nudging her arm. "Didn't expect to see you here…"

"Oh, hi." Eden frowned, clearly in a world of her own. "I didn't know you were coming today."

"I'm here most weekends. And I couldn't miss today's quarterfinal. Grace would kill me with her huge, bare, goalkeeper hands."

Eden wore a shy smile, holding up her umbrella. "How are you feeling this morning?"

"Tired, but otherwise fine. You?"

"So-so."

"I know you wanted to walk home last night, but I couldn't let you. I'm sorry. And I know I probably overstepped when I decided to call that cab, but I wanted you to get home safe."

"Thank you for being so concerned. I got ahead of myself. I'd enjoyed some good company *again*, so thanks for entertaining me week in, week out."

"Any time," Aster said, shrugging like it didn't mean a thing. But deep down, it meant a lot. She'd distanced herself as much as she could last night, but the more time they spent together, and the closer Eden sat to her, the more Aster struggled to keep her thoughts platonic.

"We have a team meeting on Tuesday if you could come along. To go over the schedule for next month. I meant to tell you last night."

"Tuesday, yes." Aster nodded, studying Eden's profile as she focused back on the game. Her boss seemed…distant. Aster hoped it was just Eden's hangover, but she got the impression that wasn't the case. "What time?"

"Ten."

"Great. I'll be there."

Eden seemed to drift off into her own world again, so Aster would let her be.

"I'll...get out of your way."

"Oh, don't feel like you need to leave. I'm only here to support Dom."

"Forgive me for being nosey, but is there a reason you're not standing with Blair?"

"She's...talking." Eden glanced over her shoulder. Aster followed, only to find Blair staring back at them. Aster smiled, and Blair returned a half-hearted one. "Or she was."

"Okay, well, I'll let you guys get back to whatever you usually talk about at the game. I'll catch up with the girls. Take care, okay?"

"I will. See you Tuesday." Eden didn't make eye contact with Aster. She wouldn't usually be concerned, but after the night they'd had last night, generally enjoying one another's company, Aster at least expected a little more from Eden.

"Bye then."

Eden nodded, her hand gripping her umbrella. "Bye."

"Okay, what's going on with you?" Blair tugged at Eden's arm as she headed for her car, stopping her dead in her tracks. This wasn't worth discussing. It sounded ridiculous enough in Eden's head. "Something is wrong. Talk to me."

Eden turned back, smiling a fake smile. "Nothing, why?"

"That's bullshit. We both know it. You've been weird since you got here this morning."

Eden wanted to get home. Was that such a crime? "Blair, go home with your fiancée. I'll speak to you next weekend."

Blair shook her head, tugging Eden's passenger side door

open. "That doesn't work for me. Get in the car. Dom isn't even finished getting changed yet. I want to talk to you."

Eden turned her back, rolling her eyes as she climbed into her Mercedes. Blair followed, reaching over Eden and pressing the lock on the driver side door once she'd cornered her inside the car. "Okay, I'm not leaving until you tell me what's going on."

Eden snorted. "Forgive me, but you haven't wanted to know much since you met Dom." Eden winced, instantly regretting what she'd just said. Still, it was how she felt. "And that's absolutely fine, you're in a different place now, but I'm not sure why you're so bothered about anything that's going on in my life."

"Ede's. I'm sorry."

"Honestly, you don't need to apologise. We're at different stages of our lives. You're back at that falling in love all over again stage, whereas…I've never even had that once. But, you know…" Eden paused, lifting a shoulder. "I guess I should be thankful for what I do have and not complain about the fact I have no love life. It's hardly the end of the world."

Except it was close to being exactly that. Eden would give anything to feel…loved.

"I'm sorry I haven't been around as much as I used to be. I'll do better, I promise. But please, talk to me."

"I'm feeling…out of sorts."

"In what way?" Blair asked, offering Eden a lopsided smile. "In your job?"

"No. My job is perfect. In life, I guess." *Aster. It's all Aster.*

"Are you and Liam having problems?" Blair placed a gentle hand on Eden's shoulder. "I thought everything was going well."

"I haven't seen him in 3 weeks. He keeps calling, but I'm always busy."

Blair sighed. "You have to make time for him, Eden. He's your boyfriend. And I know you love your business, it's been your life for so long, but you deserve love, too. And God knows you need a break. A day off."

"I...don't want to see him." Eden couldn't put into words how much she never wanted to see Liam again. And he *always* seemed to call when she was with Aster. That certainly brought the mood down.

Blair remained silent. She always was good at that.

"I feel unfulfilled with him. He wants a lavish lifestyle, and that's not me. I don't know why I keep picking the boy racers and the bad boys, but it has to stop." Eden paused, blowing out a deep breath. "I see how happy you are with Dom, and damn it...I want that, too."

"You *can* have it. You need to find the right person for you, love. And it will happen. If I can find the woman for me, you can find the man for you."

If that were true, why was Eden constantly thinking about Aster? Why, if she wasn't attracted to women, was a woman permanently on her mind? None of this made any sense.

"I don't know what I want anymore. But I plan all of these weddings, and I make sure my clients have the ultimate day, something they could have only dreamed about, and it's really rubbish when I go home alone. I mean, you know me better than anyone, Blair. You know how much I love happy endings, couples, Valentine's Day, and everything to do with love...so why am I lacking in it?"

"I don't know, sweetie. You've not found the person who makes you happy, and that's okay. It'll happen when it happens."

"What if..." Eden shook her head. She couldn't say it. Blair would laugh in her face. "No, never mind."

"Tell me. I want to know what's on your mind."

Eden swallowed, her eyes finding Blair's. "What if I've been looking in the wrong place?"

"I don't understand."

"No, me neither." Eden could only smile. Put on her best brave face. It was absurd to even consider her attraction to Aster.

It surely meant nothing. Maybe she was bored with life and she was looking for a little excitement.

But it didn't feel that way. Eden didn't for one second feel as though she wanted to experiment. No, her attraction was real. It was genuine. But she still didn't know why it was Aster who kept creeping to the front of her mind.

"Look, I should get home. I have housework to do."

"God, that's the saddest thing I've ever heard."

"Why?"

Blair laughed. "You've just told me that you want something to fulfil you. And I know what I'm about to suggest won't necessarily make that happen, but it beats going home and doing housework. What would you do after it? Run a hot bath and put your matching pjs on?"

"Uh, I don't wear pjs. You know that."

"Seven. Tonight. Be ready."

Eden's brows drew together. "For what?"

"You, pretty lady, are coming to team night. It's good fun, the girls are great, and if nothing else, it gets you out of the house for a few hours."

"I don't think I can drink again tonight."

"So don't." Blair shrugged. "I only usually have one or two myself. Even Dom doesn't bother getting drunk anymore. We have other priorities now."

"Oh?"

"Being with the team is amusing enough. And besides, I never know if I'm going to be called into work suddenly, so I don't have the luxury of being hungover on a Monday morning."

"True."

"Please? For me?" Blair stuck out her bottom lip.

Eden considered it for a moment. Having another night out wouldn't be the worst thing in the world. And who knew, maybe it'd be something Eden would consider doing again in the future.

She knew all of the players on the team, what was the worst that could happen? "Okay."

Blair leaned over, kissing Eden's cheek. "Seven. Not a moment later. I'll pick you up before we head for the bar."

"Are you sure it'll be okay for me to join you?"

Blair cupped Eden's face. "You're the sister I always wished I had. You and me together. You're always welcome in my space, don't *ever* forget that."

Eden smiled. "I'll see you tonight."

6

"I'm so happy it all worked out for you." Grace wrapped an arm around Aster's shoulder, squeezing her tight. Aster hadn't gotten the chance to meet with Grace and Mia before they came out earlier this evening, but it didn't matter. She *had* planned to talk about her feelings towards Eden but instead chose to forgo that option and drink instead. "And Eden's nice. You'll get on with her."

"You, like…know her?"

"Only from having drinks at Blair and Dom's. They're usually joined at the hip."

"That's nice." Aster wondered if she would ever hang out with the team at Blair's place. She had been invited in the past, but now knowing that Eden usually showed up, she was desperately praying for another invite in the not-too-distant future. "Hey, great game today."

"Don't change the subject. I'm trying to praise you."

"I know, but you don't need to do that. I have a steady job; it's not that big of a deal."

Grace cocked her head, smiling. "But someone has *finally* seen how amazing you are. I've been telling you this for, what? Ten years."

"You have. I guess it was a matter of waiting for the right gig to come up. And anyway, if it hadn't been for you, I wouldn't have been offered the chance to join Eden's team. So, thanks. I owe you one."

Grace waved off Aster's appreciation. "Oh, it was nothing. I'll have another pint, and then we'll say no more about it."

Aster barked a laugh. "You're so easy to please."

"Well, Bennett…that pint won't pour itself!" Grace clapped, tilting her head towards the bar.

Aster held up her hands, scrambling to her feet. "Fine. I'm going. I'm going."

She crossed the floor, reaching the bar in no time. This wasn't a usual team night. They'd actually come to a new, rustic bar. Aster loved it, but some of the girls weren't overjoyed to be here. They liked familiar, and in most cases…rough and ready.

Aster glanced back, eyeing Mia's drink. She'd order a fresh pint for Grace's girlfriend, too.

"What can I get you?" a soft voice filtered through the air, pleasant to Aster's ears.

"Oh, hi. Three pints please."

The bartender smiled, her black hair pulled up high on her head, the right side shaved. Tattoos littered her neck and exposed collarbones. She was certainly pleasing to look at. "Be right back with them."

Aster caught the nametag before the bartender turned and grabbed some glasses. *Esme.* Nice. She watched Esme work the bar, smiling when the bartender's light blue eyes caught hers. Esme's smile turned shy, her head dipped as she tilted the glass and poured a pint.

Aster turned back to her friends, waving when Dom and Blair walked into the bar. Blair always looked immaculate, and Dom always looked trendy. Aster glanced down at herself; she was satisfied that she fitted in tonight. She lifted a hand, offering a drink to Dom and Blair, but then Eden walked in behind them, and Aster lost her mind. *Holy fuck!*

The door swung closed, sending Eden's hair flowing around her shoulders. A vision…that's how Eden looked. Like an absolute vision. *God, why does she have to be so beautiful?* Aster lowered her eyes, turning back to the bar. She ordered Dom and Blair their usual, Eden a whiskey—that seemed to be her drink of choice over the last few weeks—and carried the tray back to the table. Esme had given her a final flutter of the eyelashes, but Aster's head was too far up her arse to think about it now. Thirty seconds ago, she would have asked for Esme's number—it'd been a while since she'd been spontaneous—but right now, Aster was putting her all into regulating her heartbeat.

With shaking hands, she placed the tray down, handing out drinks to Grace and Mia. She turned to Dom, smiling. "Got you a beer, mate."

"Thanks." Dom took the drink, placing her hand on Blair's thigh as her fiancée sat beside her. "Aster got the drinks in, babe."

Aster offered a glass of white wine to Blair. "Good to see you both."

"Thank you." Blair wore a permanent bright smile lately. "I brought Eden with us tonight. She could do with a night out."

Aster turned to Eden. "Whiskey?"

"O-oh." Eden seemed surprised. "Thank you."

"I got you what I thought you'd like. But if it's wrong, I can grab you something else."

Eden placed a warm hand on Aster's forearm. God, it felt good. "It's great. Really."

"Well…" Aster was aware that Blair's eyes were on her. She felt them burning through the side of her face. "Have to keep the boss happy."

"Oh, yeah!" Blair laughed. "Because when you piss the boss off, punishment will follow."

Aster smiled, her nerves through the roof. Why was Blair looking at her with a stupid grin on her mouth? "I'll bear that in mind."

"You wouldn't want to be on the receiving end of a spanking, Aster. Trust me." Blair winked, sending Aster's cheeks a deep shade of crimson. "Right, sweetie?"

"Oh, give it a rest." Eden rolled her eyes, focusing back on Aster as she took a seat between Dom and Eden. "Pay no attention to Blair. She's been cooped up in an office all week."

Blair offered a single nod, sipping her wine. "This is true."

"So..." Aster paused, turning her attention to Dom. If she focused on anything other than Eden, she wouldn't have to worry about mentally undressing her. *That's weird. Don't do that!* "Who do you play in the semis?"

"Unsure at the minute. The other teams have to replay. Finished nil-nil."

"I don't suppose it matters who you end up with. Ashforth is one of the only ones in the league with a full team. Was it my poor maths, or did that other team only have nine on the pitch today?"

"They did. It's been a hard season for a few of the teams. Something needs to change because they register for cup games and end up with no players on the day."

"Ashforth is lucky they have dedicated players then, huh?"

Dom barked a laugh. "The only reason everyone shows up each weekend is because Fi threatens to knock on their door...naked."

"Oh."

"And I'd say she doesn't mean it, but she actually does. It's happened a few times now."

Aster quirked an eyebrow. "That woman doesn't give a shit, does she?"

Dom swigged her beer, her arm landing around Blair's shoulder. "She really doesn't."

"Less talk of Fi would be amazing." Blair gave them both a knowing look. "Touchy subject."

"Right. Yes." Aster couldn't help herself, her eyes flitting to Eden. "Didn't think you'd be here. You don't usually come to team night."

"No, you're right." Eden crossed her gorgeous long legs, her thigh exposed as her dress sat perfectly in place. "But Blair insisted I joined you all, so here I am." Eden turned her palms up as if she was presenting herself as a gift. And she was. The greatest gift.

"Well, it's great that you're here." And that was the truth. Two nights in one weekend with Eden…Aster was spoilt.

Eden simply smiled, lowering her head as she swirled her whiskey in the glass. Aster took that as her cue to mind her own business, so she would do precisely that.

"I'm just…going to mingle."

Eden returned to her seat, breathless as Blair flopped down beside her. "I'm not sure this is the kinda place that expects dancing."

Blair placed a hand to her chest. "We're the only ones in here. I'm sure they can suck it up."

Eden took her bottle of water from the table, finishing the half she'd left earlier in seconds. It had been so long since she'd been out dancing, Blair wasn't around for those evenings anymore. But this…it felt normal. Dom didn't hang off Blair all night, and Blair didn't pine for her when they were speaking to other people. "You know, I thought maybe I could call through the week…"

"I'd love it if you would."

"I thought I'd get in the way, I don't suppose you and Dom want to be disturbed, but you two seem to be able to separate for five minutes."

"We're not glued together, love. We do have lives, *and* friends, away from one another."

Did they? So why didn't Blair call more often?

"Still." Eden shrugged. "I don't like to show up unannounced."

Blair ran her hands through her hair. "I wish you would. At least then I'd know what was going on in my best friend's life."

"You don't need to worry about me. I'm fine."

Blair rested her head on Eden's shoulder. "Have you decided what you're going to do about Liam?"

"I have to end it." Eden had no doubt about that in her mind. There was no use in being with someone for the sake of it. And if she were being honest, breaking up with him meant she wouldn't have to worry about the incessant calls and messages. "I have my work to focus on. And I'm going to have to be on standby for Aster while she finds her feet in the team." Since Blair seemed to struggle with the knowledge that they were friends, Eden would use the colleague theory instead.

"Be on standby?"

"Be there if she needs me. I know she doesn't show it when she's with you lot, you're her friends, but her confidence is on the floor when it comes to her work."

"It is?"

Eden nodded. "Her work is incredible, Blair. But she shrugs it off and blushes if I compliment her on it. I want everyone around to see how talented she is."

"That sounds awfully nice of you."

The look in Blair's eye didn't go unnoticed by Eden, but she was barking up the wrong tree. *No, she's not. You know she sees right through you!*

"It's called women empowering women." Eden offered her best friend a knowing look. "I don't know what's wrong with you lately, but that comment you made this morning at the football wasn't cool."

"About Aster?"

"Yes."

"You may not see it, love," Blair paused, leaning in closer to Eden, "but *I* see the way she looks at you. You may be her boss, and she may know you're off limits, but that doesn't mean she can't look and dream about what she could have."

"I-I don't—"

Blair held up her hand. "She's into you. That's all I'm saying."

"Don't be ridiculous." Eden's heart fluttered a little more than she would have liked. Blair saying things like that only complicated her feelings further. Nothing good would come from thinking about Aster as anything other than her employee. "I'm straight, in case you forgot."

"And I know that…but I'm only saying. Be careful. You've no idea the effect you straight women have on a lesbian with a crush."

"Us straight women?" Eden asked, incredulously. "Don't blame me for someone else being attracted to me. I can't help it."

Blair lay a gentle hand over Eden's, squeezing lightly. "That's not what I'm saying. But you going out drinking with her and having her take you home…it could give her the wrong impression."

Had she given Aster the wrong impression? Not likely. Eden was very good at hiding how she felt.

"Then I'll make sure I don't touch her up, that should do the trick." Eden rolled her eyes, getting to her feet. "I'm going to the bar. Another wine?"

"Yes, please."

Eden crossed the short distance to the bar, blowing out a deep breath while nobody was around. Dom chatted with Mia, Blair took in the sight of the rest of the team dancing, and Eden…well, she was the epitome of confused. How had Blair noticed things she hadn't? Or was it a case of her best friend getting her wires crossed? She approached the bar, pleased to find Aster waiting for her own order.

She kept her distance, her eyes landing on Aster's profile. Her blonde hair was pulled to one side, once again exposing that neckline Eden struggled to forget. But then Eden overheard Aster asking the bartender for her number, unexpected jealousy rolling through her. She backed away a little more, not wanting to be seen as eavesdropping.

Aster caught sight of Eden in the mirrored wall behind the bar, separating from the bartender as she did so. "Oh, hey. Can I get you another drink?"

"No, thank you." Eden held up a hand. "Don't let me interrupt you."

"Oh, we were only talking. I needed a breather before someone dragged me back onto the dance floor. I'll grab my order and then the bar is all yours."

"Really, there's no rush." Eden felt awkward. She also no longer wanted to be standing there but walking away could be considered odd...or rude. "I'll use the bathroom and come back in a few."

Aster smiled. "Cool. Okay."

As Eden walked away, Aster called her back.

"Are you ready for later?" Aster asked. "The singing starts in forty minutes. You're in for a treat."

"Why is that?" Eden's forehead creased.

"You'll have the pleasure of hearing the entire team screaming the words to Bohemian Rhapsody *very* out of tune on karaoke."

Eden's eyebrows rose with surprise. "Karaoke?"

"Yep. So, I'd get the drinks in now before we all get kicked out after the first song."

"I...didn't know this place had karaoke."

"Oh, we do. But we haven't had anyone in with a decent voice in a long time, so maybe it could be considered wailing rather than karaoke," the bartender cut in. "Every bar usually has at least one good singer. But not this place."

"Mm. Well, I'm sure the team will sound great."

Eden turned and headed in the direction of the bathroom. One or two players tried to catch her hand as she rushed past the dance floor, but she made it inside unscathed. Now, her only issue was the beautiful woman at the bar. *Oh, Aster. I do wish you hadn't come into my life.*

Aster dried her hands on a paper towel, checking her hair in the mirror while she had a moment to herself in the bathroom. Several girls on the team had expressed their desire to come here again, something Aster hadn't expected. At least here, she didn't have to worry about catching a cold sore from the glasses.

Her mind instantly wandered to Eden. Was she enjoying herself? She was hard to read; Aster had come to realise that since this morning. They'd had a lovely night last night—Eden talking freely about everything Aster put to her—but today was different. Stilted. Awkward. Aster didn't know what she'd done wrong. Maybe she could check in with Eden before the end of the night. It wouldn't hurt.

She left the bathroom. Everyone had moved from the dance floor, and the most incredible sound was now filtering through the speakers around the bar. *Wow.* The hairs on the back of her neck stood on end, goose bumps spreading all over her skin. Someone—an angel—was singing Whitney Houston's *Run to You.*

Aster swallowed down the emotion she felt surging up into her throat, willing her feet to move. She couldn't see the stage, but she could see the team sitting and staring in awe at it. As Aster rounded the bar—her knees jelly-like—Eden came into view, the emotion pouring from her expressive eyes and remarkable voice chilling Aster to the bone. "Oh, Jesus." Aster was well aware that her mouth had fallen open, but the entire room had faded out, only Eden remaining in front of her.

She felt a hand tugging at her arm, Aster's body now being dragged into a seat. "Stop drooling." Blair's voice penetrated her thoughts momentarily, but Aster didn't respond. She couldn't. Everything within her begged to reach out and touch Eden, to hold her as the pain in her voice became almost unbearable. "Are you with me?" Blair asked.

"Shush." Aster admonished, frowning as she shot a glance at Blair. "Just…be quiet."

"Oh, God," Blair whined. "I knew it. I fucking knew it."

Aster didn't know what Blair knew, but she didn't care. Eden had her wrapped up in the moment, enveloping her with a voice so syrup-like it had the ability to make her burst into tears.

"Hey," Aster said, leaning into Blair. "Who the hell hurt her?"

"What?"

"Eden. That's a voice of pain. Surely you see that…"

"I-I…" Blair frowned. "Shit."

"You see? Or rather, hear?"

"I do." Blair nodded, dropping her head to her hands. "I've been a rubbish friend lately. And I only noticed that she was…not doing too well earlier."

"She seemed fine with me until this morning. So, whatever happened, it happened very recently." Aster knew something wasn't right, but was she the person to question it? She'd only known Eden for a month or so. But now that Blair recognised it, she could work through it with Eden. "Maybe she needs a friend right now. I'd offer, but I don't think I'm the right person."

"Why?" Blair turned side on, shooting Aster a questioning look.

Aster lifted a shoulder. "Because I don't. Now, I'd like to enjoy the rest of this." She tilted her head towards Eden, smiling as her eyes flitted away from Blair. "I'd *really* like to enjoy it."

"Okay, but can I speak to you when Eden has finished?"

Aster simply nodded. She didn't want to waste another second, not when Eden was serenading the bar. *God, I wish she was serenading me.* Aster smiled when Eden looked directly at her, that piercing stare holding her against the booth they were seated at.

But then the song came to an end, leaving Aster more than disappointed. She wanted to listen to that voice all day, every day. She wanted to wrap herself up in a warm blanket, Eden beside her, while her soft breath washed over the side of Aster's face, sweet lyrics slipping from Eden's mouth.

Eden lowered the microphone and handed it back to the guy taking care of the music. The team erupted into cheers and whoops, but Aster remained silent and still. She had no words to describe what she'd just witnessed. She knew a few people who had a lovely voice, but that wasn't lovely…it was extraordinary. Haunting. Special.

Eden dipped her head, smiling as a blush crept across her chest. The team were all up on their feet, crowding around Eden while they congratulated her on such a beautiful performance, but Aster wanted them all to piss off. She wanted Eden to herself. She wanted to pull her to one side, tell her how exquisite everything about her was, and kiss her until this night was over.

Get real. Never going to happen.

Eden flopped down beside Aster, blowing out a deep breath as she reached for her glass of white wine. "Wow. It's been a while since I did that."

"It was great," Aster said, aware that Blair was watching. "Really nice."

Blair snorted. "Nice? Great? It was fucking amazing!"

Aster winced. Yes, she was aware how stupid her own description was. But she didn't want to seem too enthusiastic. Because in her mind, she wanted to get on her knees and kiss the ground Eden had just walked across. "Well, yeah. It was amazing."

Eden offered a shy smile. "Thanks, Aster."

"I think you may have put everyone else off." They all

laughed, and Aster was thankful for the reprieve. Blair would be lurking, no doubt about it, but for the time being…laughter was the best thing for everyone involved. "They'll slowly slope off to the stage and cancel their tracks."

"Oh, I'm sure they won't."

Aster relaxed, sipping her beer as she rested an arm along the back of the booth. "No, you're right. We're not that lucky."

7

"Hey, I'm getting some air." Aster eyed Mia as she pushed Blair's patio door open, stepping out and closing it quietly.

She didn't know how the entire team had ended up back at Blair's, but Aster was impressed. The house Blair and Dom had was everyone's dream home. Yes, Aster knew how Blair had acquired it, but wow…it was amazing. And as incredible as it was, she didn't suppose Blair wanted to go through divorce proceedings to get it. From what she'd heard, Blair had been through hell with her ex-husband.

She rested her forearms against the railing around the decking, looking out at the clear night sky. The stars were breathtaking tonight, but Aster's heart wasn't quite where it needed to be. Honestly, she wanted to call a cab and go home. It would be better for her sanity if nothing else.

All night, she'd gravitated towards Eden. From the moment she stepped foot inside the bar, Aster had struggled. Add in the voice of an angel, and Aster was completely lost for words. She'd never met anyone quite like Eden. She had a quiet presence, but one that had the power to make your knees tremble when she looked at you in a particular kind of way. And lately, Aster was *only* seeing that look. It was her mind working overtime—Eden wouldn't ever contemplate someone like her—but for a brief second this evening, she felt one hell of a connection. Unfortunately, it was only getting worse.

It's all in your head.

Aster gritted her teeth, clasping her hands behind her neck. "Shit!"

"Oh dear. What did you do?" Blair's voice travelled low through the air before she came to stop beside Aster.

"What?"

"You seem…bothered."

"Blair, is there something you'd like to say to me?" Aster straightened, turning to face Eden's best friend. The other woman was significantly taller, but she wasn't intimidated. "You've been making sly comments all night, and I really don't know what I've done to upset you."

"How long?" Blair cocked her head, smiling gently. There was no denying that Blair Harrington was incredibly beautiful, but Aster was tired of all the stunning women around her. She only paled in comparison.

"How long what?"

Blair rolled her eyes, folding her arms. "How long have you been attracted to my best friend?"

"I-I…"

"Please, don't deny it. I'm not stupid."

Aster pulled her shoulders back. "I'm not attracted to her. She's my boss, and we're friends. That's all."

Blair took Aster by the elbow, moving out of earshot of the door. "I wasn't born yesterday, Aster. I like you, you're super lovely, but Eden is straight. You do realise that, don't you?"

"Of course I know she's straight. I'm not as stupid as I *obviously* look."

"I've been watching you all night. *Nobody* has ever looked at my best friend the way you do. You're waiting for every word that falls from her mouth. Even Dom has noticed, and she doesn't usually notice what's right in front of her."

"Look, Blair, I know you mean well, but if you're worried about me getting into Eden's pants, you needn't bother. I'd never do anything like that. I have too much respect for her."

"So, you *are* into her?"

Play it cool, Bennett. "Who wouldn't be? Have you seen her?"

"I'm not talking about appreciating her beauty. I'm talking about everything else I'm seeing."

"You're seeing things that aren't there. Trust me." Aster backed away, returning to her previous position at the railings. She couldn't look Blair in the eye and lie to her. She wasn't that person.

Blair stepped forward, her body painfully close. "Don't hurt her, Aster. She deserves so much more than that."

"I'd never hurt her," Aster whispered. "She means too much to me."

"Then we're on the same page. That satisfies me for the time being. But I'm watching you. I'm watching everything."

Aster scoffed. "Eden's a big girl. She doesn't need you flaunting what you have to remind her of what she doesn't." *Ouch, that was harsh.*

"What's that supposed to mean?" Blair's hands landed on her hips, a scowl now covering her usually pretty face.

"It doesn't mean anything. But she's definitely not in a good place. I think we all know that from listening to her singing earlier. If you don't want me within ten feet of her, you'll have to take it up with your best friend. I'm just the colleague who is slowly turning into a friend."

"She's not in a good place?"

"I can't be the only one who saw the tears in her eyes tonight. She's very good at wearing a mask, but I saw right through it."

"I-I don't…" Blair lowered her eyes. "She's been off with me. She doesn't call as much as she used to. I don't know what I've done wrong."

"Maybe she's trying to let you get on with your life. I know what you've been through, Blair, and I'm sorry about that. But you've recently got engaged to Dom, so maybe Eden is taking a step back, I don't know."

"I don't want her to step back. There's plenty of room in my life for both of them."

Aster shrugged. "I'm trying to be her friend, Blair. I'm not lucky enough to be anything more."

"You've fallen for her, haven't you?" Blair's eyes softened, and her arms wrapped around herself.

Aster couldn't hold it in much longer. Grace would hit the roof when she found out that Aster had confided in Blair before her, but Aster needed to speak the words to someone. "I think I fell for her the moment I walked into her office, Blair. But I've managed this long, so I'm sure I can keep it to myself and take it to the grave with me."

Blair's hand covered her mouth, a tear slipping down her cheek. "Oh, Aster."

"Please, don't." Aster held up her hands. She didn't want someone to cry for her. She wanted to forget about Eden Kline. It couldn't be that hard to do. It wasn't as though anything had happened between them. "It doesn't mean anything, okay?"

Blair shook her head when Dom stepped up behind her. "God, I don't know what to say."

"About what, babe?" Dom cut in. "What's going on? Did something happen?"

Aster watched Blair intently, silently begging her to remain quiet about this. "Blair was having a gushy moment about you." She switched her gaze to Dom, wearing her best fake smile. "You've made this woman's life, mate."

"Aww, you big softy." Dom got to her tiptoes, kissing the side of Blair's neck. "I love you."

"I love you, too." Blair side glanced at Dom, her eyes glossy.

"Hey, what did you think of Eden's voice tonight?" Dom relaxed an arm around Blair's shoulders.

Aster cleared her throat. "Amazing."

"She plays guitar too. You should ask her to show you one night."

Aster's entire body buzzed. How could a woman who looked swanky and professional possibly lounge around with a guitar? Aster blew out a breath. She couldn't hang around here much longer. "Yeah. Maybe."

Eden sat comfortably, snuggled up with Blair as the team told their latest stories of one-night stands and bad mistakes. She'd been here once before when the girls were invited over, and this night was living up to be as good as the last. The major difference this time around was that Aster was here too. *She looks cute tonight...*

"What time are you working tomorrow?" Blair asked, twisting Eden's hair around the tip of her finger. It was a habit Blair hadn't been able to shake since they were kids. "Early start, or?"

"Nope. No work tomorrow. Tuesday, I have the entire team in for a meeting. I almost forgot to tell Aster."

"I think she's going to thrive with you, Eden."

"I hope so," Eden said, her head falling to Blair's shoulder. "I should show you some of the images she took when I called her in last minute. Maybe you could use her for your wedding."

"I'm trying to avoid using anyone we know."

"Why?" Eden glanced up, frowning. "I mean, don't you want me involved?"

"I do, but I also want you to be a huge part of our day. I don't want you working behind the scenes, and I don't think Dom would want Aster to, either. You're there as guests, not staff."

Eden hadn't thought of it that way. She could see what Blair was saying, but how was Eden supposed to sit back and allow some random event planner to take charge of her best friend's wedding? No, it simply couldn't happen.

"What if I got someone from my company to oversee everything?"

"I'll speak to Dom."

"You'll…speak to Dom?"

"Mmhmm. We discuss everything. It's a good thing to do. Stops me from panicking all the time that I'm doing something wrong."

"As if Dom would ever think you'd done anything wrong. She worships the ground you walk on."

Eden caught Blair's eyes as she focused on her fiancée standing in the kitchen. "She does."

God, why doesn't anybody look at me like that? Eden scanned the room, thankful when she found Aster standing with Dom. While they were together, she'd get away with staring. Really, this evening had been everything Eden could have hoped for. Long overdue time spent with her best friend, Aster in the same room as her, and a bout on karaoke. Yeah, it was definitely a night she'd needed.

Aster glanced in Eden's direction, smiling when she caught her eyes. Eden's stomach rolled, the intensity pinning her to the couch. Aster had beautiful dark eyes. When she looked at you, you felt safe. Comforted. Cared about. But that was Aster. A kind soul…

Eden snapped herself from her thoughts, sitting up on her elbow. "What time does this usually wrap up?"

"Whenever Dom kicks everyone out." Blair yawned.

"Right, well I'm probably going to call a cab soon. Get out of the way. I could do with a decent night's sleep."

"You're not staying here? The spare room is made up for you."

"No, I'll go home. I want to be in my own bed. I have an important day tomorrow…"

Blair's forehead creased. "You do?"

"Yes. I'm calling Liam. I'll ask him to come over so I can talk to him."

"You mean…end things with him?"

Eden sat up fully, tugging her dress down her thighs. "Yes, so I can end things with him."

"Are you sure you want to do this?"

"Blair, I'd rather be single. It's easier for me. He's…always there. Wanting to see me. Needing to see me."

"Isn't that what he's supposed to want?"

"Maybe, but it's not for me. *He's* not for me."

Blair nodded. She had a look in her eyes that acknowledged Eden not wanting to be pushed on this. "Fair enough."

"I'm going to start saying goodbye to the girls. I'll call a cab while I'm doing the rounds."

"Are you sure you don't want to stay? I hate the idea of you taking a cab home alone."

"I'll be fine." Eden leaned in, kissing Blair's cheek. This night had been perfect for them. She wouldn't wait so long to do it again. "Hey, I'm so proud of you."

"Huh?"

"Just…because of everything. I'm so happy you're settled and you're marrying the woman of your dreams."

Blair eyed Dom again. "I'm so happy she found me."

With tears in her eyes, Eden got to her feet and pushed her emotions aside. She'd had a million and one heart-to-hearts with Blair since she met Dom; it didn't need to be repeated this evening. She approached the kitchen, placing a soft hand on

Dom's shoulder. "I'm ready to head home. Thank you for inviting us all back."

"I thought you were staying?"

"According to you and Blair, yes. But I had no intentions of staying the night."

"Oh, well…do you want me to see if any of the girls are going the same way as you?"

Eden shook her head, thankful for Dom's concern. "No, it's okay. I don't think anyone else is ready to leave yet. And that's fine; I'm a lightweight now."

"Will you text us when you're inside with the door locked?"

"I will." Eden smiled, and then her gaze fell to Aster. "Goodnight, Aster."

"I could share a cab with you. I'm ready to leave."

Eden scratched the back of her neck. "I mean…if you're sure?"

"One hundred percent. I've been ready to go home since the club."

"Thanks," Dom said, scoffing. "You'd better look after her, Bennett. I'm watching."

Aster rolled her eyes, the same reaction Eden often had around Dom and Blair. Their concern wasn't necessary. "Settle down, Dom. You'll see Eden again. I'm not going to kidnap her."

Oh, I wish she would. Eden's eyes suddenly widened at that thought. *Curb it, right now!* "Okay, well I'll call a cab."

"No, I'll do that. You say goodbye to the girls."

Eden offered a single nod, turning around to tackle the team in Blair's living room. She said her goodbyes to everyone seated on the couches and floor, returning to the kitchen as Blair followed her.

"Did you call a cab?"

"Aster's doing it…"

A smirk played on Blair's lips. "Hmm. Interesting."

"What is?"

"You're going home with Aster."

Eden straightened. "Actually, we're sharing a cab, and I'll drop her off first."

"All done. Cab should be here in a few minutes. They said to wait outside because it wouldn't be long."

"Aster?" Blair stepped forward, linking one arm through Aster's. Eden had no idea what was about to happen, but she cringed nonetheless. "You make sure she gets home, okay?"

"I will. I'll walk her to her front door."

"Hello? I'm still standing here," Eden cut in, her jaw clenched. "And I'm perfectly capable of looking after myself."

"Still," Aster said, shrugging. "I'd like to walk you in for my own peace of mind."

Eden noted the smirk on Blair's mouth. "Such a gentleman. Now, leave. The cab will be outside before you know it."

Eden and Aster headed for the door, waved away by Dom and Blair. Eden wouldn't let it fester, but she was getting sick and tired of the snide remarks from Blair. Her best friend couldn't possibly know how Eden was feeling, everything was hidden deep down, so why did she insist on making comments at every turn? *Claims she sees how Aster looks at me. Don't make me laugh!*

They reached the gate, stepping out onto the pavement as it closed behind them. Neither spoke, and Eden just shifted from side to side as the cool air hit her bare legs. She shivered, releasing a shaky breath.

"Here." Aster shrugged her blazer from her shoulders, wrapping it around Eden. "It's not much, but it might take the chill off."

Eden should have insisted Aster take her blazer back, but the warmth of the jacket followed by a subtle perfume had Eden melting. Her knees weakened so much that she had to lean back against Blair's fencing. If she remained upright, she'd slide to the ground. "Thank you."

Aster shrugged. "No reason to be cold."

"Aren't you?" Eden asked, her voice booming in her ears.

"No, I'm good. And you…" Aster paused. "Well, you have significantly less clothes on than I do."

Eden grinned. "I didn't anticipate standing around waiting for a cab to collect me tonight. Sorry."

"You look great."

"T-thank you." Eden frowned as she stared at Aster's back. Nobody had said she looked great in a long time. Not even Liam when she met him at a local restaurant or bar. "So do you."

"I always choose comfort over everything else." Aster shoved her hands in the back pockets of her jeans, leaning heavier on one leg. The stance had Eden admiring Aster from behind, her jeans hugging Aster's perfectly rounded backside. *Oh, no. No. No. No.*

Eden opened her mouth to speak, but then Aster turned around, her eyes penetrating. "And tonight…wow. Your voice was incredible."

"Again, thank you." Eden dipped her head, reddening. She didn't take well to compliments. They were always few and far between.

"I mean, I didn't expect that *at all*. Not even a hint of it."

Eden shrugged. "Why would you?"

"You're right. We've been spending time together, but I don't really know you. Even though I feel like I do. You're so easy to get along with."

"I try to be," Eden said.

"And Dom says you play guitar?"

Why would Dom say that? Unless they'd been talking about Eden, that piece of information couldn't have possibly come up during conversation. "I…do."

"Could I maybe hear you play sometime?" Aster asked, her eyes brightening ever so slightly. "If you wouldn't mind?"

"Oh, I don't know. I don't usually play for anyone. Not even Blair. Guitar is my personal downtime."

Aster smiled faintly. "That's a shame."

"But, never say never." Eden pushed off the fence when a car pulled up outside Blair's. "After you…"

Aster shook her head, opening the door as Eden stood painfully close. And then Eden saw it. The look Blair had been talking about. The supposed attraction. God, that look *was* intense. "After you."

Good Lord. I could get used to her company…

8

Aster eased into her seat, swivelling as she looked around the bright white room. This place was something else, and she had full reign over it. *Okay, kid! You landed on your feet this time around.* She smiled, eyeing her camera bag sitting next to the iMac. When she was positioned in this spot, she had a panoramic view of the Three Graces. It was an astonishing sight. When she arrived early enough, she was in time to catch the sun rising and breaking through the sandstone buildings. They always looked so perfect next to one another. None of them matched, the symmetry completely non-existent, but they looked ideal side by side.

She sighed, rocking back in her office chair. Yesterday, this room had been unveiled to Aster, and Eden's eyes had lit up as much as her own. Aster truly couldn't believe her luck. "How the hell did you end up here?"

She truthfully had no idea. While she'd spent her life making sure she had what she needed, this was entirely different. And to have gotten this position on her own merit…she'd never felt so proud of herself before today. *I should call Dad.* Ted would be thrilled to hear Aster's news. They hadn't spoken in a couple of weeks, but Aster had been busy with scheduling. *Not too busy to check in with him.* Lily had moved back home almost two years ago when her relationship ended, and Rose visited every weekend. So, he wasn't completely alone. Still, Aster knew she should make more time for him. She made a mental note to call over at the weekend.

And then her phone buzzed in her pocket. When she removed it, she was thankful to see Grace's name.

G: Tired of waiting for an answer so I've booked your flight for Pride.

Shit. Aster had completely forgotten about Gran Canaria Pride. She wanted to go, but it wasn't the wisest of choices she could be making. Two weeks had passed since she heard Eden's incredible voice at the bar. Throw in this new editing suite, and Aster was struggling more than ever before. Nothing good could come from Pride. Nothing *at all*.

A: I don't even know if I can get the time off work.

G: Eden is coming. Why wouldn't you be able to?

A: She may need me for a job while she's away.

G: And you're being a miserable arse. Have a look at the accommodation. If you don't like it, book somewhere you do.

Aster sighed, lowering her phone for a moment. Could she go on a trip to a hot country where her boss would likely be lounging around in a bikini? *You're making a huge mistake…*

A: Fine. I'll look tonight.

G: Come over. I'll help you. Mia is at her parents tonight.

A: I'll come straight over from work. Love ya!

G: See you tonight. Love ya!

Well, that was that. Aster couldn't back out now, Grace had already put the final nail in *that* coffin. But maybe it would be good. Aster sure could do with some sun on her skin, so what's the worst that could possibly happen?

A gentle knock on the door caught her attention. She turned

in her chair to find Eden staring back at her. "Hi. How's the suite?"

"Um, amazing."

"I'm sure you have all your own stuff at home, but this is here if you ever want a change of scenery, okay? I had it all fitted a year ago with the hopes of finding someone permanent...so here you are. It needed a few bits and pieces finishing before I could show you."

"I didn't think I'd be working in a room like this, so if it's okay with you, I'm going to take full advantage of it."

"It'll be nice to see a friendly face around the office. You're more than welcome to spend as much time as you like in here."

Aster smiled, her eyes almost straying to Eden's chest. She managed to keep them where they should be, but it was a struggle. "Thanks. You've set me up with *everything*."

"Good." Eden pushed off the doorframe. "Maxine is going out to lunch now. Can I have her bring you anything back?"

"Oh, don't worry. I'm fine."

"She's only going to come in here and ask you herself anyway..."

"Okay, I'll have a coffee please. Cappuccino."

Eden quirked an eyebrow. "That's it?"

Aster nodded. She'd been so excited to get into work this morning that she'd prepared a packed lunch last night. "I have lunch with me."

"Okay, well I'll be in my office if you need anything."

"I think I may have some images for you to take a look at soon from last week's wedding. Should I pop in to you?"

Eden's eyes lit up, sending Aster's entire body alight with nervous energy. "Yes. Absolutely. I'm looking forward to it."

Aster glanced over Eden's shoulder, wearing her best poker face as a smart, handsome man walked towards them. "I...think somebody is here to see you."

Eden's forehead creased, and then she glanced behind her. "Oh, for the love of God!"

"Everything okay?" She noted the disinterest in Eden's eyes as she focused back on Aster. "Eden?"

"Yeah. It will be. Ex-boyfriend…Liam."

Aster was taken aback. She didn't know Eden had left Liam. "You split up?"

"Two weeks ago. I'm surprised it took him this long to show up here." She backed out of the room. "Hopefully, this won't take a minute. Come and find me when you have some things to show me. I'm *more* than happy to be interrupted." Eden's bright smile lit up the suite, but it quickly faded when Liam stepped up behind her, a controlling hand settling on Eden's hip. "Have a good day, okay?"

Aster watched Liam intently. Did he have to be so…vile? "Sure. You too."

"Don't ever walk into *my* business again and take a hold of me like you own me!" Eden slammed her office door shut, the walls shaking as she marched across the floor. "Who the hell do you think you are?"

"Babe, I'm sorry." Liam held up his hands, genuine remorse in his eyes. "I didn't mean for you to feel like that. But I wanted to talk to you, and I've missed you."

"Liam, I have work to do. A business to run. You can't show up demanding that I talk to you."

"Why not? I thought you loved me!"

Eden pursed her lips. Did Liam truly believe that? "I've never once told you I loved you."

Liam frowned, taking a step back. Eden didn't know why he was so shocked; they'd *never* discussed love. Not once. "Well, I mean…"

"No. You don't get to assume you know how I feel. It doesn't work like that." Eden paused, running a hand through her hair. "Do you have *any* idea how busy I am here?"

"M-maybe I could see you tonight? Come over to my place, and I'll order in."

Order in. That's all they ever seemed to do. Eden didn't want someone who constantly ordered in. She wanted someone who would take the time to cook for her. She also wanted to return the favour. Liam, in the six months they'd been together, hadn't once asked Eden to come over because he'd cooked dinner. It was takeout or it was a restaurant. And while Eden loved to be wined and dined in a restaurant that offered good food, she'd rather be at home with her…lover. She wanted—no, she *craved*, that intimacy.

"No."

"What do you mean no?"

"I mean…no." Eden glared straight through Liam, willing the door to open and end this discussion. "I called you and ended this, Liam. Please respect that."

"You expect me to walk away from you?"

"I do, yes. Surely you saw this coming. I mean, it's taken you two weeks to show up." Eden knew Liam had to be out of his mind if he believed they were happy.

"I…thought you were busy."

Eden nodded, resting back against her desk. "I am busy. But this also isn't working for me. I'm sorry."

A light knock on the door almost produced an audible sigh of relief from Eden. If it was Aster, her legs may just turn to jelly. "Come in."

"I'm talking to you," Liam said, frowning. "Tell them to wait."

Eden pushed off her desk, walked towards her ex, and stepped past him. "I think it's time you left, don't you?"

"Not really, no."

"I'm not feeling this attitude; I don't like it. I'm asking you to leave. Do so, or I'll remove you myself."

Liam snorted, folding his arms across his chest. He wasn't intimidating in the slightest. Eden, herself, had more intimidating tendencies than Liam ever would.

"Please. Don't make a dick of yourself."

The gentle knock on the door from before was this time stronger. Eden gripped the handle and opened it. Relieved when she found Aster standing on the other side, a shy smile playing on her lips, she tilted her head and smiled. "Come in."

"Oh, I can wait if this isn't a good time."

Eden took Aster's arm and pulled her inside. "It's the perfect time. Have a seat; I'm just seeing my visitor out."

Aster slowly moved through the office, stopping as she stared out at the water through the window. Eden turned her attention back to Liam, clearing her throat. "Now, it was lovely to see you, but I'm busy."

"Come over tonight. Please?"

Eden pinched the bridge of her nose, gritting her teeth. "Liam, what part of no don't you understand?"

"All of it. None of this makes any sense," He lowered his voice. "I thought we were good together."

"If this, what we've been doing, is your idea of 'good together'…then I had other expectations."

"So come over and we'll discuss them. Every last one."

Eden was done with this conversation. Liam had never been this vocal in the six months they'd been together; why was he now demanding one thing or another? "Please leave. And don't come back here. This is my job; I don't want to see you in this building again."

Liam's shoulders slumped, his phone gripped tight in his hand as he walked through the door. Eden should feel some kind of sorrow for how this was ending, shouldn't she? She glanced back at Aster…that was who she wanted to be spending her time with.

Satisfied that Liam was actually leaving, Eden closed the door and turned back to her employee. She didn't like to think of Aster in that way, but it beat thinking about her in *other* ways. Ways that could get her into a lot of trouble. "So…"

"Sorry. I heard you call for me to come in, but he didn't sound like he wanted me to do that."

"He's…the least of my concerns. Did you bring me some images?"

Aster grinned, holding up a USB stick. "I did. Want to take a look?"

"Let me make us some coffee and then we'll sit down and go through them together," Eden said, busying herself away from Aster. When she beamed that smile, it was hard to focus on anything else. And those long, dark lashes…divine. "Cappuccino?"

"I thought Maxine was bringing me one back?"

"She is, but she'll be gone for the hour. You can wait until then if you want?"

"No, it's okay. I'll drink coffee with you instead."

Eden's chest expanded. Aster was going to become a major issue in her life. If she allowed that, of course.

"You're still going to Pride, right?"

Eden turned, allowing the coffee machine to work its magic. "I am. And I can hardly wait."

"You know we spoke about it when I started working for you? Well, I was wondering if it was still okay for me to come along?"

Eden narrowed her eyes. "They're your friends, Aster. I'm only tagging along for some sun."

"I know, but I wasn't sure if you needed me to work while you're away."

"We have no events for those two weekends. There is no reason why I'd need you here."

Aster nodded slightly. "Okay. Well, Grace booked my flight earlier. I have no choice but to tag along, too."

Okay. This changed *everything*. Eden had initially invited Aster to share a room with her before all these feelings came to light. Now that she found herself drawn to Aster, it made life that little bit more difficult.

"I can find my own accommodation. It's no problem."

Eden looked up to find Aster chewing her lip. Her silence wasn't helping, that much was clear. "No. Sharing a room will be fun. I haven't had a girly holiday in forever."

"Right, well…"

The coffee machine beeped, and Eden took their drinks from beneath the spout. She set them down on her desk, getting comfortable in her seat. "Pride is going to be great. Now, pull up a chair and show me the work of art you likely produced."

Aster blushed, handing the USB over.

Eden focused her eyes on the screen. Being alone with Aster was much more pleasing than being alone with Liam. *Ordering in.* She scoffed inwardly. Aster probably didn't order in. No, she probably took the time to prepare dinner when she was dating. Or perhaps she didn't and ordering in was just what couples did these days. Maybe Eden was setting her evening expectations too high. Suddenly, her interest was piqued. "Hey, I have a question for you…"

"Okay, shoot!"

Eden cleared her throat, enjoying the warmth of Aster's body beside her. "How do you feel about ordering in?"

"Ordering in? Like, takeout…at home?"

"Mmhmm." Eden didn't stray from the computer screen. Sitting beside Aster was becoming painful. "Just a random question. I'm not expecting any kind of life changing answer."

"I don't mind it when I'm home alone. You know, if I'm not dating."

"And does that happen much at all, or?" Eden should have

clamped her mouth shut, but verbal diarrhoea was about to commence. "I mean, do you have a partner at the minute? You said you didn't, but things change."

"Nope. No girlfriend."

"Okay, so ordering in works for you when you're alone."

"Yep. Absolutely. But if I had a girlfriend, I wouldn't insult them with takeout. I mean, not regularly. I'd cook dinner. Whatever they wanted. I make some mean Italian dishes, and I'm a dab hand when it comes to putting some tapas together. But that happens *very* rarely. You know, cooking for someone else…" Aster trailed off, shaking her head. "Sorry. Way too much information."

Oh, no. That was the perfect amount of information. Eden would love nothing more than to show up at Aster's, dinner waiting with a glass of wine. God, she really *would* revel in that. "I asked."

"But why?"

"Intrigued."

Aster cleared her throat, the file on the screen coming to life. "Okay, well…now that you know my takeout routine, should we do some work?"

Eden felt a swell of something unfamiliar in her chest. "Y-yes. We should do that."

9

Aster blew out a deep breath as she knocked on Grace's front door. She'd driven here tonight with the intention of discussing what was going on with her best friend, but she suddenly felt herself backing out. As she had a few weeks ago. Aster knew this was the perfect time to talk to Grace since Mia wasn't around to influence anything Grace said about it all, but the thought of laying her feelings bare sent a wave of anxiety through Aster.

It's only Grace. You've been best friends for a long time. She wouldn't judge you. Aster straightened herself, gripping a bag of popcorn and various other treats in her hand. When the hallway light flickered on, Aster swallowed hard.

The door opened, instantly settling Aster when she saw Grace's kind face. "Hi. Come in."

Aster stepped past her. "Okay, look. I'm here tonight because I need to talk to you about something. It's a mess, at least in my head it is, and I could do with some advice. But if you don't think you can give me advice, it's fine. I'll figure it out myself. It's stupid to even think what I'm thinking; I don't even know why I'm here."

Grace placed her hands on Aster's shoulders, tilting her head. "Maybe we should go into the living room and sit down before you explode."

"I think exploding is what I'm hoping for. At least then I wouldn't have to deal with all this shit."

Grace remained silent, taking the bag from Aster's hand and resting it at the side of the couch. "Sit. Calm down. It's nothing that can't be fixed."

If only that were true. Aster blew out a shaky breath, listening to Grace moving around in the kitchen. When she returned with a huge bowl, emptying the popcorn into it, she relaxed into the couch, sitting beside Aster. "Okay, what's going on?"

"I think I'm falling for someone…"

Grace's entire face lit up, her hand stilling in the popcorn. "Oh my God! This is amazing news. I'm so happy for you."

"No. It can't happen. It's…not possible."

"Okay, I need more to work with."

"Eden." Aster said her name as though she was the only other living, breathing being on the planet. And at times, in Aster's world at least, she was. "It's Eden."

Grace's shoulders slumped as her face fell. That excitement in her eyes had turned to terror. "No. No, no, no."

"So you see my issue?"

"Issue? Oh, this is more than an issue, Aster. How the hell could you be falling for Eden? She's straight."

"I know." Aster gritted her teeth. "I'm well aware of that shitty fact, but it doesn't change how I feel, Grace. It doesn't stop me from thinking about her from the moment I wake up."

"Have you had like…a thing with one another? Did she lead you on? Is that why you're feeling like this? A one-night stand gone wrong…for you."

"No, not at all. I'd never go there. I'm not that stupid." And Aster meant that. If there was *one* no-go, it was dating a straight woman. "I don't even know why I'm feeling like this. It's not like she's even looked at me that way."

"Sometimes the heart wants what it wants. Maybe it's more of a gratitude thing because she saw something in you and took a chance."

Could it be that? It felt like more, but perhaps Grace was right. "Could be."

"I'm sure it'll all wear off before you know it. And Pride… that's a place you could let your hair down."

That wasn't Aster's style. Sometimes she wished it were, but the idea of sleeping with someone she'd never see again didn't appeal to her. She wasn't sure it ever would. "I don't know."

"Nobody on the team you like the look of?" Grace wiggled her eyebrows.

"Nope."

"No, I don't blame you. I mean, there's always Fi."

Aster wrinkled her nose, horrified her best friend could insinuate Aster pursuing something with Fi. "Fi has slept with *all* of Liverpool. I don't think she's my type."

"What *is* your type?" Grace rested her head in her hand, her elbow propped up on the back of the couch. She sat with her legs crossed, their bowl of popcorn cradled.

"Eden. She is completely my type."

"Successful, power suit, dominating personality."

"No," Aster said, smiling weakly. "Interesting, missing something in her life, genuine."

"Okay, maybe this is more than gratitude." Grace sighed. "But I don't know how you tackle that. Because whatever you feel, it doesn't change the fact that Eden *isn't* likely to be interested. And if she was, would she stick around? Or would it be the good old 'experiment' we all hate? I'd be *very* careful."

"I don't think she's that kind of woman."

"But you don't know her, Aster. It's been two months since

she had her PA call you, and I know you've become friends, but I don't want to see you hurt."

Aster was well aware of everything Grace was saying. But she couldn't change the fact that she was into Eden. Unless she left her job, and probably the city, she couldn't change any of this. Eden wasn't a woman you simply stopped looking at and that was the end of it. She had too much to say behind those piercing eyes of hers. "How do I be her friend when I feel the way I do?"

"I...don't know. Being her friend outside of work could turn into you torturing yourself."

"You're right. This is completely ridiculous. Eden Kline...and me?" Aster barked a laugh. "I realise how stupid it sounds."

"I know you have feelings for her, I can see it in the way you speak about her, but I need you to be careful, Aster. I don't want to see you getting hurt by *anyone*, least of all someone who probably only wants a night of no strings sex *if* it ever happened."

"Thank you," Aster whispered, her emotions threatening to tip over. "For being here for me. For not laughing in my face but working through it with me instead."

"You know I'm always here for you." Grace lifted the popcorn from her lap, setting it down on the table. "Come here. Give me a hug."

They embraced, and Aster relaxed against her best friend. This was exactly what she needed. A stern, but supportive voice. Someone who would discuss it with her rather than talk *at* her. "Thank you. Seriously." Aster pulled back. "But I need you to know something else..."

"What?" Grace wore a look of fear.

"I'm sharing a room with her when we go away."

"You are joking!"

Aster winced. "No. I wish I was. But she asked me months ago when she found out I was a regular at the games. I told her I wasn't going because I didn't want to third wheel with you and Mia. But she said we could hang out and enjoy ourselves."

"Uh-huh. I bet she's planning to enjoy herself. Why is she even coming? It's not like it's her sort of scene."

Aster shrugged. "Blair invited her."

"And are you *actually* going to share a room with her? You can always book your own. Maybe that would be for the best."

"I was planning to, but I don't know." Aster was torn. She'd love to spend her holiday in a five-star boutique hotel, it beat the other accommodation on offer, but could she manage the entire holiday with Eden in the next bed to her? "What do you think?"

"I think you need to seriously consider all of this, Aster. Because all it takes is one drunken night, and the rest is history. If she breaks your heart…"

"She won't." Aster lay a gentle hand on Grace's knee. "It's not going to come to that. Eden has no interest in me. It's just a holiday with friends, nothing more. I know what I'm doing, okay?"

"If you're sure."

"I…am." Aster hoped she sounded confident as her voice betrayed her. But as Grace looked at her, studying her, she knew Grace saw right through her. "Honestly, I'm sure."

"Be careful."

Discussing Eden with Grace had really helped. Aster had just needed someone who could help her to see sense. To remind her that falling for someone like Eden could only end *one* way. With heartbreak. Thankfully, Grace would always give it to her straight.

"Anyway, enough about me." Aster waved off Grace's concern, it was all she could do. Because while everything Grace had said was absolutely true, Aster still wished things could have been different. "How's life living with Mia?"

Grace grinned as she sunk back against the cushions, that familiar twinkle of love in her eyes. "Oh, where to begin…"

10

Aster grinned as she moved through the swathes of people on the dance floor. A week on from telling Grace everything, she felt less inclined to seek Eden out at any given opportunity. She'd also made a promise to herself that Eden was low on her list of priorities. Not in terms of friendship, but she was kicking all thoughts of her in any other way from her mind. Eden was her boss only; it should remain that way.

And the benefit of coming to the club midweek was that Eden wouldn't be here. There wasn't a single world in which she would drink on a school night, so Aster had freedom over the entire bar tonight. Not that Eden would care if she *was* here. But Aster couldn't focus when her boss was around. It felt wrong to flirt with other women when the one woman she'd once wanted was in the same room as her.

She moved towards the bar, checking the clock on the back wall. Esme, the bartender and her date for the night, was about to finish her shift. They'd spoken over the weekend, made plans for during the unexpected Wednesday team meet up, and now here she was. Ready to hopefully spark something between them.

Because she needed *something* to spark with *someone* soon. The longer she was hung up on Eden, the worse it would surely be. And in the two and a half months that she'd known Eden Kline, Aster had come to realise that she was only torturing herself. Eden, as beautiful as she may be, was entirely oblivious.

"Hey," Esme said, removing her badge from her shirt. "Let me change quickly and then I'll be back."

"Sure. I'll be around and about."

Esme smiled, nodding as she brushed past Aster. Esme seemed nice whenever they spoke on the phone, and she didn't come across as someone who would mess Aster around. *That* was just what she needed. Fun and easy.

Aster turned, watching Esme walk away, only for her eyes to land on her best friend. Grace hadn't known if she could make it tonight, something about meeting with Mia's brother, but Aster was certainly happy to see her.

"Aster Bennett! Have I just caught you checking out one of the ladies?"

Aster grinned. "You have. And you'll be pleased to know that she's my date tonight."

Grace wrapped her arms around Aster, then pulled back and studied her eyes. "Really? You're serious?"

"Don't sound so surprised. I'm not that bad at this, am I?"

Grace gave her a knowing look. "You know that's not what I'm talking about. But you know…with what we discussed when you came to mine?"

"That is all in the past," Aster said quietly. "For my own mental health and because it was a ridiculous thought to begin with."

"So, you're not into her anymore?" Grace arched a brow, one hand on her hip. "Don't lie to me. I want the truth."

"I wouldn't say I'm *not* into Eden, but I'm getting there. It's only been a week since I spoke to you, but the next morning I felt better for it. When I got into work, I felt different."

"Different how?"

Aster shrugged. "I don't know exactly. But I do realise that I'm wasting my time. And you were right, I don't want to get hurt. And especially not by Eden of all people."

"Then I wish you well with tonight's endeavour." Grace winked, squeezing Aster's shoulder. "You know I want the best for you. I'm glad you've realised that it's not Eden."

"No, I know." Aster lowered her eyes as Grace turned and walked through the crowd of people milling about. In her heart, she would drop everything and *anyone* for Eden, but it simply wasn't to be. And she couldn't hold onto something that was unobtainable. It wasn't realistic.

"Hey, mate." Dom nudged Aster's shoulder, grinning. "See anything you like tonight?"

"I…have a date."

Dom's eyebrows rose with surprise, and then she swigged her drink. "So, everything you told Blair is over and done with?"

Aster scoffed, scanning the room for Blair. She could throttle her. "She told you?"

"Of course she did. She's my fiancée."

That made sense. If the shoe were on the other foot, Aster would one hundred percent expect her partner to be honest. So long as Dom didn't let it slip, everything would be okay. "You won't say anything, will you?"

"No, mate. That's not my style. Your secret's safe with me."

"T-thanks." Aster's stomach swirled with anxiety. She'd never been in this position before and now that Dom knew, she felt like the ultimate fool. The more people who knew about her feelings for Eden, the more likely it was that the team would find out. And while Aster could deal with being the butt of their jokes, she would *never* want Eden to be subjected to that. "I'll bet you two had a good laugh at my expense, didn't you?"

"Quite the opposite actually. Blair felt sorry for you when you told her. But she was also concerned about Eden, which I'm sure you can understand."

Aster nodded.

"I mean, we could have both told you to go for it, but I've never gotten the impression that Eden is gay, mate. With Blair it was kinda obvious, but Eden is the total opposite."

"I know she's not gay. I was letting my thoughts get the better of me. But that's over now. I have a date tonight, and I'm happy. Eden is a good friend who I don't want to lose."

"Good for you." Dom smiled. "I hope it all works out for you. I'd better go and find Blair before she threatens to divorce me again."

"You're not even married yet."

"Oh, she's still threatened to divorce me before the day comes." Dom laughed, shaking her head. "Women, eh?"

"Y-yeah."

Eden rushed through the doorway of the club, lowering her umbrella as the rain pelted the pavement. Tonight wasn't supposed to be spent at a bar. She should have been home with a cuppa and the worst TV imaginable, but Blair had twisted her arm earlier when she explained that tonight was more of a meeting between the team and their new manager than a regular night out.

So, here she was, standing in the doorway to a club in the pissing down rain. Blair owed her one. And she would make sure her best friend knew that once she was inside.

Eden shoved her umbrella into the stand near the door, shaking the rain from her knee length coat. She spied Blair at the bar, rushing to catch her before she placed her order. "Hey! I'll have a large white wine since you've dragged me out in this weather."

"Nice to see you too, bestie." Blair grinned that stupid grin she always wore when she got her own way. "One large white wine, coming up."

"And I want another after it," Eden said, glancing around the dancefloor. Truth be told, she was looking for one person in particular. "Everyone here?"

"Yep. The whole team. Which is surprising since half of them said they couldn't be arsed showing up."

"You said they have a new manager?"

Blair nodded in the direction of a tall woman with cropped hair. She looked nice enough. "That's her. *Zoe*. Mark had other commitments, so he handed the team off to her."

"Well, I'm sure Zoe will be welcomed with open arms."

"Mmhmm. I'm sure she will." Blair rolled her eyes. "She's gorgeous. I'm sure they'll *all* want their arms around her."

"Maybe they will." Eden shrugged.

"No, that's not what you're supposed to say. Because what if Dom falls for her? What if *she* falls for Dom? She's the star striker, and I cannot for one second think about the possibility of 'extra practice' and all that shit."

Eden pressed a hand to Blair's shoulder. "You're not serious…"

"Deadly."

"Blair, Dom is so in love with you that it's actually sickening at times. I mean, how could you even *think* she'd do something like that to you?"

"I don't mean that it would be intentional," Blair said, turning to face Eden with a large glass of wine. "But you never know. I'm way past my prime. Dom could fall for *anyone* at *any time*."

And Eden knew that was the truth about most people. But not Dom. She was thinking about her own recent experiences. "Do you think that's possible? For someone to fall for *anyone* when they least expect it?"

"I think it's perfectly possible." Blair guided Eden towards a table, sitting down with her own glass of wine. Eden sat beside her, confused by Blair's sudden worries. "I mean, you could fall in love with the woman behind the bar. Anything is possible."

"Well, I think that's unlikely. I'm not attracted to the woman behind the bar."

"But it could happen. You never know."

"I wonder if people actually do that." Eden knew she should have kept that thought to herself. Aster wasn't here tonight; there was no use thinking about her. "No, I don't suppose they do."

"Do what?"

"Fall for someone they never thought they'd fall for."

Blair eyed Eden suspiciously. "*Anything* is possible. And that's that."

Eden held up a hand. "Okay. I'm only saying."

Silence settled between them, Blair focusing on her glass as the team sat around with Zoe. Eden couldn't comprehend what Blair had just said. Dom would never do anything to hurt her. And in Eden's opinion, Blair was ten times what Zoe was. "You good?" She settled a hand on top of Blair's. "You're not thinking she would do something like that, are you?"

"No." Blair smiled weakly. "But they don't usually have new people come into the fold. And Zoe is going to take a shine to Dom; she's the best player."

"And for all we know, Zoe is in a relationship already. Married with kids. Maybe not even gay."

Blair snorted. "She's gay."

How did Blair know that? She was about to ask her best friend when she saw Aster on the dance floor. Her pulse quickened. Aster looked exceptional tonight. *Wow. I need to find a hobby.* Eden cleared her throat, shaking her head slightly as she focused on her glass of wine. "Well, I know Dom would never do anything to hurt you. And you're a fool if you think otherwise."

"I know she wouldn't. I'm being stupid." Blair straightened, crossing her legs as she turned her attention to Eden. "So, how's work?"

"Okay, I guess. But Aster has been a little quieter than usual."

"Oh?"

"And those Saturday nights we've been spending together came to an abrupt end." Eden frowned. Why *had* that happened? "But I guess you were right. As usual. I'm her boss and that's that."

"Well, I know she's here tonight on a date. So maybe that has something to do with the Saturday cancellations."

Those words cut deep through Eden. It hadn't occurred to her that Aster would one day be unavailable. But it made total sense. Aster was a dream. God, she'd certainly been Eden's dream. "O-oh. Well, that's nice."

"Are you okay?" Blair narrowed her eyes. "You seem a bit shocked by that."

"Shocked? No. Aster is lovely; she deserves to find a partner. I hope it all goes well for her." Eden swallowed down the emotion in her throat, her stomach lurching at knowing she couldn't even entertain the idea of them together any longer. But it didn't matter. Aster wasn't looking in her direction…and she never had been. "I'm going to use the bathroom. Can I get you anything from the bar on the way back?"

"Are you working tomorrow?" Blair asked.

She was supposed to be, but something told Eden she wouldn't leave her bed tomorrow. "No. I have the day off."

"Then I believe some midweek shots are appropriate."

The team meeting had ended no sooner than it started, but that made life easier for Eden. It meant she could chat with everyone, avoiding the space Aster was sharing with her date. Upon closer inspection, Eden had discovered that it was the bartender who worked here that was accompanying Aster this evening. That only made this all worse. Because not only did Eden feel dreadful seeing them together, it meant she wasn't on an even footing. This was Aster's date's territory, not Eden's.

But she'd taken her mind off it by dancing with the team and Blair. This wasn't her first outing here, but it could be her last. If Aster fell for the woman she currently had her arms around, Eden wouldn't step foot inside this bar again. She couldn't face seeing it all play out in front of her.

"Hey, Eden." Fi approached her, a fresh bottle of beer in her hand. "How's your night going?"

"Okay. I was catching my breath before I went back into the pack." Eden threw her thumb over her shoulder, directing Fi towards the team. "How's the new manager?"

"She's…nice. I don't think she's going to take any shit from us."

Eden laughed. "She's going to have her hands full with you lot. Does she know what she's getting herself into?"

Fi smirked, edging a little closer to Eden. "Maybe. But she's not much of a worry for me right now."

Wow. Fi had intense eyes. And yes, Eden knew all about the player she was, but they seemed to pull you in unexpectedly. "N-no?"

"Wanna dance?" Fi held out her hand, grinning when Eden took it.

"Sure. Everyone else seems preoccupied, so why not?"

"Don't worry, I'll keep you busy." Fi led Eden onto the dance floor and away from the team. They moved towards a less chaotic area, Fi's hand instantly falling to Eden's waist. "You seem to be around a lot lately."

Eden smiled, moving to the beat of the music. "Blair keeps dragging me along. I should say no, but she's very hard to turn down."

"Oh, I know." Fi grinned, stepping closer.

As the music changed, Rita Ora's *Only Want You* now playing, Fi placed her beer on a nearby table, her other hand now settling on Eden's waist. It didn't mean anything. She was simply dancing with one of the players…the same way she had since the meeting finished.

She caught Aster's eye as Fi pulled their bodies flush, a hint of sadness sitting within them. She offered Aster the slightest of smiles, unsure if that was okay to do now that she had a woman in her life, and lowered her gaze. God, it was painful seeing Aster with someone else. Much more painful than Eden had anticipated.

"You know," Fi paused, her lips moving closer to Eden's ear, "there's a lot of women in here who have their eye on you."

Eden found Aster staring at her again, her eyes teary. Was she…upset?

When Eden considered moving towards Aster, her heart crumbled in her chest as Aster's date turned her head and kissed her.

Oh, no. That pain in Eden's chest was intense. It left her breathless. Unable to take her eyes off what was playing out in front of her, Eden felt a swell of emotion in the pit of her stomach.

"Did you hear what I said?" Fi's lips brushed Eden's ear, but it did nothing for her whatsoever.

"I'm flattered, but I'm not interested." Her voice sounded like it didn't belong, as though Eden was underwater.

Fi pulled back. "No?"

"No. I'm not looking for—"

Eden was suddenly grabbed from behind, Blair now coming face-to-face with Fi. "Don't even fucking try it," Blair spat. "She's not interested. And even if she was, *you* would be the *last* person on her list."

"Back up, honey." Fi smirked, throwing a wink in Eden's

direction. "Eden is a big girl. She seemed happy enough with my hands all over her."

Eden frowned. Was this a game to Fi? God, she could barely keep up when she was around the team. Honestly, it was all too much drama for Eden.

Blair grabbed Eden's wrist, pulling her through the crowd. "Outside, now!"

Eden almost fell out the door as Blair forced her through it, a look of complete disgust on her features when Eden turned around. "What the hell is your problem?"

Blair pointed towards her own chest. "My problem? Are you fucking serious?"

"That was rude. And obnoxious. I don't know what's going on with you tonight, but I think you need to go home."

"And you seriously need to get a grip of your life. I mean, Fi? Are you for real?"

Eden didn't understand this anger from Blair. Yes, Blair had made a mistake and slept with Fi way back, but Eden wasn't about to fall into the same trap. "I was dancing with her. I'm not sure what the issue is."

"That's not cool you know, Eden." Blair gave her a knowing look. "I know you're here with all of us, but you've been invited. You're a guest. You have no right to play with her feelings like that. It's *not* your place to flirt with the lesbians. Not if it doesn't mean a thing to you."

"What are you talking about?" Eden swayed. She knew she shouldn't have had that last shot. "I'm not playing with anyone's feelings."

"Do you know?" Blair asked. "Do you know and you're trying to cause a reaction?"

Did Eden know what? This was all…confusing. "I don't know where you're going with this, but you've lost me."

"You need to back off. Maybe stop coming here with me. I shouldn't have invited you tonight."

That hurt. It really hurt.

"You know what, forget it. Forget all of this." Eden needed her belongings and then she would be on her way home. "You've changed since you met Dom. And you know I love you both, but I don't like this. You're not you anymore."

"I think you need to take a look at yourself, Ede's. You're the one throwing yourself at people in a gay bar. I told you not to push it, and I told you she was into you. But you wouldn't listen."

"What? You've never once told me Fi was into me. And correct me if I'm wrong, but she's into *everyone*."

"I…I'm not talking about Fi." Blair cast her eyes on the floor.

"Okay, then I'm even more lost than I was before."

Blair threw her hands up. "It's Aster, okay? She's trying so hard to not be into you, and God love her, it's breaking my heart."

Eden's world stopped momentarily. They'd been here before with this conversation, but it had never been so intense. So… confrontational. "You keep saying this, but if you opened your fucking eyes, you'd see that Aster has a date."

"And if *you* opened *your* fucking eyes, you'd see that she is trying to protect herself and let you go."

No. This was complete rubbish. "No. That's not right."

"Except it is. She told me a few weeks ago." Blair swallowed hard. "I know I should have told you, but I thought it would all fizzle out."

"Well, it clearly has." Eden scoffed. "She's on a date with someone."

Blair's right eye twitched as she focused on Eden. "You seem bothered by that."

"I'm not. Why would I be?"

"You're not being honest with me. And if you can't do that with your best friend…then there's no hope for any of this." Blair walked away, turning back momentarily. "You need to decide what you want. If it's Aster, you need to move your arse and stop denying how you feel. I've asked you on multiple occasions, but you keep shooting me down. I know you though, and I think you forget that."

"Blair."

"I don't want to know anymore." Blair held up both hands. "But if you continue with this, you're going to break her heart and lose the one thing you want all at once. And to think I was worried about *her* hurting *you*. I've been trying to protect you because you're sweet, and my closest friend, and I know that you'd feel dreadful if she got too close and you had to let her down."

"Blair, I—"

"Go home, sweetie. This place really isn't where you should be."

11

Eden cleared her throat as Blair welcomed her into her home. Four nights ago, she'd discovered that Aster was attracted to her, but Eden's mind hadn't quite taken control of the fact yet. She'd gotten her handbag and coat and left the club quickly after Blair's little outburst on the street.

And until now, she'd laid low. It seemed easier. Nothing had to be done at the office, and after taking a few days on sick leave, Eden was finally prepared to sit down and talk to Blair. She knew it was too late, Aster was dating another woman, but discussing it could be good for Eden. A kind of closure she hadn't expected she'd need. And if nothing else, Blair may be able to explain why Eden was feeling the way she was.

"Did you want a coffee or something stronger?"

Eden knew she would be wise to insist on something stronger, but she wasn't sure what would come out of her mouth if she had liquid courage.

"Ede's?"

"Coffee is fine, thanks."

Blair popped her head around the wall separating the mostly open plan area. "You in your own head tonight?"

"A bit, yeah." Eden smiled weakly, wringing her hands in her lap. "Nothing that won't blow over, though."

"I'll be in now. Just waiting for the kettle to boil."

"Okay. And, Blair?"

"Mm?" Blair stood in the space between the kitchen and the living room.

"I'm sorry about the other night." Eden offered an apologetic smile.

Blair held up a hand. "I'm not fighting with you. We've been friends for too long. We'll talk in a minute."

Thankful when Blair disappeared back into the kitchen, she flopped back on the couch, sighing. Could she be honest with her best friend about the feelings she had? They'd been through so much together, but this? A possible change in Eden's sexuality? No, this was new territory.

"Dom was gutted she couldn't be here tonight. But with the cup game coming up, she couldn't miss training."

"Oh, it's fine. I'm sure she's sick of seeing my face."

Blair lowered the cups to the table, taking Eden's face in her hands. "It's a very beautiful face. Don't talk rubbish."

"How are you both getting on? Still in the honeymoon stage, so to speak?" Eden needed a moment—normalcy—before she laid everything bare.

"I don't know," Blair said, relaxing beside Eden and curling her legs to the side. "I just know that all of this feels a million miles from what I ever knew. But I wouldn't change it. It gets overwhelming at times, you know, realising that I'm going to marry a woman after being with…well, *him*."

"But it's what you want, right?" Eden knew it was pointless asking; Blair's happiness was written all over her face. "I mean, I know it is, but Dom makes you happy, doesn't she?"

"Incredibly."

"When did you first know you were a lesbian?" Eden asked,

shocked that she'd actually gone there with that question. Blair quirked an eyebrow, smirking. "Sorry, that was rude."

"Not at all. I've always known I was into women. Since I was probably around fifteen…give or take a year either side."

"That early on in life?" Eden suddenly felt deflated. If Blair had known since her teens, Eden was obviously not attracted to women. She was 42. She should have known long before now. "That's…wow."

"Everyone is different," Blair said, reading Eden's mind. "Some know early, some discover it later on in life, and some never come to terms with how they feel…"

"It's fascinating, don't you think?"

Blair shrugged, cradling her coffee in her lap. "It's not something I think about. Now that I have Dom, I don't need to think about what I'm missing anymore."

"But you did? You thought about it while you were married to Barrett?" Eden could barely stomach his name. The way he'd treated Blair, how he'd abused her over the twenty years they were married, she could kill him with her bare hands.

"Almost daily," Blair said quietly. "It was torture for the most part, but I had to keep it in my mind that one day my situation would change. I mean, Mum never really recovered from discovering I was gay before I married Barrett, so it didn't matter when I called her to tell her I was with Dom. You know the reaction she had, but it's her own issue to deal with. If she can't be happy for her daughter, that's her own tough shit."

"Oh, could you imagine my mother? I'd never hear the end of it."

"Is this a hypothetical, or?" Blair narrowed her eyes, watching Eden suspiciously.

"Oh, it wasn't anything. I was speaking in terms of parental reactions to that kinda thing."

"Eden, sweetie, I love you to death…"

"I know. You're forever telling me this."

Blair held up a hand. "But something is going on with you lately, and you're asking me all these crazy questions and throwing 'imagine ifs' at me...so what's going on? Is this about Aster?"

"What?" Eden snorted, pushing down the desperate need to yell YES! "Why would it have anything to do with Aster? I was simply asking a question."

"Mm. But you never ask things like that, so forgive me for being suspicious. I know I blurted out how Aster felt, but you don't have to feel the same way."

This was a waste of time. Blair would never believe for one second that Eden could be attracted to women. Because she never had been...so why would that suddenly change now? It was way too far-fetched in Eden's mind, so Blair would go into overdrive. "Never mind. Sorry. I was taking an interest. It won't happen again."

"Oh, love. I'm sorry. I wasn't suggesting that it's none of your business. But I know something is going on in that beautiful mind of yours, and I'm worried about you."

"It's okay." Eden turned her watch towards her. She'd only been here for half an hour, but she was thinking of leaving. She couldn't sit here and lie to her best friend, so leaving was the next best thing. "I should head home. Busy day tomorrow."

"What? You haven't touched your coffee."

Eden lowered her eyes, sitting forward on the couch. "I'll finish it and then get out of the way. Dom will be home soon."

"Look at me right now." Blair sat forward, placing a hand on Eden's shoulder, but she couldn't meet her eyes. "Eden?"

Tears welled, her bottom lip close to quivering. "I'm okay." She shrugged Blair's hand from her shoulder, clearing her throat. "I think I need some sleep."

"No. I'm not doing this anymore. If you have something on

your mind, come out and say it. Please, you know I support everything you do."

The words were on the tip of her tongue, but Eden couldn't bring herself to say it. She wasn't ashamed of how she felt about Aster, not at all, but she didn't know how to come to terms with it. It was…not what she expected. "I know you do."

"And I'll always support you. If you told me you wanted to throw yourself out of a plane tomorrow, I wouldn't agree, but I'd support you."

"This is more complicated than that."

"So, talk to me. You helped me through so much when I decided to divorce Barrett. Let me be there for *you* this time."

"Blair…" Eden's voice trembled as she shook her head ever so slightly. She'd never felt so apprehensive about her life or what she wanted before. But it was fear of the unknown that had Eden unable to say the words out loud. And then she looked into Blair's eyes. Eden was safe here. "I-I…I have these feelings for Aster. And I don't know what any of it means. She's so wonderful and genuine a-and…addictive."

"Addictive?"

"God, I can't stop thinking about her. She's constantly on my mind. And I don't know why." Eden took a breath. "And this has nothing to do with how she feels. I'm actually relieved now that I know, but…"

Blair wrapped an arm around Eden, pulling her against her. "Eden, this isn't the end of the world you know."

"None of this makes sense. I've never looked at another woman in my entire life. I mean, I spent years knowing you were gay. You're every woman's dream, so why wasn't I attracted to you?"

"Because that's not how it works."

Eden smiled, wiping a tear from her cheek. "I'm sorry I wasn't into you. It's not that you're not gorgeous, you really are, but—"

"Don't even finish that sentence. We're best friends, sisters, whatever you want to call it. You have no reason to explain anything to me, but you do need to decide how you feel…and what you want."

"Mum would have an aneurysm."

"Your mum isn't the one feeling like this. And I know you watched my mum hit the roof time and time again, but that doesn't mean you'd receive the same treatment. Your parents are much more laid back than mine are."

"But it also doesn't mean they wouldn't freak out, and I don't want to risk that. I have a hard enough relationship with Mum as it is."

Blair turned Eden to face her fully. "I've spent my life watching you grow up with me. You've never been content with who you were with. And maybe I should have questioned that, but it seems to me like this is the first time you're feeling this way."

"It is."

"So do what *you* want to do. If Aster is who you're attracted to, then so be it. You could certainly pick worse people."

"She's sweet."

Blair grinned. "Yeah?"

"When she took a cab home with me from here last weekend, she handed me her jacket outside because she saw that I was cold. Nobody has ever done that for me before. And she told me I looked great." Eden paused, aware that it all sounded a bit sad. "I'm not attracted to her because of those things, but it certainly makes it easier for me. She's just…not like anyone else I've met before."

"When did you know?"

Eden ran a hand through her hair. "The day she came to my office. The first time I met her."

"Sometimes it just happens, love."

"But does it? Really?" Eden wanted to believe that this thing happened all the time, but nothing made any sense.

Deep down, she knew it was the fear of rejection from Aster that had her questioning her feelings. Had it been anyone else, Eden would shrug it off and move forward, but Aster? No, she couldn't stomach the idea of rejection.

Blair ran her thumbs beneath Eden's eyes, focusing fully on her. "Answer me this. Have you ever felt that connection, that attraction, with anyone else? So intense to the point where you think about nothing else?"

"No. I haven't." Eden had never for one second considered that Aster could be the one for her; it didn't seem feasible. But with each word Blair spoke, the support in her voice…perhaps it was possible.

"And what does that tell you?" Blair asked, taking her coffee from the table.

"That I need to get out more. That maybe I'm sexually frustrated."

"No. It tells you that you may have found your person."

Eden's entire body thrummed. Was Blair right? She was gay… she must know. "I'm not sure I'd go that far yet. I barely know her; it could all fall apart."

"It could, you're right. But you won't know that unless you try."

"It's too late."

Blair shook her head and put a supportive hand on Eden's forearm. "It's never too late. You've had the realisation that you're into Aster. She deserves to know."

"Blair, she was on a date. I can't just walk into her life, lacking in probably *everything* she wants, and expect her to take me in her arms."

"Honey…"

"I've never felt this way about anyone, and when I saw her with her date, I didn't know what to do."

"I completely get that, but Fi?"

"You think I would have gone there with Fi? I was dancing, she got handsy, and before I knew it, you were dragging me away by my bra strap."

"Sorry. I panicked." Blair offered a lopsided grin. "Aster is trying so hard to not like you. When I saw her watching you with Fi, I had to step in. And you can tell me it's not my business, but I couldn't put Aster through it any longer."

Eden exhaled a shaky breath. "You're sure you're right about this? She feels the same way?"

"She does. The poor girl doesn't know what to do for the best."

Eden wrung her hands. "I feel as though I've missed my chance."

"Maybe give it some time. See how things are at work." Blair rested her coffee cup against her chin.

"You're right." Blair always was. At times it was annoying, but today her best friend had been a godsend. "I need to be absolutely sure."

"You do."

Eden never wanted to hurt Aster. Not in a million years. "Do you think I can do this?"

Blair grinned. "I've never seen you like this. You're terrified, but I can see the excitement in your eyes, too. And if Aster makes you feel that way, I'd say you can *definitely* do it."

"This isn't something meaningless for me. And I know you believe that, but do you think others will?"

"I think people will always have an opinion whatever you do."

"True." Eden relaxed against the couch, feeling entirely different knowing she had Blair's support.

"Do you want me to speak to Aster?"

Eden had to find the courage to do this herself; Blair couldn't hold her hand on this one. "No. I'll do it in my own time."

"Sure?"

"Yes. I'm not rushing this. When the time comes, I'll know."

Blair snuggled closer to Eden, sighing. "Yes, you will. Now… tell me all about how she makes you feel."

Eden's heart thundered. "God, I don't even know where to begin."

"It's intense, isn't it?"

"Very," Eden said. "I, uh…I made the foolish decision to invite her to share my room with me at Pride." Eden still couldn't believe she'd done that. "I don't think it's a good idea, but she's agreed, so what do I do about that?"

"Share the room with her. Couples are made or broken based on a first holiday together."

"We're not a couple," Eden deadpanned.

"But you could be…in time." Blair smiled, sighing. "God, I hope it does come to something and works out for you."

"Why?"

"Because I'm tired of seeing you alone or unhappy in a relationship. You deserve so much more than that, Ede's. I want you to be as happy as I am, and if Aster is the *woman* to do that for you, I'm thrilled."

"I thought you were going to tell me I was being ridiculous."

"I can't believe you were worried about telling me. I'm the most open person you know." Blair punched Eden in the arm, laughing. "Some best friend I am, huh?"

"It wasn't about that. I'm just dealing with a lot of feelings, and I didn't know how to even say the words. But I have to admit, I'm feeling better for it already."

"I'm going to invite Aster over tomorrow night. Does that work for you?"

Eden sat confused.

"Obviously, I'm going to invite you over too. I'll have Dom text Aster…"

"Oh, I don't know. She probably isn't interested anymore."

"She is." Blair held up her hands. "Don't, for one second, think that she's not."

"Blair..."

"I'll cook. Aster won't know that the team isn't invited. And then *you* will show up. Perfect."

"You can't lure her in like that. I'd kill you if you did that to me."

"Would I ever *lure* someone in?" Blair feigned offence, splaying her hand across her chest. "I'm disappointed you think that of me."

"I've known you since I was four. I think I know *exactly* what you're capable of by now. You can't pull the wool over my eyes."

Blair got to her feet and motioned for Eden to join her in the kitchen, resting back against the counter after she'd disposed of her coffee cup. "If nothing else, it'll give you a feel for what's what. You two are only ever together when the team is around or at work. But this will be just the four of us. Some adult conversation and good food. Please say you'll come?"

"Of course I will. I wouldn't miss out on a home-cooked meal."

"That's the spirit." Blair clapped, excitement overtaking her.

As much as Eden loved her reaction, it didn't change anything for her. Aster may not have the slightest interest in her anymore, and then this worry and panic would all be for nothing. "God, I feel totally up the wall with all this. It's really thrown me."

"I'm not surprised. But you have me, your favourite lesbian, and I'll be with you every step of the way." Blair stepped forward, hugging Eden. And then she pulled back. "Well, except when you find yourself in bed with her. I'll see myself out at that point."

"Don't put thoughts like that in my head."

"Eden Kline, you minx!"

Eden blushed. She couldn't believe she was discussing another woman with Blair. She certainly wouldn't have said that was her plan recently. In fact, relationships were the last thing on her mind, as always. But now, with Aster in the picture, life felt entirely different. "Let me do this slowly. I don't want to fuck it all up."

"I want so much happiness for you. Give the rest of them the middle finger."

12

Aster stared down at her phone, frowning as she read the text message from Dom back to herself. It was a wonderful offer, but Aster had no idea why she'd been invited to have dinner with Blair and Dom this evening. The rest of the team had to be involved, surely, but it was short notice, and Aster didn't take too kindly to that.

I should probably make an effort. She pushed the door open that led to the hallway, still staring down at her phone as she pressed the call button for the lift. She had an hour to herself, so she was headed out with her camera for some fresh air. The Three Graces needed some new snaps, and the dock was looking appealing this afternoon with the sun shining down on it. She would sit down to lunch there.

The bell dinged, and Aster walked straight inside, colliding with a body as she felt the suspension in the lift greet her. She looked up, startled. "Oh, I'm so sorry, Eden."

"That's okay," Eden said, taking a slight step back. "I was in a world of my own, too."

Aster flushed when her eyes landed on Eden's cleavage. It wasn't intentional; her boss was simply taller than her. Even more so in heels. "Well." She cleared her throat. "I'm headed out for an hour before I finalise the images from the Carmichael wedding. I've spoken with Jules, and she's happy with everything I've sent over."

"You're very efficient."

Aster couldn't help but notice how alluring Eden's eyes were this afternoon. If she stared long enough, she was certain she'd get lost in them. "Just doing my job." Her voice was hoarse as she spoke, but to hell with it. Her boss was drop dead gorgeous. "Can I bring you anything back?"

Eden glanced at her watch. "I have some free time. I could join you?"

"I...wouldn't say no to that offer." *Careful! That tone could be considered flirtatious.* "Like, it beats sitting alone in a bistro or whatever." Okay, being cool didn't suit Aster. She would take note of that.

"I don't want to intrude on your free time, so I can step off now and let you get on with your lunch hour." Eden offered a small smile, taking a step towards the door.

"No." Aster planted her feet in front of the open doors, aware that she probably looked slightly idiotic. They hadn't spoken since last week, Eden had unexpectedly taken time off work, but it was now Monday, and Aster knew she couldn't avoid her boss forever. "Sorry. I'd like you to join me for lunch. If you still want to."

"I do." Eden smiled, the lift doors closing. "Did you have somewhere in mind?"

"The little Italian on the dock?"

Eden licked her lips. "Sounds like my kinda lunch."

"You're into Italian then?"

"Very much so," Eden said, gripping her handbag on her shoulder. She wore a cream skirt suit, the colour complimenting her olive skin tone. "Who isn't?"

"I should cook for you sometime." Aster needed to curb her

thoughts, but they were flowing out of her without a care in the world. Why, on God's great earth, would Eden possibly want to have dinner with her? And at her own flat? *Stop falling over yourself for this woman.* Just because it hadn't worked out with Esme didn't mean Aster should turn her attention back to Eden. But it was hard not to. Eden was, well…Eden.

"That sounds lovely, but I'm not sure your girlfriend would approve. I expect your evenings are dedicated to her. A-as they should be."

"Oh, that didn't work out." Aster wouldn't explain why. Doing so would mean telling Eden how she felt about her.

Eden shifted slightly; her eyes glued to the metal doors. "I'm sorry to hear that."

"It's no big deal."

And then Eden turned around, that soft smile Aster loved playing on her lips. "I can't remember the last time someone cooked for me. Maybe we could get together one evening and discuss upcoming events that require your services."

"I'd offer you some fine food tonight, but I got the strangest text message from Dom a few minutes ago." The lift reached the ground floor, the doors opening. "I've been invited to dinner tonight. I should decline because I have stuff to do at home, but that's kinda rude, isn't it?"

"Oh, you're going tonight? Me too." They walked side by side as they left the building, taking a right towards the dock. "I was thinking of getting there around 7. Blair doesn't like it when we arrive too early; it puts her all out of sorts."

"Maybe we could share a cab? No use paying double…"

"That works for me."

"Who else is invited? I'm assuming the team will be there. I don't know why Dom would invite me but not her friends."

"You're not her friend?"

Aster shook her head, moving slightly closer to Eden. When

she did, she caught her sweet perfume. "No, I am. But the team is her base, not me."

"Right. I see. Well, I've no idea who is going. I was told to be there this evening."

"Then I suppose we should do as we're told and be there."

"Mmhmm." Eden smirked, her soft features slightly sunkissed from the early hot weather they'd had.

Aster slowed her pace, clearing her throat. "So, I noticed you haven't been at the office since last week. I was going to text you to see if you were okay, but I didn't know if you wanted to hear from me. I'm sure the rest of the staff checked up on you…"

"I'm fine. Wasn't feeling well." Eden smiled, but it didn't reach her eyes. Something was wrong.

"Right, well, it's lovely to see you back." Aster almost told Eden that she'd missed her, but that wasn't appropriate. "Lunch wasn't the same without you."

Again, another slight smile from Eden but nothing like Aster was used to.

"You left the club kinda suddenly last week. I thought you'd fallen out with Blair."

"She…didn't like the idea of me dancing with Fi." A slight blush settled on Eden's cheeks. "But they have history, so I understand. We've cleared things up."

"Yeah," Aster said, running a hand through her hair. She didn't like the idea of it either. "I *was* surprised to see you dancing with her. But it's not like you were going to go home with her." Aster laughed nervously, shaking her head. If she didn't make light of it, she was likely to vomit all over Eden's expensive heels. "You know what I mean."

Eden stopped, an eyebrow quirked. "You're rambling."

"Sorry. It's just that Fi is very unpredictable. I'm sure Blair was only protecting you. I mean, if she'd done what she usually does…kissed you…"

God, that thought weighed heavy in the pit of Aster's stomach. In a world where Eden was dancing with Fi...Aster couldn't think about it. She'd done so for days, and at more than one point, it had brought her to tears. Because Aster wanted to be that person. *Her* hands on Eden's hips, *her* lips brushing her ear. Seeing Fi with Eden had impacted Aster more than she thought it would. Honestly, she was devastated as it unfolded before her eyes. And as Eden was pulled from the bar, it was at that point that Aster decided to call it a night with Esme. She couldn't lead her on for the sake of trying to forget Eden. Because even though she knew she should move on, it was becoming increasingly clear that she couldn't.

"What would you have done?" Eden pinned Aster with her stare, one hand on her hip.

Okay, Aster hadn't expected that question. Eden was behaving strangely today. *Think! Think!* "I'd have told you to run a mile. Once Fi sets her sights on someone, she usually gets what she wants."

"Well, Fi isn't my type." Something in Eden's eyes changed. They darkened slightly, sending Aster's head into a spin. If Aster focused hard enough, she would say that Eden was mentally undressing her. *Sweet. Fucking. Jesus.*

"R-right."

And then Eden cleared her throat, gripping her handbag tighter. "Okay, so lunch. And then we'll arrange this evening?"

"Y-yes. Sounds like a good day to me."

The cab came to a stop outside Blair's gated home. Aster rushed from the car, urgently tugging Eden's door open and holding it while she stepped out. Once she was safely on the pavement, Aster turned to the driver and paid the fare. She turned back around to find Eden watching her, smiling. "What?"

"You have lovely manners." Eden couldn't recall the last time someone had held the door for her. Men…didn't do that kind of thing anymore. At least, not the ones who gravitated towards Eden.

"Sorry, it's probably annoying, but I was raised to have respect for people. And women deserve respect more than anyone else, so…"

Eden held out her arm, ushering Aster closer. It may be a bold move, but she wasn't fighting how she felt anymore. She wouldn't rush into anything, but she wouldn't hold back either. Aster Bennett made her feel good, so she would enjoy it. And knowing that she was available only stirred everything up inside Eden. "Let's walk in together, shall we?"

Aster tipped her chin slightly, sliding her arm through Eden's as though they were about to enter a black-tie event. "Yes, madam."

Eden couldn't contain the grin that spread across her mouth. "Did anyone ever tell you how nice it is having you around?"

"N-no." Though it was dark, Eden caught Aster blushing. "Thanks."

"And I don't know about you, but I'm looking forward to this evening. It'll be nice to get to know one another outside of a work setting. I mean, I know we go out to clubs together, but it's not really the same thing." *That wasn't too much, was it?*

"Yeah. You're right. We should get to know one another outside work. But I hope you realise that doing so means we'll be holiday shopping together for bikinis before we know it."

"We…could," Eden chanced, aware that she was likely overstepping. She didn't do humour and sarcasm as well as Aster did. "Although, I'm sure you have your own friends to do that stuff with."

"Hey, I'm open to the idea if you are. Maybe you could give me some tips on what's hot and what's not."

"Tips?"

"You know the trends. I don't."

Eden side glanced at Aster as she pressed the bell. God, she was striking. "Oh, I don't know. I'd say you were looking pretty dapper this evening, Miss Bennett."

"Yeah?" Aster straightened, her smile wide as they waited to be greeted by Blair and Dom. "Maybe I need to find someone who appreciates it then."

"People don't appreciate it?" Eden frowned. "Why is that?"

"No idea, but I've spent most of my life single, so I'm cocking it all up somewhere along the way." Aster slid a hand into her pocket, her navy-blue blazer and shirt *very* appealing this evening. "But at least you like it. That's something. If nothing else, I have my boss' approval."

"Ugh. Can you not call me that when we're outside the office? Actually, don't call me it at all." It had never bothered Eden before, but when Aster said it…very much so.

"No?"

Eden shook her head. "I hate it. It doesn't have a very pleasant ring to it. Call me Eden, and that's the end of it."

"Yes, Eden." Aster winked, sending Eden's heart rate through the roof.

God, why is it suddenly really hot out here? And where the hell are they? Eden rang the doorbell again, tapping her heel against the Indian stone floor.

"Think they're busy?" Aster wiggled her eyebrows.

And then Eden's blood travelled south, imagining getting busy with Aster. "I…don't know."

"Why are you blushing? Us lot are forever having sex." Aster visibly winced. "Except for me. I'm not having sex as often as half the lesbians around here." She pushed out her bottom lip, and then burst into laughter. "Which works for me."

"The team like to…put it around, don't they?" Perhaps that wasn't the right thing to say, but Eden had been shocked when Blair told her how many of the players had slept with one another as well as whoever they picked up on a night out.

"Mmhmm. And since I'm only a spectator, I thankfully don't get tarred with that brush."

"Good. You don't look like the kind of woman to sleep around."

"I have to be honest with you…" Aster paused. "You had me worried last week when you were with Fi. But I get the impression you're similar to me…"

"How so?" *This would be interesting.*

"I prefer to connect with the right person. It's important to me."

"You're absolutely right."

"And if that fails, and I want to get my kicks, I have a box full of toys under the bed."

Eden's skin had to be hot to the touch; there was no way only her core temperature was rising. Every word Aster spoke had her on pins, wanting to hear more. She didn't even have a response to the Fi comment. It was the least of her concerns.

And then the door flew open suddenly, Blair clearing her throat as she smiled. "Come on in. Sorry about the delay. Issue with the oven."

Eden narrowed her eyes, disappointed when Aster unlinked their arms. But then Aster placed a hand on the small of Eden's back, gentle and warm, and led her inside. *That* felt incredible. "It's fine. We've been talking shit out here for ten minutes."

"Oh, how terrible," Blair laughed. Eden could swear her best friend was breathless.

Eden's eyes flitted around Blair's home. "Dom not around?"

"She's…finishing getting ready." Blair looked away, her cheeks red. She'd always been a terrible liar.

"Liar," Eden whispered, spotting something on the stairs. "You may want to grab your lingerie from the bannister."

Blair's eyes widened as she suddenly backed up, almost tripping over her own feet. "Be right back. Make yourselves at home. But behave."

Eden's mouth fell open as she glanced between Blair and Aster. Did her best friend have no shame whatsoever? "Sorry about her."

"Perfectly fine. They're both good fun. Should I make us a drink since Blair has *other* things to take care of? Would that be okay?"

"Yes, please." Eden swallowed as she watched Aster move around the kitchen, her black ankle-grazer jeans and pristine white Vans complementing her casual look. But it wasn't her look that Eden was admiring. It was just Aster. All of her.

"Okay, red or white?" Aster spun around, her blonde hair falling into place.

Aware that she'd been caught staring, Eden moved towards the stools around the island and took a seat. Perhaps talking to Blair about all of this hadn't been the wisest decision in the world. When she kept it to herself, it didn't feel so intense. She'd fully expected Blair to tell her she was out of her mind, but the response had been positive, and it only encouraged Eden to want more. Throw in the intimate dinner, and Eden didn't know how to feel about anything. Yes, Blair had run it by her first, but Eden felt dreadful for duping Aster. *I want her to myself.* Was that such a terrible thing?

"Eden?"

"R-red. Sorry." She waved a hand. "World of my own again."

Aster poured a glass of wine for Eden, rounding the counter and handing it over. She stepped a little closer, dipping her head towards Eden's ear. Aster's warm breath had Eden's body on heightened alert. "Why are we the only two people here?"

Because I don't want anyone else to have their hands, eyes, or attention on you. "I-I don't know." Eden still couldn't bring herself to tell Aster that it was a plan of Blair's. It all felt wrong when she thought of it like that. "Maybe the others are arriving later."

"Yeah. Maybe."

Dinner was exceptional, but Aster didn't expect anything less from Blair. From the most incredible goat cheese and pear salad to start, the best lamb to ever enter her mouth for the main, and a salted caramel bombe for dessert, Aster felt as though she was ending her evening at a Michelin star restaurant. Blair had gone above and beyond to make sure Eden and Aster had everything they could need.

"That was…amazing." Aster relaxed back into an outside chair, the patio heaters warming her face. "Thank you, Blair."

"Any time," Blair said, her hand resting on Dom's thigh as she tipped her wine glass towards Aster. "I miss doing this, so I'm glad you could both make it."

"The team didn't want to come tonight?" Aster wasn't complaining. It was nice to have some adult conversation. And with less people around, being with Eden felt much more intimate.

"Oh, I didn't invite them." Blair said, matter-of-factly. "I don't know about the rest of you, but they don't strike me as the kind who enjoy dinner parties."

Okay, Blair made a good point. "No, they don't."

"And I love them, each and every one, but tonight I wanted something small and quiet. I'm sure I'll never hear the end of it once they get wind of it, but I'm not concerned."

"Hey, this is your place. You invite who you like. It's not as though you don't open your home to them enough as it is."

"Aster is right," Eden cut in, sitting beside Aster. As the breeze carried Eden's perfume towards her, Aster found herself inhaling deeply *but* inconspicuously.

She chanced a look in Eden's direction, immediately regretting it when her eyes landed on Eden's thighs. She had to stop looking at her boss that way. It was unprofessional, and she was fairly certain Eden wouldn't appreciate it. *What the hell is wrong with you?* She'd done so well until today.

Aster had never been the kind of woman to drool over anyone. She respected women's bodies and what they chose to wear, but Eden had a way of captivating her without Aster knowing how.

"And I've had many gorgeous meals cooked for me by Blair, but this is your first time. So, how was it?" Eden asked, her eyes landing on Aster. They were intense, alluring, and bloody gorgeous.

"It was probably the best meal I've had in a long time. Onto a winner, mate." Aster winked in Dom's direction, gaining a grin from her friend. "Do you watch and let Blair get on with it?"

"Oh, absolutely. I'd never ruin dinner." Dom held up a hand. "I know when I'm not needed, and dinner is always one of those times. I'd touch it and burn it."

"Aster likes to cook," Eden spoke suddenly. "And she's offered to make dinner for me sometime."

"Oh." The lift of Blair's eyebrows didn't go unnoticed by Aster, nor did the wink Dom threw in her direction. "That'll be nice."

Aster's cheeks immediately heated. Did that sound weird to Blair? She'd confided in her, but it was something she was beginning to regret. Aster didn't appreciate the look Blair was giving her. It wasn't fair to her that Blair was effectively dangling Eden in front of her. Still, she quickly recovered. "It's…I never have anyone over at my place. If I'm not working, I'm visiting my dad. I thought it would be nice to do something normal with a friend."

Blair's eyes shifted from Aster to Eden, a sad smile curling on her mouth as Aster explained her reasons for offering to cook for Eden. She shouldn't have to explain herself, but Aster knew Blair would only question her motives later. *And what does that look mean?*

"You're both more than welcome to come along, too."

Blair continued to switch her gaze between Aster and Eden.

Was that the wrong thing to say, too? God, she was bad at this. It was no wonder she had a very small circle of friends—if she could call them that—and nobody else in her life.

"I think I'll let Eden judge your culinary skills first. If she approves, we'll join you next time."

Eden appeared to relax next to Aster—something was going on.

Blair got to her feet, followed by Dom. "Another beer, Aster?"

Aster tipped her bottle, shrugging. "Sure. Thank you."

"And you, Ede's? Another red?"

"One more and then I think I'll call a cab. Busy day tomorrow."

Aster sat quietly when Blair and Dom vanished from the patio. This night had been wonderful, every last second of it, but she felt as though something had shifted between everyone here. Eden more so than anyone else. One minute she seemed happy, but now she looked as though the wind had been knocked out of her.

The silence was deafening. Aster didn't cope too well without noise. "Did you want to share a cab home?"

"You stay. Hang out with Dom. I think she likes having someone on her wavelength around."

Aster frowned. "I don't want you to leave on your own."

"How do you think I used to get from A to B in the past, Aster?" Eden turned, focusing fully on her. "You're very sweet, but I am capable of travelling alone."

Aster felt like an arsehole. This infatuation was getting out of hand. Yes, she wanted to see Eden safely to her door, but Eden was right. She could take care of herself. "Sorry." She winced. "You...do your thing. I'll mind my own business."

"I'll give Blair a hand with the drinks."

"Right, yeah." Aster cleared her throat, shaking her head as Eden stood and left her alone.

This had to stop. It *really* had to stop. Eden was professional, a businesswoman. Aster spent her days walking around with a bloody camera in her hand. And if she wasn't careful, she would upset Eden *and* lose her job.

It wasn't supposed to be like this.

She got to her feet, fixing the lapels of her blazer. It was time to leave and go home to have a serious word with herself. Dom would understand, and with any luck, she could sneak out the side gate without anyone noticing.

"Beer, mate." Dom tapped Aster on the shoulder, startling her. "Nice cold one."

"O-oh." Aster shoved her hands in her pockets, checking she had her wallet and her phone. "I'm sorry, but I need to get off home. I'm sure you can drink it for me."

"You're leaving?"

Aster nodded. "Yeah. I remembered I had some work to get done before tomorrow morning. Don't want to piss the boss off."

"Eden won't mind. She's having a night off herself."

"Dom," Aster said, sighing. "I just need to go home, okay?" She gave Dom a knowing look. "And I need to do it right now before your fiancée encourages me to stay."

"O-okay." Dom took a step forward. "Everything okay?"

"Will be, yeah." Aster threw her thumb over her shoulder, backing up towards the side gate. "Tell them I said goodnight, okay?"

"How are you getting home? You can't walk the streets."

"I'll walk into town. I could do with some fresh air. And it'll do me good…get rid of the twenty pounds Blair added to my waistline tonight."

"Mate, do you like need to talk or something?" Dom looked as though she had something she needed to get off her chest, but Aster didn't need to hear it. It was best to go home.

Aster held up a hand. "Nope. I'm good. Talking makes everything turn into a mess in my head. But everything is fine. Eden is my boss, and I need to remember that. It's just harder than I thought it would be."

"But I was talking to Blair, and she said Eden—"

"Dom, I'm good. To even think for one second that I would be lucky enough to discover Eden was miraculously gay was ridiculous. And you know what, even if she was…it wouldn't make any difference to any of this."

"Why?"

"Have you seen her?" Aster snorted. "I'm all for punching above my weight, but Jesus, no."

"Um, let's not forget that I was lucky enough to find Blair."

"The two can't be compared. Blair was actively looking and *is* gay. Eden isn't looking for anything at all. And certainly not a woman."

Dom chewed her lip. "Mate, I—"

"Thanks for a great evening. Bye, Dom."

Aster shot out of the side entrance, relieved when she slid out of the electronic gates and onto the pavement without being dragged back inside. She felt terrible for leaving without saying goodbye, but she needed some space and a little time to work things out in her head. Tonight was kinda special, being Eden's plus one in some way, but she couldn't do that again. It only left her longing for something impossible. Aster may have been deeply attracted to Eden Kline, but she would also be stupid to contemplate the potentials for a second longer.

13

Eden dragged her weary body into the lift, blowing out a deep breath when the doors closed. She was already running late this morning, her lack of sleep throughout the night the cause. If she could get into her office and drink some coffee, check in with Aster, everything would be fine.

She unlocked her phone. Blair had left her another message.

B: Let me know how Aster is.
E: I will. She hasn't answered any of my calls.
B: Maybe she's snowed under with work.
E: She's not. She's shit hot when it comes to work.

Eden slid her phone into the side of her oversized handbag, striding out of the lift when the doors opened. All seemed well around the office as Maxine waved from her desk, but Eden couldn't settle until she'd seen Aster with her own eyes.

"Morning, Eden." Maxine stood from her desk. "You have some enquiries to get through this morning and a note or two that have been left on your desk."

"Perfect, thank you."

She would usually hang around and catch up with her team, but Eden had zero strength for small talk today. Aster had vanished out the back last night, and Eden couldn't help but wonder if her slight outburst had something to do with it. It wasn't that she didn't appreciate Aster's concern for her, but she didn't want Aster to cut her own night short. Just as Eden suspected she had a few weeks ago when she suddenly decided she was ready to leave Blair's, mid-conversation with Dom.

But really, it was hearing Aster call her a friend that made her feel uncomfortable. Of course, they were friends, but Eden had felt special last night as they sat eating dinner together. She'd seen the look Aster gave her as Dom and Blair talked about their own relationship. She'd seen that longing in Aster's eyes. So to hear her call Eden a friend…she hadn't expected it. Then Blair's sympathetic smile had only left a dread settling within her.

Eden had well and truly blown any chance she had with Aster. She should have just been honest from the moment she knew she was into her. *Yeah, it's never that simple.*

Eden spied the notes on her desk. She would tackle them before anything else. The first was nothing too taxing. Just a call back from a regular client that used *The Garden of Eden* yearly. The second…was what she didn't want to see. A note from Aster.

Eden narrowed her eyes. That wasn't Maxine's handwriting.

All images sent electronically to the Carmichael wedding. Printed copies have been sent Special Delivery. If anything seems wrong from your end, drop me an email. Working from home on the wedding album. Jules & Barry have given me their selected images. Aster.

Eden lowered the note, sadness rolling through her. Aster had definitely taken offence to her tone last night. And who could blame her? Eden would do well to remember that there was someone out there who cared about her. Someone she cared about in return. *A lot.*

She considered her options. She could either let Aster get on with her work at home, or she could try calling her again. Aster hadn't returned a single call yet, so perhaps Eden should take Aster's address from her employee records and visit her.

Eden retrieved her phone from her bag, bringing up Blair's number. She called it, hoping her best friend was available.

"Ede's, hi."

"Well, Aster is alive and well."

Blair breathed a sigh of relief. "That's good. So, everything's okay then? She's at work?"

"N-no. I had a note on my desk when I got here. She's working from home."

"Right."

Eden chewed her lip, running her thumb over Aster's pretty handwriting. She didn't know why she needed to see the young photographer. Perhaps it was the yearning she'd pushed down, or maybe she wanted to check that everything was okay. It was the latter, without a doubt. "Should I go over there?"

"Oh, I don't know. I'm not sure she'd take too kindly to you showing up at her door."

"I know. That's what I thought."

"I could ask Dom to call her when she finishes work. Maybe even offer to go over there and hangout for a couple of hours. They seem friendly enough to do that, right?"

"No, it's okay. This is my mess to figure out, Blair. I appreciate you trying, but I'm not dragging you into this."

"I offered."

"Still." Eden slowly lowered herself into her office chair, resting back as she closed her eyes. "I think maybe it's best if I leave Aster be. She's here to work; I never should have agreed to seeing her outside of work. And you probably shouldn't have set up that dinner."

"Uh, why? If you're into her, you kinda have to be around her to be sure."

"I *know* I'm into her, no experimenting necessary, but she's *only* a friend. You say you see these things, that she told you everything, but I don't want to make a fool of myself. Not when I have to work with her."

"You're wrong, but okay."

"Look, I have you, and I have Dom. I think I've reached a point in my life where I'm not sure it's worth the hassle anymore. I've spent this long single, no marriage or kids, so I'm sure I can manage the rest of my days the same way."

"I know that's not what you want, though."

Eden had heard the whispers from their friends. She knew all about the things they said about her. How she was too busy with her own life to create a family. How she cared too much about herself to put the effort into a relationship. But that wasn't true.

"I'm sure the girls will be thrilled to gossip at your next lunch about my fleeting chances, body drying up, and the last ticks of my biological clock. I know how they all laugh at me."

"Oh, Eden."

"I have to go. Sitting here talking to you won't get my work finished, and I'm already an hour late getting here."

"Ede—"

Eden cut the call, lowering her phone to her desk. She'd become accustomed to seeing Aster's smiling face around here over the last two months or so, and now she'd made a mess of it potentially happening again. She brought up her emails, kicked off her heels, and focused on the screen. Work would always be there for her.

Aster braced herself on her hands and knees, one eye closed as she focused on the position of the image she was attaching to a wedding album. It was taking shape, she'd worked on it since this morning, and the pictures chosen by the happy couple had been the ones Aster imagined they'd pick. She desperately hoped they approved of the final product. Aster had always prided herself on getting it right the first time.

She looked up at the clock; it was almost time to put some

food in her body. She'd considered ordering in tonight—cooking was the last thing on her mind—but had decided against it when she realised she had some homemade meatballs and spaghetti prepared. She could waste money on expensive takeout food, or she could put some goodness in her body. With the mood she was in, the latter wouldn't usually happen, but Aster wasn't allowing things to get the better of her.

Eden had called several times this morning, last night too, but Aster needed to not be around her right now. It wasn't anything Eden had done, not really, but some space was ideal. That way, she didn't have to be around the woman she couldn't stop thinking about. Eden would never understand, and Aster wouldn't expect her to, so stepping away and putting distance between them was good for now. If she had to lie her way through all of this until this pathetic idea of her and Eden together had eased, she would.

Her phone buzzed beside her, but Aster's confidence didn't waver. She glanced at it from the corner of her eye, immediately stopping what she was doing so she could answer the call. "Hi, Dad."

"Hi, my love. How are you?"

Aster noted the breathlessness. As usual, it hadn't improved. "Okay. Working from home today."

"How is your new job?"

"It's...good. I have three more weddings to get through, and then I'm going away with the girls."

"Anywhere nice?"

"Spain. Well, Canaries..."

Ted coughed. "That's nice, love. You'll need some spending money."

"I'm okay, Dad. I have everything I need, don't worry." Aster loved her dad dearly, he'd raised her to be the woman she was today, but he was forever trying to hand over money. "Lily home?"

"She's been home today. She's left an hour ago to meet that boy she's courting."

"Oh. That's still going?"

"It would seem so."

Aster sat back on her knees, running a hand through her hair. "Dad, I'm sorry I haven't been to visit the last few weeks. I've been getting myself sorted at the company. But I'll visit soon, I promise."

"Don't worry about me. I'm still here."

Aster frowned. "And you will be for years to come."

"I know, I know. Well, I'll let you go so you can finish your work. I'll let Lily know that I've spoken to you, okay?"

"Yeah. Could you ask her to give me a ring tomorrow? Had a few things I wanted to run by her."

"I will. Goodnight, Aster. If you go out, be careful."

"I'm in for the night, Dad. Don't worry. I'll speak to you soon."

"Love you, kiddo."

Aster smiled, tears pricking her eyes. "I love you, too."

The call slowly cut out, her dad coughing as he disappeared down the line. She hated this. Aster couldn't bear hearing him so breathless. If she was being honest, it was the reason she didn't visit as often as she should. But that wasn't acceptable. One day he wouldn't be here anymore, and she would live to regret the time she'd missed with him.

He'd been diagnosed with a lung condition eighteen months before Aster moved into this flat. He'd insisted she go—spread her wings—but sometimes she wondered if she'd made the right decision. She'd spent the first six months in her new place waking in the night, dreaming that someone was calling her to tell her that her dad had died in his sleep. Those dreams lessened once she'd spoken with Lily and Rose, but it was still there at the back of her mind. Aster knew it always would be.

She got to her feet, satisfied that she'd done enough for today.

Aster was no longer in the right frame of mind for the happiness of weddings, not now that she'd heard her dad struggling for breath. She'd told him he should text if he wasn't feeling up to talking, but he always insisted on hearing Aster's voice. And really, she wouldn't have it any other way.

A gentle knock on her door brought Aster from her family worries, her sadness turning to a frown. Who the hell would be calling to see her? Lily had a key to her place, Grace had a spare one too, but she hadn't heard from either of them.

She crossed the living room, opening the door. "Oh."

"Hi," Eden said, holding a bouquet of flowers to her chest. "You're probably mad at me for showing up like this, but you've ignored my calls since last night."

Aster smiled weakly, a tear gliding down her cheek. She quickly wiped it away, lifting her head to find Eden with a look of concern in her eyes. "Come in." She stepped aside, clearing her throat. "I wasn't expecting anyone. You'll have to excuse the mess." Aster glanced down her body; she looked like nobody owned her. "And please, excuse the state of me."

Eden turned back around, smiling. "You look comfortable. And your flat looks lived in. I wish the same could be said for mine lately."

"Maybe you need to work less and enjoy life more." Aster instantly regretted saying that. It was none of her business what Eden did with her time. "Sorry, that was rude."

"No, it was honest. And I have to agree with you." Eden cocked her head, smiling weakly. "Are you okay? You seem upset."

"I'm fine. I was on a call with my dad."

Eden's concern grew. The lines in her forehead deepening. "Oh, is everything okay?"

"Yeah. No changes." Aster realised she was talking to her boss and not one of her friends. Eden had no idea about her dad's condition. "He's not very well. When he calls, he always sounds like he's getting worse. It's hard to hear." Aster paused, watching Eden as her face morphed into one of sadness. "It's just Dad and us. Mum died when I was seventeen."

"I'm sorry."

"I came to terms with the fact that I'll lose him sooner than I'd like a long time ago. But we're a strong family, and I know that he's okay for now. He's quite amazing, really."

Eden shifted slightly. "May I sit?"

Aster nodded. "Sorry. I'm not very familiar with having guests over. It's usually only me. Can I get you a cuppa or something?"

"If I'm not interrupting anything…"

"I was finishing for the day and then making dinner. But you're welcome to stay for a bit if you want to."

"You answered the door and let me in. I'm not leaving yet." Eden stepped forward, handing the flowers over. "They're my poor attempt at an apology. For last night. I'm sorry."

Aster frowned. "Sorry?"

"For brushing off your concern about the cab. I never meant to make you feel as though you were being too overbearing. Not at all."

"It's okay. I forget that I should mind my own business. But I'll try to remember in future." Aster didn't make eye contact with Eden. It was one thing that the object of her affection was about to sit on her couch. Getting caught up in those eyes wouldn't be wise. "If I've *ever* made you feel uncomfortable, Eden…"

"Uncomfortable?" Eden shrugged her coat off, resting it over her lap as she sat down.

Good idea. Now I can't glare at your legs.

"You know," Aster said, lowering her eyes to the flowers. "I don't want you to think I'm trying to flirt with you or anything. I'd never disrespect you or do anything to upset you. I thought that with us both living in the city…the cab thing…it—" Aster sighed. "Never mind."

"Aster, that's not what I thought."

"Maybe not, but I wanted you to know that I haven't been cabbing it with you hoping that you'll invite me up to your place. I like to know that my friends get home safe. It's something I've always done."

"And I appreciate that."

"But I won't do it again." And Aster really wouldn't. Because even though Eden claimed she didn't feel uncomfortable, she knew there was a fine line. And she was close to crossing it as each day passed. "Tea or coffee?"

"Coffee, please."

Aster brought the flowers to her nose, smiling as she inhaled. "Thanks for these. They're lovely. They'll brighten the place up."

"Again. I'm sorry."

14

Aster pushed the door open to Eden's office, grinning as she balanced coffees and donuts on one arm, her phone in the other hand. While she waited in the queue at the local coffee shop, she'd browsed the internet for some holiday attire. Today on the list…bikinis. Aster couldn't say she was a bikini kinda girl, but she was willing to try one out. She had the figure—she thought—but she always felt as though people were staring at her. And not for good reasons.

"What time do you call this? I'm glad you're not my assistant!" Eden grinned as she peeked over her computer monitor. "I'm famished."

"Then you should probably eat something more substantial than a donut." Aster snorted, setting it all down on the desk. They'd become good friends since Eden turned up at Aster's flat. Three weeks on from the sweet bunch of flowers, and she was finally coming to terms with their friendship status rather than anything else. Eden, when she wasn't being all sexy and sultry, was a lot of fun. And it beat losing her entirely. "And before I forget, I found a bikini online I'm considering buying."

"Why are you only considering it?"

"Um, because it might not look good on me."

Eden beckoned Aster closer, waiting expectantly for her phone with her palm held out. "Let me see. I'll tell you."

Aster swallowed, handing her phone over. "Be honest. I don't want to look a state while I'm away."

Eden tapped her chin, adding in the occasional 'hmm' as she looked at it from different angles. "I think it'll look great on you."

"Really?" Aster deadpanned.

"I wouldn't tell you to wear something if I didn't think it'd look good. Don't forget, I have to walk around with you."

"Ah. Cramping your style am I, Miss Kline?"

Eden arched an eyebrow, smiling. "Not likely."

Aster took her phone back, adding the item to her online basket. As she eased into her seat, kicking her feet up onto Eden's desk, she sighed. Could she buy this bikini? Would everyone think she was out of her mind for attempting to pull off such a style? "Maybe I should order some shorts to go with it…"

"Why? You've got great legs."

Aster bookmarked that response for a time when she was feeling shitty about herself. When Eden complimented her, life felt amazing. And that seemed to be happening more often than not recently. They'd spent so much time together lately that Aster had to call Eden this morning and ask her to bring the clothes she'd left at her apartment through the week. She was yet to cook for Eden, but she wasn't pushing it. They'd eaten out a handful of times though, and it was pleasant. *It's enough. Remember that.*

"Anyway, never mind planning holidays." She held up a hand as she flipped the lid on the box of donuts. "I can't believe we don't have any work on this weekend."

They didn't usually work at the office on weekends—events happened mostly—but Eden had some things to take care of, so Aster decided to make full use of the editing suite. She would only sit at home in her pyjamas otherwise. Funnily, she was yet to do any work.

"I know. I can't remember the last time I had an entire weekend to myself."

"You coming out tonight?"

Eden stopped typing. "It's Saturday. I thought the team went out on Sundays?"

"Usually. Unless the Sunday game gets cancelled, which is what's happened. They prefer a Saturday because then nobody is hungover for work on Monday morning."

"Ah. That sounds more like my kind of night out. I can't abide a hangover on a Monday morning. It ruins my week."

"So?" Aster shoved a donut into her mouth, moaning as she got a hint of the custard filling. She didn't usually eat donuts, but it was Saturday, and she was in a good mood. "Mm. That's divine."

Eden watched Aster as she licked her lips, and then she suddenly frowned, clearing her throat. "Okay. If you're going, I'll be there."

"Don't pretend you're only coming out for me. Blair and Dom will probably be there, too. And Grace...with Mia."

Eden's eyes twinkled. Aster hadn't realised it at first, but Eden lived a simple life. And the more time they spent together, the stronger their bond became. "I know. But I prefer your company. You're the only one who makes sense during a conversation most of the time. I like that. I *prefer* that."

"Well, thanks." Aster grinned. Seemed she wasn't so boring after all.

Eden busied herself on the computer. "So, what time should I be ready?"

"Whatever time you want to meet us there. Early, late, it doesn't matter."

"Oh."

"What?" Aster spoke with her mouth full, almost choking on

her sweet treat.

"I hoped we could head to the club together. But if you already have plans, I can arrive alone."

Okay, that sounded terrible. She didn't want Eden to arrive alone *anywhere*. And certainly not at a club. "I'll pick you up. I… wasn't sure if you wanted me to or not. It's your first Saturday off in a long time; you could have a hot date planned before."

"Get ready with me," Eden said, glancing up over her screen and totally dismissing Aster's comment about a date. "I'll make us some cocktails while we get sorted and all that."

Aster's insides swirled. This was the feeling she'd been avoiding since she resigned herself to the fact that Eden wasn't available weeks ago. It bubbled up now and then, more often than she'd like, but she was managing it. "Want me to bring anything over with me?"

"Just whatever you need."

"Should I get there for around six? Is that too early for you?" Aster was trying to play it cool, but the idea of actually preparing for a night out with Eden wasn't great in her mind. Well, it was, but it was the effect this woman would likely have that she was struggling with. Dressing, undressing…God, her head was spinning.

Eden appeared to be lost in her own thoughts.

"Eden? You there?"

Eden shook her head. "Sorry. Yes. Six is perfect."

"Great." Aster wore a wide grin, but one that had mixed feelings weaved through it. This wouldn't be any different to them hanging out after work. It was the same as when they went shopping together. And it certainly couldn't be any different to the night they sat around the dining table until after midnight while they sorted through images from an event they'd run. No. Nothing could be different…it'd all be fine.

"Right, I'm off." Aster popped her head through the door, her hair now pulled up on her head. Eden could only admire her. Her soft skin, that dark blonde hair. All of her. *This is painful.* "Need anything before I go?"

"No. Nothing." Eden powered down her computer, sitting back and crossing her legs. "I'm leaving in the next hour. Should I check in with Blair? See how they're getting there?"

Aster shrugged, moving further into the doorway, her hip holding the door open. "Up to you. They could pick us up on the way. I assume they're going, but I don't know for sure."

"I'll call her. But I'm still up for a night out regardless."

"Good. That's what I like to hear." Aster threw a wave over her shoulder as she left. "If anything changes, let me know. See ya, boss!"

Eden watched her leave, her hips swaying ever so slightly. Aster had a curvy figure, one that had been tempting Eden more and more as the months passed. When Eden had gone to apologise a few weeks ago, she hadn't expected them to become such good friends. But in her mind, it was more than that. They were simply dancing around one another, waiting for the right moment. Eden felt it every time they were alone together. The fire she felt burning was becoming unbearable.

And Eden had decided that tonight would be the night she told Aster everything. She couldn't wait much longer. Aster needed to know how she felt. Even if it turned to shit, Eden still had to say the words out loud to her. Because if she didn't, she would lose her mind.

Every morning, she woke up thinking about the previous day they'd had together. Every night, she wondered what Aster would enchant her with the following day. All in all, Aster Bennett was all Eden thought about. But it was a nice place to be in her head. If Eden was being honest, she hadn't ever thought so much about another person. She'd certainly never felt this was about any of the men she'd dated in the past. It was nothing more than going through the motions so people didn't talk. But they talked anyway, regardless of what Eden chose to do. She was done with people and their opinions. This was her life and if she wanted Aster in it, she would make sure that happened.

But first, she needed to speak to her best friend. If Blair thought for one second that it was a bad idea for Eden to lay it all out, she needed to know now.

She picked up her phone and dialled Blair's number.

"Hello, this is the happiest woman in the world, how may I help you?"

Eden snorted. "You've just had sex, haven't you?"

"Maybe." Blair sighed as Dom whispered beside her.

"You're in bed, aren't you? For God's sake. I need your full attention for five minutes." Eden didn't need to hear how happy her best friend was right now, and she also didn't need to hear the post sex bliss either. "I'm sorry to disturb you, but I need some advice."

"Lesbian advice?"

Eden paused. Was that what she needed? Was that what she was? God, this was all so confusing. "Just…advice."

"Okay, go!"

Eden released a slow steady breath, exhaling deeply through her nose. "I'm going to tell Aster how I feel tonight."

The line silenced. Not a single breath could be heard.

"Blair?"

"Eden…"

"Yes?" Eden rolled her eyes.

"I'm not sure that's a good idea right now. You two are becoming friends. At least wait a while and see how it flows."

"I can't, Blair. I feel like I'm going to combust. She's been sitting here today talking about holidays and bikinis, and I'm losing my fucking mind!"

"I don't know, love. Are you going to do it when you're alone?"

"Yes. Before we leave to meet you lot."

"Y-you're coming out?" Blair almost choked on her words. "I didn't think it was your thing." Eden hadn't ventured out since the episode with Fi. She didn't want to come across anything Aster could be getting up to. It was better…not knowing.

"It's not. But Aster invited me, and I feel like we're in a good place at the minute."

"Don't you want to stay in that good place?"

Eden sighed. "I want to be in a better place with her. An honest place. I can't keep pretending to be her friend. It's not fair to either of us. I can't keep acting like her bestie when I want more."

"What if it goes wrong?"

"You seemed adamant not too long ago that it wouldn't. Right?"

"Yeah."

Eden heard the shakiness in her best friend's voice. That was never a good sign. But Blair was preoccupied so maybe it was best if Eden left her and Dom alone for the rest of the day.

"You know what, it's okay. I'll figure this out myself. Enjoy the rest of your afternoon, and say hi to Dom for me, won't you?"

"Eden, I'm free to talk to you. But I…I don't know what to say for the best. I want you to take the chance, but I'm not sure now is the right time."

"Okay." Eden suddenly felt despondent. She'd been building herself up for days, and now Blair was putting her off the idea. "Okay. I'll wait. Maybe once the holiday is over and everything, I can sit down and talk to her. She probably thinks I'm only looking for a quick hook-up anyway."

"I don't think that's the impression you give her at all. We'll discuss this tonight, okay?"

Eden sighed, her mind swirling with the decisions she had to make. "Sure. Yeah."

15

Music played through Eden's apartment, the sound of laughter coming from her bedroom as Aster thumbed through a box of old photos on Eden's bed. They'd discussed going through them for a laugh last week, and since Aster had arrived pretty much ready, she was keeping herself busy with a good twenty years' worth of pictures.

Eden stood in front of the mirror, smoothing her dress down at the sides. She looked impeccable—nothing new there—but Aster had seen her in better dresses. Even arriving at work, Eden looked as though she was getting ready to leave for a red-carpet event.

"Can I be honest?" Aster said, glancing up from the pile of images in her hand. "About your choice of dress tonight?"

"You can."

"Red looks great on you, but black..." Aster eyed the little black dress hanging over the mirrored wardrobe doors. "Black is your colour."

"I agree. I was only trying something different."

"I mean, you go with what you prefer, but black looks incredible on you."

Eden's cheeks flashed red; her palm settled against her stomach. "The heels? Will they do?" Eden looked down at her feet, turning to the side. "Or should I choose another pair?"

"The heels look great. But they'd look even better with that dress." Aster pointed to the dress she'd been drooling over for the last few minutes. "I feel awful for telling you what to wear. That's not what I'm doing at all...just giving you my opinion."

Eden suddenly turned her back. Gripping the hem of the red dress she wore, she lifted it over her head. Aster's eyes widened, her hands shaking as she dropped the photos into her lap. *Sweet. Fucking. Jesus.* Aster's eyes grazed the entirety of Eden's body, her black lace underwear barely hugging her ass cheeks, the backs of her tanned thighs toned and smooth. "I-I can leave the room if you want me to…"

Eden turned, frowning. "You don't strike me as a pervert, Aster."

"I'm not." *Then why are you looking at her like you're about to fuck her against every wall in this apartment?* "But I can still leave while you finish up here."

Eden laughed, shaking her head. "Aster, do I make you nervous?"

Yes! "No."

"Then I don't know why you're even suggesting leaving the room." Eden took the dress from the hanger, slipping it over her shoulders.

Aster's eyes followed the hem as it brushed Eden's cleavage, finally covering her beautiful body. She released a slow breath, focusing back on the images that had fallen into her lap. Eden was watching her, she felt the burn of her stare, but Aster couldn't meet her eyes. She couldn't bring herself to look up again, because the arousal she felt would be written all over her face. "Is this Blair?"

Eden approached, leaning down as she braced her hands

against the mattress. *Fuck, she's too close.* Aster had to concentrate. "Yep."

"Who is she with?"

"Her bastard ex-husband," Eden spat, the venom in her tone startling. "I think she was pregnant with Harry in this picture."

"She looks so young."

"She was. Twenty-one." Eden pushed off the mattress, fixing her dress around her thighs. Aster watched out of the corner of her eye, Eden's perfume making everything ten times worse than it already was. "The day she called to tell me she'd left him was probably the first time I slept fully in twenty years."

"Really?"

Eden cleared her throat, her eyes filled with tears. "He was evil. And she couldn't see it for a long time. But then everything got worse. She'd turn up to events in the winter wearing sunglasses, and in the summer, she'd cover up. She felt she had no way out. But he made her feel that way."

"When did she meet Dom?"

"It's coming up to two years, I think. And even when she met Dom, I still had a bit of worry at the back of my mind. I'd spent so many years fearing for Blair that I couldn't possibly understand why Dom wanted to be with her. Before I saw the love they shared, my mind was stuck on the money side of things, the big house and the car. You know?"

"Understandable. She's your best friend and you only wanted to protect her."

"No. I should have protected her from Barrett, not Dom," Eden paused, taking a seat beside Aster. "I sometimes wonder if she hates me for that. But I tried, more than once. She cut me off whenever I did."

"I know it's hard seeing your friend going through something like that, but nobody knows how Blair was feeling at the time. And she had Harry to think about. You have to remember that it all worked out for her in the end." Aster chanced her luck, placing her hand over Eden's. "She got out. And look at her now."

"God, I'd give anything to have what they have…"

Aster's heart beat harder; it was almost slamming against her chest. Eden was looking at her as though she was the only woman in the world, but they were simply in a moment of reflection, so she wouldn't allow it to consume her. Eden's eyes often had this effect on her. She'd managed on numerous occasions before. But the truth was, this felt different. The intimacy, how Eden turned her palm upright to meet Aster's…it *all* felt different than before.

"You will. I'm sure of it."

"A-Aster…" Eden chewed her bottom lip, her long lashes fluttering slightly as Eden drew in a shaky breath. "Could we talk about something in the next few days?"

"Sure. If you need to talk, you know I'm here for you." She squeezed Eden's hand. "I'm your friend."

Eden smiled weakly. "Yeah."

"Why don't we get this show on the road? I'll make us a cocktail while you finish up in here. I'm only keeping you from getting ready. We'll never get out at this rate." Aster needed to distance herself once again.

"Wouldn't be the worst thing in the world," Eden muttered.

Aster loosened her grip on Eden's hand, searching her face. Had Eden agreed to this night out only to appease Aster? "Did you not want to go out tonight?"

"I did. I mean, I do." Eden shook her head, the slight curl in her hair bouncing as it fell around her shoulders. "You make the drinks. I'll be five minutes in here."

Aster smiled, offering a slight nod as she stood and collected the photographs into piles. Once she'd put them safely away, leaving the box for Eden to put back, Aster moved towards the door. She turned back momentarily, surprised to find Eden staring at her. Through her. Just…staring. "You good?"

"Perfect. Yes."

Aster faltered when Eden continued to eye her. She threw a thumb over her shoulder, her entire body heating. "I-I'll be out here, okay."

"Mmhmm."

Eden scanned the club, spying Aster at the bar with Grace. She smiled, watching as Aster wiggled her bum to the beat of the music. This bar was nothing like the last one they'd all gone to, but Eden was enjoying a change of scene. She could certainly see the appeal with Blair and her decision to suddenly love team nights.

Women danced with other women, grinding while they shoved their tongues down one another's throats. Eden would usually be unnerved by that, public displays of affection wasn't something she was used to, but tonight she felt different. Because the women who were dancing with one another appeared happy. They were carefree and enjoying their night out. Nobody was sitting around judging anyone else, and that was something Eden could get on board with.

Aster turned, silently offering Eden a drink. Eden lifted her glass; it was still full. She was taking it slow tonight, since she didn't need anything to go wrong. Mouthing 'no thank you' to Aster, Eden turned her attention to her best friend. "This place is great."

"Babe, this isn't your scene. You don't have to pretend."

"Blair, I'm serious. I like it in here."

"Okay." Blair paused, holding up a hand. "This is an *actual* lesbian bar. Do you realise that?"

"No. I had no idea." Eden rolled her eyes, sipping her glass of wine. Okay, the wine wasn't the best she'd had, but she could always change her drink next time around. "Of course I know it's a lesbian bar. I mean, it's full of lesbians, so…"

Blair turned in her seat, propping her head in her hand as she smiled at Eden. She hated that smile. Blair was about to talk down to her. "How do you think you identify, love?"

"I don't know." Eden really had no idea.

"Could you see yourself dating women for the rest of your life? Do you still find men attractive?"

Eden didn't know how to explain how she felt. She hadn't thought about labelling herself. Did she have to? "Blair, I know that I'm attracted to Aster. I haven't looked at a man or even any other woman since she showed up in the picture, so I couldn't possibly say. But what I do know, is that sometimes *someone* comes into your life and makes you feel things in a matter of days…that you never felt in a number of years with anyone else."

"Oh, honey. You're preaching to the choir."

Eden smiled, then lowered her eyes. "I did something stupid before."

"What?"

"Aster came over to get ready for tonight. We were in my bedroom, and she mentioned that she preferred a different dress to the one I'd decided on."

"O…kay." Blair narrowed her big blue eyes.

"I stripped off in front of her to see if she had any reaction. And now I feel awful for doing that."

"You stripped off?" Blair barked a laugh, shaking her head. "I have to admit, you're definitely not what I expected you to be. You've always been so…straight."

"I know this is probably confusing for you, but it is for me, too. I need your support on this, Blair. We've been through everything together, and I don't know my arse from my elbow lately."

Blair offered a sympathetic smile. "Look, you're into Aster. So what? Who says you have to conform or fit into one particular box? If you want her, go and get her. Ignore me and anything I say. It's just taking me a minute to see you like this. To understand that you're into a woman. But…I support you, okay?"

Eden glanced towards the bar. Aster had gone.

"If you're looking for her," Blair whispered as she leaned in, "she's on the dance floor."

"I don't know what I'm supposed to do." That admission sent a wave of anxiety through Eden. How could she show Aster how she felt when she didn't know the first thing about women? "I mean, if *that* time ever came…what do I do?"

"Trust me, it all falls into place. Don't even worry about that."

Eden reddened. She couldn't believe this was the kind of conversation she was having with Blair lately. "Has Dom mentioned anything about Aster to you?"

"She told me that you and Aster have to figure it all out yourselves. She's not getting involved, and she's not being a go between."

"Smart girl."

"That may be true. But it means I don't get the gossip from her if Aster *has* discussed you. Which seems kinda unfair."

Eden grinned. "Dom doesn't trust you to not tell me. And I don't blame her. If you knew something I didn't, you'd be on the phone to me within seconds."

"This is true." Blair nodded, swirling the last of her wine in her glass. "Get your drink down you and then we're going to dance. Dom is amongst that crowd somewhere."

"Dance?"

"Mmhmm. You'll just happen to find Aster, and then your arse will 'naturally' fall into her lap."

Eden couldn't do that. Could she? She knew she wanted to, to feel Aster's hands on her body as the beat took them away, but would Aster be into that? God, she hated all this uncertainty. She'd never done well with not knowing.

"Stop overthinking it. If you do, it'll go wrong. And us lot are like cats…we sense fear."

Eden's mouth fell open. Would Aster sense her lack of experience? "Okay, I don't think I can do this. She's going to laugh in my face, Blair."

"No, she won't."

Eden looked down at her glass, blowing out a deep breath as she brought it up to her lips. If she was going to do this, it had to be tonight. And with Blair close by, nothing could go wrong. Eden had felt it earlier in her bedroom. Aster may not know it, but she'd heard the photographs fall into her lap, she'd heard the sharp intake of breath, and she couldn't mistake the way Aster was looking at her. That surely meant Blair was right, didn't it?

"You're overthinking," Blair cut into Eden's thoughts unexpectedly.

"I'm not. I'm remembering how nice my life was before I fucked it all up." Eden downed her glass of wine, wincing as the mediocre taste reached her throat. "Okay, the wine in here is terrible."

"Mmhmm."

Eden's eyes widened as the burn slid down her throat. She looked over at the dance floor; Aster was throwing her head back as she laughed. Eden couldn't see who she was dancing with, but she would find out sooner rather than later. "Okay, let's get a shot or two from the bar, and then I'll be fine."

"Sure?" Blair got to her feet, dragging Eden up with her.

Eden gripped her best friend's hands. "Please tell me I'm not making a mistake."

"I...can't do that, love."

Eden nodded. "No, I know. But if she rejects me—"

"She won't. Everything is going to be fine."

Eden held her head higher, forcing herself to feel more confident than she did inside. She could do this. And if it did turn out that she'd missed her chance, Aster would be a sweetheart about it. Eden had no doubt about that. "Let's dance."

Blair threw her best friend a wink, guiding her towards the

bar. Once they'd knocked back a couple of shots, Blair danced her way towards Dom, and Eden was thrilled to see Aster close by.

The music drowned out every thought that whirred through Eden's mind, but it was absolutely what she needed in the moment. She couldn't think too much about how she would approach Aster, and she couldn't dwell on the possibility of being rejected. Nobody ever got anything they wanted in life by panicking, so Eden wouldn't allow her fears to take over everything else she felt.

Aster made eye contact with her, her deep brown eyes dragging her nearer. She smiled, holding out a hand, and pulled Eden closer. "Thought you two would never make it over here."

"Discussing some stuff. Sorry." Eden gave herself a moment to adjust. While she'd spent many a night in a bar or a club, she'd never enjoyed a night out in a place like this.

Aster was into the music here, her hips moving incredibly well. Eden had never seen this side of Aster, not a care in the world, but she loved it. If she could capture this moment and frame it, she would remember the good times. Because as Eden moved ever so slightly closer, she felt her confidence crumbling. She'd never been in a position like this before.

But then Aster grabbed Eden's hips, pulling their bodies flush as she swayed to the music. One leg landed between Eden's, and then Aster's breath tickled her ear as she leaned in closer. "You're really tense. Loosen up. It's just me here."

Oh, Lord. When Aster said things like that, Eden could drag her home and have her way with her. Her heart raced, her hands clammy as she placed them on Aster's waist. She felt Aster smile against her ear, and then something incoherent followed.

"Hey…" Eden turned her head slightly, and their cheeks pressed together as she inhaled Aster's scent. A mixture of perfume and whiskey. It was strangely sexy and arousing. "I'm so into you, Aster."

Aster pulled her head back slightly, their bodies still flush. And then she stopped moving as she frowned. "Sorry, what?"

"You…" Eden smiled, her voice more certain than it had ever been. "You're so beautiful, Aster. Gorgeous. And to be perfectly honest, I can't think straight when I'm around you. I just…I'm *so* into you." She switched her gaze from Aster's eyes to her lips, licking and wetting her own. Eden may have been worried before, but the hundred plus people around them faded out, and only Aster remained. Eden leaned in, her eyes focused on soft plump lips. Another fraction of a second, and she would be kissing Aster Bennett.

That was, until Aster turned her head away, blowing Eden off immediately. Her hands left Eden's hips, one now gently placed against Eden's shoulder. "N-no."

Eden's stomach sank. She was almost certain that if she looked down at the floor, she would find her beating heart at her feet. Not knowing where to look or what to do, she wrapped her arms around herself and took a step back. Her entire body felt weakened, but then the pressure in Eden's chest reminded her to take a breath. She hadn't expected to feel so devastated…but she was.

"No. We're friends. You're my boss…who *isn't* into women." Aster took a step back, creating more space between them. "And I'm flattered, *really*, but…no."

Eden needed to recover. She didn't know how, she wasn't sure it was even possible, but she had to hold onto some element of control. "I'm sorry. I shouldn't have…"

"It's fine." Aster shoved her hands in her pockets, confusion in her eyes. "Let's not make a big deal of it."

"I shouldn't have said anything. It's unprofessional, and you're right. We're friends."

Aster nodded, plastering a beaming smile on her mouth. But that only made things worse. Eden wanted Aster to be smiling for other reasons. "I, uh...I'm going to grab a fresh drink. Can I get you one?"

"No, thank you." Eden couldn't stay here a moment longer. She wasn't pouting, far from it, but she knew she had just humiliated herself for an entire club to see. She looked to her right; Blair and Dom were watching on with bewilderment. She offered her best friend a sad smile, and then cleared her throat as she turned her attention back to Aster. "You enjoy the rest of your night. I'll see you Monday at ten. Goodnight, Aster."

Eden spun on her heel and left the dance floor. She heard Blair and Aster calling her name, but the dread she felt rolling through her body was enough to bring tears to her eyes. Perhaps she'd been foolish to think for one moment that someone like Aster would be attracted to her. But then she also knew Aster must be feeling uncertain. When they'd met, Eden had a boyfriend. And before that, a line of men. Never a woman. Not once.

She took her coat from the seat next to Grace, her handbag from the floor, and smiled at Aster's best friend. "Thanks for a great night. I'm headed home."

"Oh." Grace frowned, turning her watch towards her. "It's only nine."

"I know, but I'm not feeling well," Eden lied. She couldn't contain herself for much longer. Within the next thirty seconds, she would be a sobbing mess. "Would you make sure Aster gets home safely for me?"

"Of course, yeah." Grace stood, wrapping her arms around Eden. "Thanks for coming tonight. I can't believe you enjoy our nights out."

Eden pulled back, holding Grace at arm's length. "You're all lovely. But I'm not sure this is my scene, so I'll see you around. Probably at the football."

"Goodnight, Eden." Grace glanced over her shoulder, frowning.

When Eden followed her line of sight, she found Aster, Blair, and Dom all staring back at her. She shrugged her coat on and stepped forward to kiss Blair on the cheek. "I'll call you through the week."

"Love, wait."

"I can't." Eden focused on Blair; the tears wouldn't hold off much longer. "I need to leave."

"Eden—"

She leaned in closer to her best friend. "You told me this would all be okay. I've never felt so stupid in my life. I...I need a few days to myself. I'll call you when I get the chance."

And then the embarrassment truly kicked in, her heart beating rapidly as Eden swallowed repeatedly. She needed to shift the lump in her throat.

Before Blair could respond, Eden was stepping out onto the street, the cool air hitting her face. As it did, tears fell down her cheeks, unrelenting as she took a left with no idea where she was going. But one thing was for sure: Aster wasn't by her side.

Aster sat at the curb, her hands clasped behind her neck, her head between her legs. The last ten minutes or so had been a complete blur to her, but the one thing she couldn't get off her mind was the look of complete devastation in Eden's eyes. Aster hadn't ever experienced heartbreak, not really, but Eden had shown her what it looked like tonight.

She lifted her head, tears falling freely down her face. How could she be so stupid? How, in any world, could *Aster* reject *Eden*? It didn't make sense. But at the same time, it made total sense.

Aster had been holding everything back, and over the last couple of weeks or so, had been detaching herself from how she felt about Eden. She didn't want to, and it wasn't working, but as

Eden moved closer tonight…it hit her like a train. The one woman she wanted…wanted her back? *Wow*.

Had she ruined everything between them by turning Eden down? Had she lost her friendship, her job, and the one woman she spent every waking moment thinking about all in one fell swoop? It certainly felt like it.

She placed her palm against her forehead. How could something so unexpected like this happen? Yes, they'd had a *kinda* moment in Eden's apartment earlier, but it hadn't felt like *this* was about to happen. Eden…was going to kiss her. Eden…was into her. Eden…had gone. Aster hit her palm against her forehead repeatedly, gritting her teeth. "Stupid, stupid, stupid!"

"Whoa, calm down." Dom dropped down beside her, wrapping an arm around Aster's shoulder. "Don't go hitting yourself."

And then tears fell hard and fast. Tears Aster didn't know she was capable of producing. "I've fucked everything up."

"Mate, women are complex. We both know that."

"But…Eden isn't." Aster had never felt so at ease around anyone else before. Okay, she felt a little tense when Eden was close by or when they were alone, but that wasn't because Eden made her feel that way, it was how Aster chose to deal with her emotions. It was her way of holding everything back.

Their eyes finally met, and then Dom spoke. "So, why did you turn her down then?"

"Panic? Sheer surprise? I don't know."

"All perfectly fine in my book, mate." Dom offered an understanding smile, but it didn't quell Aster's fears. "I mean, Blair is like a raging bull in the club, but I'll deal with her later. She'll be fine."

"She hates me."

"Who?" Dom asked. "Eden or Blair?"

Aster snorted, embarrassment rolling through her. "Both."

"Blair is protective. And I love that about her. But Eden is old enough to deal with her own relationship problems. And so are you."

"You should get back inside. Blair will hit the roof if she finds you out here with me. I don't want to come between anyone."

"Blair can do as she pleases. She's seething, yes, but that's her own fault for putting the idea in Eden's head that you wouldn't turn her down."

Aster furrowed her brow. "What?"

"Eden confessed everything to her several weeks ago. How she felt about you." Dom looked as though she shouldn't have revealed that piece of information, but Aster appreciated it. It meant she had something to work with. Didn't she? "I did try to tell you when you came over for dinner. Eden wanted to do it in her own time, which I completely understand, but you were upset."

"How long ago was this?"

Dom blew out a deep breath, her eyes wide. "Maybe a month ago?"

"Before or after the dinner party?" Aster needed to get this all straight in her head. "That she told Blair how she felt?"

"Before. Definitely before."

"So that's why the team wasn't invited but me and Eden were? We were Blair's little experiment?"

"No, it wasn't like that." Dom held up a hand. "And I'd appreciate it if you didn't insinuate that my fiancée is causing trouble. Blair wants the best for Eden. She thought that was *you*."

Aster's stomach lurched. Blair had been playing matchmaker without telling her that her *straight* boss was into her. She could have at least given Aster the heads up. After all, Blair knew *exactly* how Aster felt. "Where is she?"

"Who?"

"Blair."

Dom stood, wiping the back of her jeans. "She's inside, but I wouldn't approach her. It won't be pleasant."

"Nope. That doesn't work for me. I want to speak to her."

And then Blair landed on the pavement outside the club, her eyes filled with anger. "Are you out of your mind? I mean, that was your chance. You…you turned her down. Are you fucking stupid?" Blair raged. "And don't dare tell me you don't want her. Anyone within a ten-mile radius can see it!"

"I didn't say I didn't want her."

"You didn't have to. I think she got *that* memo."

"Did you not think that it would have been a good idea to tell me?" Aster's entire body shook, the city around her slowing. Dulled. "What was I supposed to do? You told me she was straight!"

"I also told you not to hurt her! But here we are."

Aster's forehead creased. "Don't dare stand there and yell at me. You're the one who fucking caused this."

"Alright. Now wait a minute," Dom cut in.

"I've spent the best part of two months trying to get her off my mind. I wanted to do the right thing. I thought she was straight, and when I met her, she had a boyfriend. I knew she wasn't happy, and even though I wanted her to be happy with me, I had no right to go in there all guns blazing. Because she's my boss and now my friend." Aster took a breath, tears falling down her face. "You two have no idea how I fucking feel. You don't know how hard it is to walk into work every morning and see her gorgeous face. You don't know how much I desperately want to see her each night when I go home alone. Neither of you have a fucking clue. And the reason you don't is because it's not your business."

Blair opened her mouth to speak, sighing as she fell short of any words.

"The times I've wanted her to know how I feel are too many to count. I've sat at home begging myself to pick up the phone and call her, so I could be honest. I was even willing to tell her how I felt so she could decide if she still wanted me to work with her, because deep down, I knew I couldn't hold all of this in forever. But this is all a mess now, and while we're standing here arguing about who is right and who is wrong...Eden is home, *alone*."

Blair offered a sheepish smile. "So what are you going to do about it?"

"I don't know." Aster sobbed into her hands, immediately enveloped by more than one pair of arms. "I don't want her to be sad, and I never meant to make her feel this way, but I didn't expect any of this tonight. You have to understand that."

"I do," Blair spoke quietly. "I'm sorry."

"I-I was getting over the idea," Aster whispered, her stomach continuously somersaulting. "I was trying to stop looking at her as though she could be mine."

"Aster, you have to go to her."

"I can't. You didn't see the look in her eyes when I pushed her away. She just...God, I've hurt her. I *never* wanted to hurt her." Aster's emotions overwhelmed her, her knees almost giving out. "Blair, I've fucked up."

"No. I have." Blair sighed. "I should have told you. Eden asked me not to, but I should have. Then none of this would have happened."

Aster's head spun. This night could have been ending differently. God, she could have been in Eden's arms right now.

Don't torture yourself.

"Could you give me some space to figure it all out myself?" Aster wouldn't usually ask that of someone, but this meddling had been going on behind her back, and it wasn't okay. "I need some time. I need to maybe leave the city and visit my dad for a while. I'm pretty sure I'm the last person Eden wants to see anyway."

"If you turned up at her door right now, I know she'd see you."

"But I can't do that. I have too much to work through in my

head. I've spent every moment since I met her pushing down how I feel. You can't expect me to throw it all away because *you* told her to kiss me."

"I didn't tell her to kiss you. She said she was going to tell you how she felt. Anything that happened afterwards is down to Eden."

"Still, I need to be alone right now. I mean, how do I know I'm not some experiment to her? How can I be sure that she'll still be here three months down the line?"

"She will be…" Blair eyed Aster.

"Maybe. Maybe not." Aster held her thumb out as a hackney cab approached. She only lived ten minutes away, but she didn't have the energy to walk tonight. "Please, mind your own business in future. The mess you've created is one *I* now have to fix." Aster climbed into the cab, not bothering to say goodbye to the team. Really, they were the last thing on her mind. And Grace, the one who mattered, would understand.

Oh, Eden. Why didn't you give me a hint of how you felt before now?

16

With a shaking hand, Aster keyed in a code she knew she probably shouldn't use. It was the code that would grant her access to Eden's apartment building. Yes, she'd snuck a look one evening when they'd come back here together. She wasn't proud of the fact, and she'd never had any intentions of using it without her boss' say so, but Aster wasn't sure Eden would answer a call from her, let alone invite her up to her apartment.

She'd checked the car park when she arrived here; Eden's Mercedes was in her numbered spot. How did that make her feel? Honestly, Aster half wished that Eden wasn't home. Then she wouldn't have to see her. But the other half was glad she was home because Aster needed to collect her belongings from yesterday, including her camera kit. It went everywhere with her; she never knew when she may need it.

As the lock clicked, the door seemingly less heavy than usual. Aster quickly slipped inside and stood in front of the lift. Two floors up, and she would be standing outside Eden's door. Thirty seconds more, and she would see the woman who tried to kiss her last night.

That moment had played on Aster's mind from the second it

happened, the tiredness evident in her eyes as she swilled her face this morning in the bathroom mirror. She hadn't slept…not a wink. She lay in bed, the same music playing in her head that played last night as Eden gripped her hips, the vividness of the memory sending every hair on her body on end. God, the emotions were powerful. Almost too powerful to deal with.

Aster stepped forward, pressing the call button for the lift. She had no intentions of bothering Eden for any longer than necessary, so it was best to get this over with. She would take her things and allow Eden to get on with the rest of her Sunday.

But then her phone pinged in her pocket.

It was Dom.

D: Checking in with you this morning. How are you?

Aster appreciated Dom's concern, but she was okay. That wasn't strictly true, but her friends didn't need to worry about her. She'd always figured life out by herself.

A: Good, yeah.

D: Are you sticking with that story?

A: Really, I'm okay. I'm leaving the city for a few days. I have to visit my dad.

D: Eden wouldn't appreciate you running away.

A: I'm not running away. I'm visiting my sick dad. Stop trying to make me feel guilty for something I had no knowledge about, Dom. I'll speak to Eden about all of this when I'm ready to.

D: Sorry, mate. Give me a call if you want to talk.

Aster shook her head, locking her phone. She didn't need people to be nice to her today. She needed her camera kit, her phone charger, and then she would be driving away from Liverpool. It was that simple.

As the lift arrived, Aster's knees weakened. She knew she needed to do this, but it suddenly didn't seem like a good idea. Eden was a private person. Showing up here was going to anger her.

Too late. You're here now.

The lift whooshed to life, shooting Aster up to Eden's floor far too quickly. But maybe that was for the best. She'd planned to arrive here over two hours ago, but she'd talked herself out of it. As Aster stepped off the lift and moved towards Eden's apartment, she froze.

The sweetest sound filtered through the tiny gap at the bottom of the door, the strum of a guitar taking Aster's breath away. And then Eden started to sing, her voice husky and enticing.

She curled her hand and lifted it, only to refrain from knocking on the door. Instead, she placed her palm flat against the wood. "Oh, God." Aster rested her forehead beside her hand, her eyes closing as she listened to Eden serenade her. The swell of emotion that rose in her throat was difficult to curb, but she managed to block the sob that desperately wished to escape. Tears fell, but the silence of the hallway kept her grounded.

Eden's choice of song was both beautiful and heartbreaking, and Aster immediately recognised it as Sara Bareilles *Send Me the Moon*. The lyrics, the pain in her voice…Aster could barely contain herself. She needed to be on the other side of the door; she needed to be with Eden.

But everything felt so uncertain, and Aster had no idea the kind of welcome she would receive. Last night, she'd asked that they didn't make a big deal out of Eden's sudden attempt at a kiss. She'd shrugged it off so she didn't hurt Eden's feelings, but deep down Aster knew she'd done exactly that. The thought of Eden blowing her off left a heavy dread in her belly, so she couldn't imagine how Eden must have felt last night.

As the song started to near the end, Aster cleared her throat and knocked on the door. The guitar stilled, and Aster's heart rate shot up to an unimaginable tempo. Her mouth ran ridiculously dry.

The lock on the door clicked, and then Eden's face came into view. Eden frowned, opening the door a little further. "How did you get in here?"

Okay, this was awkward. How did she explain to Eden that she'd basically stolen the code for the door? She could lie and insist that the main door was unlocked but lying had never been her thing. And Eden didn't deserve lies. Aster had hurt her enough already. "I knew the code."

"You *knew* the code?"

"I saw you putting it in last week." Aster chewed her lip, shoving her hands in her pockets. "But that doesn't matter right now."

Eden quirked a brow, her usually alluring eyes tired and puffy. "No?"

"Could I come in for a moment? I had some stuff I left last night."

Eden stepped aside, holding the door open. "It's there." She nodded towards the small pile on the floor. "I was going to drop it off to you, but I hadn't gotten around to doing it yet."

"That's okay." Aster turned, studying Eden's body language. She appeared uninterested, perhaps busy with other things. "H-how are you?"

"Fine. Why?"

Aster huffed out a breath. She knew exactly where this was going. Maybe she'd blown this all out of proportion in her own mind, because Eden didn't seem to care about what had occurred between them. "Just…last night, you know?"

"Oh! That?" Eden barked a laugh, waving a hand between them. "I'm so sorry I threw myself at you. I was drunk."

"You *were?*" Aster's brows drew together. Eden hadn't seemed drunk.

Eden nodded. "I was. I didn't realise how much until I tried to kiss my lesbian employee. How embarrassing." Eden's cheeks didn't heat, something Aster expected *would* have happened if Eden was embarrassed. "Thanks for pushing me away. Imagine if

I'd *actually* gone through with it. We'd have been the talk of the office."

"R-right." This didn't make any sense. Blair had told Aster that Eden was interested in her, but as she stood here this morning, she wasn't getting that impression at all. "Well, so long as we're cool?"

"Of course we are."

These basic responses from Eden weren't what Aster expected. She couldn't read this woman at all. "Okay, well I'll be out of the office this week, but I'll be back in time for the twilight wedding on Friday."

"Aster, if I've made you feel bad, I'm sorry." Eden hesitated as she stepped forward, lingering somewhere in between.

"No, you haven't. I'm visiting my dad. I've told him I'd be there this week so Lily could have a break. But he knows I'm working Friday."

"Look, if you need me to find someone else for Friday, I can do that."

Aster frowned. "You want to replace me?" Her heart sank, she couldn't do this right now. She'd come here, listened to Eden pour her heart out via song, and now she was being given the cold shoulder. If Aster got a hint of how Eden was feeling—truthfully—she'd tell her everything she was feeling herself, but this was all completely odd. She didn't know what the truth was anymore. "I mean, if you want to do that for your own reasons, you know? I'd love to remain an employee, but if you want me to leave, I can do that. F-for you. I'd do it for you."

"I want to do what's best for you."

Aster grabbed her camera bag from the floor and shoved her phone charger into a side pocket. "I want to further my career and do the best job I can. I'll plan to be at the wedding on Friday, but if anything changes, let me know."

"Aster…"

Aster backed up towards the door, blindly gripping the handle behind her. "Nice song, by the way. Sounded great."

"Y-you heard that?" Eden asked, tears welling in her eyes as her bottom lip trembled.

Why is she suddenly so upset?

"I did. Whoever you were singing about is one lucky bastard." She knew she should leave, but Aster's feet wouldn't move. Instead, she cast her eyes on the floor, shifting slightly.

"Aster?" Eden spoke with such softness that it brought tears to Aster's eyes. "Are you okay?"

"You have a beautiful voice," she said, her voice low. "And I don't only mean when you're singing. I mean all the time. But I love it most when you laugh. I wanted…*needed* you to know that."

"Th-thank you."

Aster considered running out, but instead, she removed her hand from the door handle and lowered her camera bag back down to the floor. She had the chance here to be honest with Eden, and even if it came to nothing, Aster could walk away knowing she'd put her heart—her feelings—out there. Being honest could never be wrong. And yes, she was probably going to lose Eden as a friend, but Aster knew deep down that she couldn't keep this up. She wanted so much more than a friend in Eden. God, she wanted to show this woman what being loved felt like.

"How you've brushed last night off, how you said that you were drunk…" She swallowed, finally meeting Eden's eyes. "Well, did you mean it? Were you trying your luck with me last night?"

Eden watched her, while she watched Eden.

"I'm quite happy to walk away right now if that's what you want, but I would like you to be honest with me. I have people telling me one thing and then you telling me another." Aster blew out a breath, her mouth awfully dry. "And I don't think I can handle it much longer."

Eden frowned, wrapping her arms around herself. "I-I don't…"

Aster's stomach rolled. "Is there any chance I could get a small glass of water? I didn't think this would all be so hard to say."

Eden remained silent, fetching a glass of water for Aster. She handed it over, her own hands shaking.

"Thanks." Aster gulped it down, placing the glass on the kitchen island. She opened her mouth to speak, but Eden held up a hand.

"Aster—"

"No. P-please. Let me speak."

Eden nodded, resting against the counter. Aster took a moment to admire her in casual clothing. Yoga pants, an oversized off-the-shoulder jumper, and barefoot. It wasn't often she was blessed with such simplicity, and her heart *almost* settled.

"Last night shocked me," Aster explained. "And while I've been waiting for that moment since the day I met you, it doesn't change the fact that I hurt you. Which, by the way, I *never* wanted to do. I just…I didn't know. I wish I had and then this could have all been different, but I didn't know there was even a possibility that you felt the same." Aster focused fully on Eden; she needed a hint of whether what Blair said was true or not. "I've been pushing down these feelings since day one, terrified that you would find out and ask me to leave. Or worse, laugh at me. I considered telling you, but then I couldn't do it. Because you knowing and nothing coming of it would have meant that there wasn't a single chance I could ever call you mine. And I guess, deep down, that was the hope I was clinging onto."

Eden sniffled, wiping a tear from her jaw.

"And then you tried to kiss me last night, and I freaked out. I knew it could never be, that you'd never want me…how I want you. So when you did that, I'm sure you can understand why I pulled back." A sob escaped Aster's mouth; this was useless.

Eden was giving her nothing. "I think this conversation alone has shown that Blair was talking rubbish. Y-you've never told her you were into me, have you?"

Eden squeezed her eyes shut, exhaling a deep breath. Her mouth tried to move, but nothing came out.

"That's all I need to know. But maybe it's a good thing that this happened, because now you know how I feel. I know this means nothing to you, but I need you to know that *you* mean a lot to me, Eden. Probably more than I should admit. And working with you has been a dream for me," Aster said, retrieving her camera bag. "But I don't think I can work with you any longer." She backed up, sadness rolling through her. "Kissing you is *all* I've wanted to do since I laid eyes on you, so turning you down is something I'm going to regret for the rest of my life."

"Aster…" Eden's voice trembled, her feet moving as she finally found her voice. "You…"

Aster stared; she had nothing else to say. She was all out of words and almost all out of caring.

Eden lifted her hand, brushing Aster's hair from her face. The touch was gentle, feather-like, a shiver travelling throughout her entire body. "I don't know what happened the moment you walked into my office *and* my life, and I'm sorry it's taken me so long to find the courage, but I wasn't drunk last night."

Aster's pulse quickened. "N-no?"

Eden's hand settled against her cheek as she stumbled back, connecting with the wall.

"I don't know what I'm doing from one day to the next when I'm around you, but you make me feel some kind of way, and I had to tell you. Perhaps at a bar wasn't the greatest idea, but I have all these feelings building up inside of me, and I don't know where to direct them or how to deal with them."

"Y-you feel the same way?" Aster wasn't sure if she'd spoken those words, but then Eden nodded, the gentlest of smiles curling on her mouth. "I mean…y-you really do?"

Eden pressed her body to Aster's, her light breath tickling her face. Aster's palms, clammy and itching for something more, tentatively settled on Eden's hips. Just the sensation of Eden's body beneath her fingertips sent a rush of energy through Aster. God, she'd dreamt of this moment.

It didn't matter that she was supposed to be leaving, and it was irrelevant that she was in some ways angry with Eden for leading her to believe she didn't mean last night. What mattered was that Eden's supple body was pinning her to the wall, ultimately grounding her once and for all.

"You know that kiss you refused?" Eden whispered, her hand slipping around the back of Aster's neck.

"Foolishly, yes."

"I think it's time you made up for it. Because the more I look into your eyes, the harder I'm finding it to let go of you."

Aster didn't need any other invitation than that, and she was done holding back on how she felt.

Their lips met in the most passionate dance Aster had ever been subjected to. With knees already weak, she held onto Eden as though her life would end the moment she let go. Eden, her lips, nothing would ever be the same again. This woman was devastatingly beautiful with the ability to break Aster's heart in mere seconds. But if she pushed that from her mind, arousal flooded her body. Because Eden also had the ability to make Aster come alive. And in the months since they'd met, Aster had never felt this alive. Eden…had the power to change Aster's life.

Eden pulled back, her breathing laboured. "I…want you."

"I want you, too." Aster curled her fingers under Eden's chin, her heartbeat beginning to adjust. Had Eden's voice always been so alluring? So…sexy? "You've no idea what you do to me. And I'm starting to wish I didn't have to leave." Eden evidently felt the same way, judging by the sadness in her eyes. "Hey."

"Yeah?" Eden dipped her head, a blush settling on her cheeks.

"Thank you. For being honest with me," Aster paused, unable

to comprehend the fact that she'd just kissed Eden. "It means more than you know."

"I...had to. I couldn't hold it in any longer. But last night, I shouldn't have told you. It wasn't the right time or the right place."

Aster wanted to spend the rest of this day kissing Eden. Honesty, in Aster's book, was sexy. "Don't worry about it. It's out there now."

"God, I thought I'd lost you in every way possible last night when I walked out of that club." The pain in Eden's eyes was devastating to Aster, as was the tremor in her voice. If she'd known just how much she was hurting, Aster would have been here sooner. "But I should have been honest with you before now."

Aster leaned in, her lips ghosting over Eden's. She held back the urgency she felt. If she didn't, this could run out of control far too soon. "I'll be gone all week, but I'm *so* coming back. For you."

Eden sighed. "If you get back earlier, will you call me?"

"I'm about to add you to my speed dial."

Eden grinned, leaning back in and pushing Aster harder to the wall. Her expressive eyes showed how much she wanted to say, to do, but Aster would never leave if she didn't do so right now. "I have to be at the venue early on Friday."

Aster feathered her thumb across a soft cheek, smiling. "I promise to come and find you."

17

Okay, this was it. The first time Eden would be alone with Aster since the kiss. No distractions, no need to cut things short. Only the two of them. They'd spoken briefly while Aster was home with her dad, but Eden was pacing herself. At least, she had been until her eyes landed on Aster this evening during work.

Both knew they had to remain professional, and that was Eden's saving grace all night. Because the times she'd thought about dragging Aster into a corner were too many to count. But now, five days on from the most earth-shattering kiss, Eden was truly ready to try. If she wanted a happy ending, she didn't have time to waste.

Eden turned her key in the lock, pushing the door open with her shoulder. Aster followed behind her, the camera bag weighing her down during the walk back, but she was thankful Aster had decided to come back with her after work. She could see how tired and worn-out Aster was this evening. It had been the longest day.

Now, Eden just had to figure out where they went from here. She was hopeless when it came to dating.

She turned around, taking Aster's camera bag from her. "Let me put that somewhere safe. You're like a cart horse with it."

"Thanks." Aster's right shoulder sagged as Eden lifted the weight from it. "I'm so used to it that I don't realise how heavy it is until I take it off."

"You're joined at the hip. I'm not surprised." Eden gave herself a moment for some small talk. She needed to get everything right this evening. Aster was here. There was no rush to get carried away.

They were both shattered, it'd been a long night, but as Eden had walked through the door, she felt wired. If Aster was sitting on her couch, she would always be alert. She placed the camera bag down on the counter, pushing it away from the edge. She wouldn't be responsible for it toppling onto the marble floor below; that really would be the end of any and all relationships between the two of them.

"Can I get you anything? I could make a snack…it's up to you."

"No, I'm okay. I picked up a bowl of chips between the speeches and the meal."

Eden hadn't thought to do that, but she rarely had the time anyway. She had to be on hand for any issues that may arise. It didn't happen often, but she knew her luck would fail her when she wasn't around and ultimately needed. "Okay, well something to drink then?"

"Sure. What do you have?"

"Anything you want. I have that Irish whiskey you like. I picked a bottle up a few weeks ago after we'd hung out a bit. Figured it would be handy to have a bottle in for you."

Aster shrugged her blazer from her shoulders, untucking her shirt from her pants. "Okay, that's kinda nice."

"It's only whiskey."

"I know, but it's still a nice thing you did."

Eden glanced around the kitchen, trying not to think too

much about Aster or how she'd looked at her all evening. When she did, she couldn't concentrate. "Or I have different teas. Coffee. Whatever."

"I think coffee is best for now," Aster said, kicking off her shoes and easing onto Eden's corner couch in the window. "Alcohol doesn't do either of us any favours."

Eden had to agree. Before she joined Aster, she had to stand for a moment and appreciate the scene playing out in front of her. Aster was here, and it was as though she always had been. She was lounging on the couch, her legs crossed, thumbing through a magazine from the coffee table. "I'll be over in a few minutes. I'll get the coffee."

Aster didn't respond; she was engrossed in whatever she'd found in the magazine. But that was okay. It gave Eden a moment to gather her thoughts *and* herself. Because she had no idea what this night would result in. They may end up in a better position, but it could also go the opposite way and ruin whatever was budding between them. Eden didn't want that outcome. Of all her failed relationships, this couldn't become one.

While she desperately craved something more with Aster, Eden didn't have a clue what was and wasn't on the table. Could she touch her, hold her hand? Should she refrain from getting too close? *God, I hate this.* She exhaled a steady breath, gripping the counter as she calmed her nerves. Maybe if they'd had a real chance to talk last week, this meeting may have felt less intense.

A sudden hand placed on her shoulder had Eden's body pin straight, Aster's breath tickling the back of her neck. "Need a hand?"

Eden dropped the spoon she was holding to the counter, the clatter bringing her right back into the room. "N-no. I've got it."

"Turn around, Eden."

Eden did exactly that, breathless when she found Aster closer than she expected, her eyes holding her in place. "Is everything okay?"

Aster shrugged. "You tell me…"

"I want it to be." Eden paused. "God, I want *everything* to be okay, but is it? Can it be? I feel so out of my depth with this."

"You're scared, and I completely get that, but I need you to always be honest with me, okay?"

"Last week when you came over was probably the most honest I've been with anyone." It was true. Eden never discussed how she was feeling. And she certainly never took the first step with someone else like she had at the club. Maybe that was where she'd gone wrong all her life, waiting for the right person and the right moment. But with Aster, it was all different. She felt as though they were on an even footing in some ways.

"How do *you* want to do this, Eden?" Aster tucked Eden's hair behind her ear, smiling as her fingers grazed her skin. "I mean, you're not out. Nobody knows about this. Is that something you want to do? To be out?"

Dread filled Eden's entire body. She hadn't thought about that moment until now. "Shit. I don't know."

Aster offered a sad smile, nodding slightly. "I didn't think you would. But I had to ask."

"It's not that I don't want to be out, but can I do that? I don't even know how I'd label myself."

"Don't label yourself. Nobody is asking you to." Aster's body heat relaxed Eden, her muscles less tense as she rested back against the counter. "But I would like to know how you want to play this."

"Y-you mean…" Eden stammered, pointing between them. "There's potentially an us?"

"I thought I'd made that clear last week before I left."

Eden gripped what she could before her knees gave out on her. Why did Aster mean so much? Why did she have this effect? Nothing made any sense. "Oh. Wow."

Aster furrowed her brow. "You sound surprised."

"I am. I hadn't anticipated this moment. It's not something

I've thought about. It didn't seem possible, even as you were kissing me."

"Then don't think about it. Not right now." Aster curled two fingers under Eden's chin, lifting her head ever so slightly. "Right now, it's you and me. Nobody else. No best friends or acquaintances. Just us, Eden."

Oh, boy! Didn't Eden know it.

"And as much as I've tried to distance myself from you, I can't. I spent the week at home with Dad and all I thought about was you. You're everywhere, but that's what I want. If I'm going to be serious about someone, having you everywhere is *exactly* what I want."

Eden swallowed, her hands clammy as she gripped Aster's hips. She pulled Aster closer, desperate to taste her.

Aster leaned in slowly, smiling as Eden's breath came in short sharp bursts. Was this the moment that Eden would realise everything she'd been missing in her life? Would kissing Aster again bring everything together for her once and for all?

"I need to know that you want this, Eden," Aster whispered, switching her own gaze between Eden's eyes. "I know you say you do, but I need to know you're sure."

Eden gripped the front of Aster's shirt, pulling their breasts together. "I want this. No doubt about it."

"Yeah?" Aster's husky voice only heightened everything Eden was feeling tonight. She'd fully expected to be home alone after work, but here she was, about to kiss one hell of a woman.

Eden didn't need to explain anymore. She needed to be kissing Aster Bennett. She surely couldn't get that part wrong. Kissing was…just kissing.

You make the first move this time. Show her you want it!

Until Aster's lips met hers and Eden was reminded that kissing really *wasn't* just kissing. The softness, the light breath, the audible moan from Aster. God, the arousal that pooled between Eden's legs was off the scale unexpected. Nobody had ever made her feel that way from a simple kiss. But this wasn't simple, and it wasn't anybody. It was Aster.

"Breathe," Aster said, pulling back. She swiped a thumb across Eden's bottom lip, relaxing her. "If we're going to do that more often, I need you to breathe for me."

Eden brought her fingertips up to her lips, pressing them against the moistness she felt. "Jesus."

"The name is Aster, babe." Aster suddenly leant back in, devouring Eden as she pressed her body harder against her. "I never knew that kissing someone could feel so fucking good," Aster said, her forehead resting against Eden's. "I mean, I've thought about last week's kiss every minute of every day, but I'm surprised all over again."

Eden wrinkled her nose. "It was okay?"

One of Aster's hands slid to Eden's ass, cupping it as she pulled her away from the counter, her own back connecting with the opposite side. "Okay?"

"Y-yeah." Eden swallowed, trying to read Aster's eyes. All she found was arousal. Deep, dark eyes.

"I think we may need a separate hotel room for Pride. Because if I manage to have my way, we'll never leave the one we're supposed to be sharing."

Those words sent Eden into a frenzy. Not only was Aster the greatest kiss of her life, she was saying *all* the right things too. "Oh, I'm sure we'll manage."

Aster's world was spinning. Not out of control, but on its head. Eden was sitting beside her, the taste of her still on Aster's lips, her legs pulled across Aster's lap. Yeah, there was no doubt about how much it was spinning. But it felt good. After the week she'd had, missing Eden, she truly believed she'd made the right decision to come back here tonight.

Okay, they had a way to go before anything significant would happen, but the first step had been taken, and that was the most important thing. If Aster cast her mind back to last Sunday, that unease remained. The disinterest in Eden's eyes was startling considering she'd been lying. Did that make her good at fooling people? Aster hoped not. She also prayed Eden hadn't had much experience in doing so, because even though she was thoroughly enjoying being here this evening, Aster did have some reservations.

She wanted to go hell for leather with this, to enjoy every last second of it, but what if Eden changed her mind? What if they had their fun and then went their separate ways? Eden didn't give off that impression, but Aster still didn't know much about her. She didn't know what made her tick, the relationships she'd been in before, or why on earth she'd taken an interest in Aster.

But maybe that would be discovered in time. Maybe Aster had to allow Eden the chance to understand it all herself before she threw herself at her. "Do you have any plans to speak to Blair?"

Eden feathered a fingertip over the back of Aster's hand. "I haven't thought about it. I know I can't avoid her forever, and I know that she was technically right, but she's only going to push this. And I don't want that."

"I know you have…issues. I mean, this is potentially going to shock a lot of people, you know, but I'm okay with keeping it all quiet. For now, at least."

"I appreciate that." Eden shifted closer, resting her head on Aster's shoulder. This moment was the moment she'd been daydreaming about from the second she'd discovered her attraction towards her boss, but Aster understood that nothing could be rushed. If she fell hard, something she fully expected to happen, it could become too overbearing for Eden. "I want to enjoy you for a while before I deal with the backlash of all this."

"The backlash?"

"My mother," Eden said. "I don't think she's going to hit the floor when I tell her, but I'm sure she'll have something to say. She *always* has something to say about my life."

"And if she does have a problem with this?" Aster asked, turning her hand over and lacing her fingers with Eden's. "Would it change anything for you?"

"I hope not." Eden spoke with honesty. And honesty was important to Aster. "It's not going to change how I feel about you or the fact that I want to be happy. That's not something you have to worry about."

"I'm...surprised."

Eden turned her body towards Aster. "About me?"

"About all of this." Aster ran a hand through her hair. She didn't know how to explain all of the thoughts running through her mind. "I noticed you the day I met you, but to be sitting here with you now..."

Eden cleared her throat. "My biggest concern is making you happy. I'm not sure I've *ever* made anyone happy before. And the girls back home always laid the blame at my feet, so it was easier to agree. And after a while, you start believing the things your supposed 'friends' are saying behind your back."

"What do they say?"

Eden's skin flushed, her eyes lowering to their hands. "They like to have an opinion on my life. Everyone else is married with kids, but I'm not."

"Blair isn't..."

"Blair is different. And she was at one point. But they all had an inkling about her when she was married to Barrett anyway. Whereas I've always been single and childless. They blamed my career. They blamed me for wanting what was best for myself. And they even suggested that I was too cold hearted to raise a family."

"They sound like shitty friends to me," Aster scoffed, angered that Eden's friends would say such things about her. "Just because you don't mirror their lives doesn't make you any less deserving of whatever you want."

"I tried to find the perfect man, and I tried to date whenever I had spare time. But nobody ever did it for me. Poor Liam was another in a long line of failures. But that was my fault for staying with him. I'm not sure I'd ever felt a connection with him, but it seemed easier to plod along than call it a day."

"Have you thought that maybe you've never really been into *only* men? Or not as into them as you thought you were?"

Eden shrugged. "It wasn't something I considered. Whether it was a man or a woman, I wasn't paying full attention. Liam always wanted to be out eating or drinking. But this...*this* is what I want. To be alone, relaxed, in your arms."

"You want a simple life, don't you? Work and a relationship to come home to at night."

"I've spent so much time dreaming about that kind of life, Aster. And when you walked into my office...I don't know. Something clicked together for me. I was drawn to you before you'd even opened your mouth to speak. What does that mean?"

"I'm not the greatest with relationships so I can't say, but in my opinion, we just found one another. And maybe that was always supposed to happen, I don't know, but I feel like I'm in the right place. With you. Like this."

Eden leaned up on her elbow, her lips ghosting across Aster's. Those lips, the gentleness, it almost had Aster melting into the couch. "I'm so sorry I lied to you last weekend. And I'm sorry for leading you to believe that I was trying my luck with you. I've never felt that way about you, Aster. And I never will."

Aster swallowed as she cradled Eden's jaw gently in her fingers. "Please don't take this the wrong way..."

Eden frowned.

"But are you entirely sure you want to do this with me?" Aster didn't lose her focus on Eden's eyes; she needed the absolute truth tonight.

"You mean, am I bored and looking for something to take my mind off things?" Eden didn't sound offended, but it was hard to be sure. "Aster, is that really what you think of me?"

"N-no. It's just…I've always been hopeless with relationships. They never last. And I really want this one to last because it means so much to me."

"Aster—"

Aster snorted. She really couldn't believe she was lying here with Eden Kline. Of all the women in the world, it was the attention of this particular one that Aster *never* thought she'd catch. "I can't even get the lesbians to look my way. I'm sure you can understand my uncertainty."

"I have no answers for you, but I *know* that I'm certain. This isn't me looking to get my kicks somewhere new. I wouldn't do that to you."

Aster nodded, wrapping an arm around Eden's shoulders. They slouched against one another, the slightest sound coming from the television. "I know."

"Let's figure this out together, okay?" Eden nuzzled into Aster's shoulder, sighing. "Because I want to get this right."

"Me too."

Eden glanced up, her eyes bright. "I thought maybe…if you're not busy tomorrow, I could take you out to dinner."

Aster leaned down, kissing Eden's forehead. "I'd love to go to dinner with you."

18

Eden shook her hands at her sides; she needed to get rid of the nervous energy she'd felt all day. She wasn't worried about dinner with Aster, but where it would go, she had no idea. Aster had hung around last night for a few hours, not leaving until after 1 a.m., but Eden hadn't heard much from her today. Was Aster nervous, too? Was she standing in front of her own mirror, panicking about dinner? Eden hoped not. They needed to remain calm.

She held up a blue dress, wrinkling her nose as soon as she pressed it up against her. It didn't do it for her. Not today. "Nope."

Then she picked up the one Aster had insisted she wear last week. It was a no brainer. This was the one that caught Aster's attention, and while it had brought her bad luck in terms of being rejected, Eden planned to change that tonight.

Don't walk into the restaurant and throw yourself at her. Be you.

Eden sighed. What if she couldn't do this? She'd failed time and time again when it came to relationships, and women were even more complicated than men.

Eden eyed her phone on the bed as she stood in her lingerie, debating whether she should call Blair. They hadn't spoken since last weekend when she left the club, but Eden was slowly coming to terms with the fact that Aster had just panicked, so the humiliation didn't feel so severe anymore. She cleared her throat and dialled Blair's number.

"H-hello?" Blair spoke quietly.

"Hi, it's me," Eden said. Maybe she'd been a little harsh in not calling sooner. "Are you free for a few minutes? I understand if you're not."

"No, I'm free."

"Right, well, I was wondering if I could speak to you about something?"

Blair remained silent. Well, this was awkward.

"Blair?"

Blair sighed. "Go on. I'm here. What do you need?"

"Are you mad at me?" Eden asked, her stomach lurching. She had every right to be upset with Blair last weekend, but she knew Blair would have been worried this week without hearing from Eden.

"No, I'm not mad. Just...thought you may have called before now."

"I know. I needed space."

"Well, I hope you found some. How are you?"

"I'm okay." Should she tell Blair that she was going on a dinner date tonight? She felt as though she should, but Blair wouldn't be impressed with the fact that she hadn't told her about her meeting with Aster last night *or* last week. They shared *everything* with one another.

"Good. I never meant to make you feel as though I was humiliating you. Aster told me she was interested. More than interested. So, I don't understand what happened. I am sorry it didn't work out for you."

"I'm going to dinner with her tonight."

"O-oh." Blair's surprise wasn't unexpected. Eden still couldn't quite believe it herself. "Well, that's nice. I hope you have a lovely night."

"Honestly, I'm terrified." Eden dropped to the bed, placing her head in one hand. A cold sweat developed across her skin, the air in the room thick with uncertainty. "What if she wants more tonight? As much as I'd love to get my hands on her, I don't think I'm there yet."

"I don't think Aster is the type of person who wants a shag on the first date. She's too respectable."

"But, what if she does?"

Blair laughed. "Then you tell her it's too soon and that's that. But I don't think you need to worry about her dragging you into bed. And if I'm not wrong, she's probably feeling exactly how you are."

"You think?"

"I'd be very surprised if she wasn't."

"Blair, I really like her. But I mean, *really* like her. And I know I'm nervous about tonight, but God, I can't wait to see her."

"Maybe now she'll give you that kiss she turned down."

Eden's face heated. "That kinda happened already..."

"Oh, it did now?"

"She showed up last Sunday. God, she was breaking my heart with everything she said to me. And it just happened. I told her how I felt, but then she had to leave to visit her dad."

"Okay. This is good."

"Why didn't you tell me how amazing it was kissing a woman? You've been keeping that a secret for too long!"

"She's good then, huh?"

Eden's insides swirled. "Oh, you've no idea." If Eden had known how last week would have felt, she'd have done it much sooner than now. The longing, the desperate need to be with Aster, it could have been averted. But then wasn't that part of the thrill? Didn't it add to the excitement when that time finally arrived? "Tonight is everything I've been praying for. I didn't think I'd see her again. My worst fear was that she'd leave the company and then I'd be left in the dark, but she came back with me last night when we finished working…"

"And?"

"And it felt so good to be alone with her. She just held me, Blair. We lay on the couch and relaxed with one another."

"I like her. I think she could be good for you."

Eden smiled. "I'm glad to hear that."

"She certainly put me in my place last weekend."

What did that mean? "How so?"

"I was angry with her when she turned you down. I found her outside talking to Dom, and we may have had words. There was some yelling involved."

"Blair." Eden sighed.

"Oh, she held her own. And the only thing she was concerned about was the fact that you'd gone home alone, and you were upset. She didn't care about what I had to say, which I admire since it's none of my business, but she was worried about you above all else."

"I know I'm doing the right thing. Any consequences can be dealt with another time."

"Consequences?" Blair asked.

"Any that may arise. Family, friends…you know."

"Honey, they are the least of your worries. If they can't accept the fact that you've fallen for a woman, simply don't invite them to the wedding." Blair laughed, and Eden followed. "But in all seriousness, I hope tonight is something beautiful for you both. Enjoy every moment of it."

Eden exhaled a slow breath. "I only called to ask what dress you think I should wear. But it doesn't matter. The fact that we're sharing the evening together is the most important thing."

"Correct. Call me tomorrow."

"I will."

Blair cleared her throat. "And I'm sorry. I never meant for last weekend to happen."

"It doesn't even matter anymore. I'll call you. Love you."

"I love you, too."

Aster blew out a shaky breath, turning her watch towards her. Eden was due at the restaurant any minute now, but she had a sinking feeling that her date wouldn't show. Aster had insisted she pick her up on the way, but Eden was determined to arrive alone. She shouldn't think too deeply into it, but Aster's mind had run into overdrive. If Eden didn't show…devastated wouldn't come close to how she'd feel.

She'd built herself up all day, had numerous pep talks from Grace, and now here she was. Waiting. Just…waiting. And this was the part she hated most. Standing around with no idea what would happen. And then Aster's attention turned to how remarkable Eden would look tonight if she did show up. In all honesty, she wasn't satisfied that she looked good enough to be on Eden's arm.

Will I be on her arm? Would that happen? Could they walk into the restaurant as a couple, or would Eden prefer a more subtle entrance? As friends, perhaps? Aster had it all planned out in her head. The hand on the small of her back, the eyes across the table, the innuendo. But what if Eden didn't want that? What if Aster was getting way ahead of herself? God, this wasn't good. The feeling she had inside didn't feel as wholesome as she'd like it to.

She'd never dated someone who wasn't out. And she'd always told herself she wouldn't. Aster liked to show off the woman she was dating. She wanted the entire restaurant to know that she'd bagged someone beautiful, someone who made her heart sing.

But tonight, that may not happen, and it was something she

would have to accept. She'd agreed to give Eden time to figure this all out, to process it all when she was good and ready, but she already itched to kiss her in the street. Slip her hand to Eden's backside as they walked together. Public displays of affection didn't frighten her in the slightest.

Okay. Play it cool. Go slow. Give her time. That was the logical thing to do. If Aster got too comfortable with this, Eden could break her heart. Yes, this was a date—she assumed—but it was also a chance to get to know one another on a different level. Something more intimate. It didn't mean they were together or that they would end up marrying one another. It meant that they wanted to eat dinner together. Maybe see where things went. *You have to remember that. Protect your heart…while holding hers.*

A white cab pulled up outside the restaurant. Aster couldn't see who was inside, the windows were tinted, but her body told her it was Eden. It told her that she was about to go on a date with a woman who was a million miles from what she thought she'd ever be lucky enough to date. The door opened, and Aster knew immediately who those slender, tanned legs belonged to.

H-holy shit. Eden stepped out, her long dark tresses flowing down the front of her shoulders. And she wore *the* dress. Aster swallowed hard before Eden caught her eyes, smiling as she gripped her clutch bag in her hands.

"Hi." Eden had gone for false eyelashes tonight. But they weren't too much. Just the right length. They only brought out the definition in her eyes further. The dark makeup surrounding them had Aster squeezing her thighs together. She was a sucker for a woman with *come to bed* eyes. "I'm not late, am I?"

Aster distracted herself, looking at her watch. "Nope. Right on time."

"Okay, good." Eden stepped closer, pressing a kiss to Aster's cheek.

Okay, not what I was hoping for…but it'll do.

"You look remarkable." Aster refrained from taking Eden's

hand, instead shoving her own in her pockets. If she didn't keep them out the way, they would be trailing Eden's body for the world to see. "And you don't know how happy I am that you actually showed up."

Eden wore a slight frown. "You thought I'd stand you up?"

"I...can't believe we're going to dinner together. So, yeah. It kinda was at the back of my mind."

"Well, I'm here. And I'm looking forward to having dinner with you. Should we go in?"

"Definitely." Aster opened the door, holding it for Eden. "After you." Eden offered a shy smile, passing by Aster. But it hadn't been the best idea. Aster's eyes were now firmly glued to Eden's arse. "Did, uh...did you go into the office today?" She shook herself from her thoughts, aware that she was almost drooling.

"No. I stayed home and got ready for tonight." Eden glanced over her shoulder as they waited to be seated. "I may have had a slight panic, but I'm fine now."

"Why did you panic?" *The same reason as you. Don't pretend you've been cool all day.*

"This is all very new to me. I've never been to dinner with a woman before. I mean, I have, but not like this." Eden smiled, interrupted by the waiter.

Once seated, Aster lifted the menu, unsure as to what was and wasn't acceptable this evening. If Eden wasn't worried about people seeing her, she surely would have taken Aster's hand, perhaps linked arms as they made their way inside. The not knowing was frustrating.

She lowered her menu. "Hey, so I was wondering what's what with us tonight?"

"I don't understand." Eden's eyes remained on the menu.

"Like, are we here as friends, so to speak? A business meal, I don't know..."

"A business meal?" This time Eden did look up from her

menu, confusion etched on her face. "Why would we be having a business meal?"

"What I'm asking is…am I to keep my hands to myself? Do I have to avoid anything that would be considered flirting?"

Eden's face morphed into a look Aster wasn't sure she recognised. Fear? Apprehension? "I-I…" She looked around the restaurant, and then her eyes landed back on Aster. "I don't know. I hadn't thought about it."

Aster held up a hand. It didn't matter. What counted was that they were here at all. "You don't need to worry about it. I completely get it."

Eden sighed. "It's not that I don't want to…"

"Eden, it's okay." She offered a genuine smile. She didn't want Eden to feel uncomfortable. "Should we order some wine?"

"Yes, okay." Eden lowered her eyes, closing them momentarily as she shook her head. Aster knew she wasn't supposed to notice it, but she did. "You choose. I don't mind what we have."

Aster cleared her throat, sitting up straight. "No pressure here, okay?"

Eden nodded, the smallest of smiles playing on her lips. "Thank you."

"Now. Let's eat, drink, and enjoy ourselves." Aster took the lead. She had to remember that Eden was putting things on the line here tonight.

"You look gorgeous, by the way." Eden's eyes pinned Aster, her focus not wavering.

"Thanks."

Eden slid her credit card into the leather wallet, placing it on the edge of the table. Dinner had been exceptional, the company even better, but now it was over. What was she supposed to do? She didn't want it to end. Aster had been the perfect date, and the fact that she was willing to understand Eden and her predicament meant the absolute world to her. It hadn't gone unnoticed.

"Eden, let me at least pay for half of it." Aster slid her hand across the table, pulling it back when she realised what she was doing. Eden would love to hold her hand, but she wasn't quite there yet. Not in public, anyway. "Sorry."

"I asked you to dinner. That's the end of it."

Aster smiled. "Well, thank you. It was lovely."

"So you know, I'm fully expecting you to invite me to dinner in the not-too-distant future." Eden sat back in her seat, her fingers stroking the stem of her wine glass. "Since I'm not impressed that this date is over."

Aster shrugged. "Doesn't have to be."

Oh, God. She's going to suggest her place…or mine. "I have an early start tomorrow." That was a complete lie, and Eden felt awful as it slid so easily from her mouth. *Don't do that. Aster wouldn't appreciate it.*

"Oh." Aster sunk back against her seat. "Well, maybe another time then. I was looking forward to a walk along the dock."

Eden's eyebrows rose with surprise. "You wanted to take a walk?"

"Mmhmm. But I'm sure we can do it again. Maybe I need to check you don't have plans the following morning first…"

Could she backtrack? Take Aster up on her offer of a walk? "I mean, I could walk with you."

The waiter appeared, a single nod in Eden's direction as he took the leather wallet. Eden focused back on Aster, watching her intently.

"You said you needed to get home."

"I suppose I should take what I can get with you. I have a packed week coming up, and I'm away for four days of it."

"Anywhere nice?" Aster asked, her tone holding an element of disappointment. But Eden felt the same. Not seeing Aster through the week was kinda shitty in her book, too.

"Business trip."

"It'll be nice to get out of the office." Aster pushed her chair back when the waiter returned with Eden's credit card. "You must get bored sitting there all day."

"Until recently, yes."

"Something changed around the place?" Aster asked, her eyebrow quirked as she stood. She never once took her eyes off Eden.

"New staff. Kinda nice. *Very* pretty. I have a bit of a thing for them."

Aster smirked. "Well, I hope they treat you right."

"So far, so good."

They left the restaurant together, side by side as they crossed the road and headed for the bright lights of the dock. The temperature was around the average for the time of year, but Eden had brought a wrap with her this time. She wouldn't have Aster shivering again.

"Maybe we could walk along the front?"

"Okay." Eden followed, careful of her heels on the cobbled pavement as they entered the dock gates. As they reached an even surface, the sound of the water lapping against the wall, Eden linked her arm through Aster's. It was quiet with not many people about. "Thanks for a lovely evening, Aster."

"Thanks for inviting me to dinner."

"I'd like to think we can do it again, but if you don't want to, that's perfectly fine. I wouldn't expect you to hide who you are for me."

"It's not about hiding who I am," Aster explained. "And yes, it's different for me, but I'm respecting what you want. That isn't an issue for me. At least, not right now."

"No?" Eden studied Aster's profile and smiled.

"I mean, you may decide next week that you're not actually into me. You could decide that it's not worth the hassle in your life. So, I'm not getting my hopes up."

"That wasn't in my plans, if that means anything to you."

"I know you're not out to intentionally hurt me, but you don't know how you'll feel down the line. And I understand that. I've always known who I was. This must be difficult for you."

Difficult? No. Different and unusual, yes, but not difficult.

"I want you to know that it's totally fine if you change your mind. I'd be hurt, but I'd get over it." Aster stopped and winced. "Wait, that sounded terrible. But I'm not very good at explaining what I mean."

"It's okay. I know what you mean."

Aster smiled weakly. "But do you?"

"I do." Eden guided them off the path and towards a wall. She wasn't overly keen on looking down at the water; it made her queasy. And when they moved away from the streetlight, Eden felt much braver. "I know it's going to take time for you to trust me. To trust that I'm genuine."

Aster sighed. "It's not that I don't trust you."

"Then what is it?"

Aster looked up at Eden, fear in her deep brown eyes. "I don't want to be a mistake to you."

Eden's heart constricted. Aster could never be a mistake to her. Instead of trying to explain to Aster how she was feeling about her, Eden dipped her head, her lips pressing softly against Aster's. A strong hand gripped Eden's hip, a breathy moan escaping Aster's lips as Eden pulled back, smiling. "You're not a mistake. You'll never be a mistake. And if you need some space while you think this all over, I understand."

"I don't know what I need," Aster spoke, her voice thick with emotion. "I want to be with you. God, I do. But the thought of you never truly giving me all of you…it scares me."

"Y-you mean…sex?"

"God, no. No, it's not about sex." Aster shook her head, running a hand through her hair. "I worry that we'll have our fun, I'll fall for you, and then you'll realise that this wasn't what you wanted. I can deal with the secrecy and the hidden intimacy, but I can't deal with you turning your back in the end."

Eden reached out a hand, feathering her thumb across Aster's cheek. She completely understood. "Why don't we take this slow. Really slow. And then down the line, when it feels right, we can try again."

"You're already having second thoughts, aren't you?"

"Quite the opposite, actually. But I don't want you to feel like you have to do this because you know I'm attracted to you. I know you willingly came back with me last night, but was that because you thought you had to? So as not to hurt my feelings?"

Aster stood tall, pushing off the wall, no longer slumped against it. She looked Eden dead in the eye, her focus intense. "I want you. I want *all* of you, Eden. But you're right. I think we have to take this slow. The last thing I need is for you to feel overwhelmed by it all and then I get complete radio silence. Just promise to talk to me. If things get to be too much, I need you to be honest. Okay?"

"Okay."

"Because if we can communicate, nothing can go wrong."

Eden knew Aster was right. Here she was, offering Eden time to work out this new life in her head. To decide if she was truly sure. That meant a lot.

"Why don't we have a great holiday with the team and see what's what when we get back? I'll take a separate room, you can have your fun. And if when we get home, you still want this, then we will work through it together."

"Have my fun?" Eden's eyebrows rose.

"You never know, someone else may catch your attention."

Oh, no. That wouldn't happen. Not in a million years. "I think you forget that I explained myself last night. I'm not attracted to multiple women, Aster. I'm attracted to *only* you."

Aster smiled, a blush flashing on her cheeks. "Yeah. I

remember that bit. Still hard to believe that of all the women in the world, I'm the one you like."

"Take a bit of credit. You're one of the most wonderful people I've ever met. You make me smile. You make me laugh like nobody else ever has. You just…I still haven't figured out what it is I saw in you. Perhaps it's your natural beauty. Or it could be the incredible eye you have for the things around you. I only know that when I'm with you, I'm happier than I've ever been." Eden paused, frowning. "Does that make any sense to you at all? Or am I talking complete rubbish?"

"No." Aster took Eden's hand. "No, you're not talking rubbish. I feel the same when I'm with you."

"Then…that's what counts, right?"

Aster grinned, pulling Eden closer to her, their bodies flush. "It's the only thing that counts right now." Their lips met, a surge of emotion rushing through Eden's body. Aster's hands held her waist, one slipping around her back, the gentlest touch she'd ever felt. "I'm not doubting you, Eden. I want you to be sure."

"I know." Eden chanced a kiss. "Come on. We'll go back to mine for coffee if you like?"

"You have to be up early."

Eden cleared her throat. "That was a slight white lie."

Aster stopped in front of her, looking expectantly at her.

"Don't be offended, but I thought you were expecting more tonight. You know?"

"Ah. You thought I was going to get my lesbian hands on you and keep you up all night." Aster nodded, laughing. "Trust me. When I want you…you'll know."

A rush of arousal had Eden's body throbbing. Aster, when she was being herself and confident, was something to admire. "Oh?" Eden started to walk, but Aster tugged at her wrist, pinning her to the wall.

"One more kiss before we leave." Aster pressed her body

against Eden, the warmth of it inviting. "There's something about you and those eyes in the moonlight."

"Yeah?" Eden's skin flushed hot and cold, Aster's leg between her thighs.

"Oh yeah. Makes me come over all funny."

Eden grinned, gripping Aster's face. Aster pressed her hand to the wall beside Eden's head, capturing her lips with a hunger that almost knocked Eden off her feet. God, she could kiss. She could *really* kiss.

Aster pulled back breathless, taking her bottom lip between her teeth. "Shit, I could kiss you all night long."

"All in good time." Eden leaned in once more, smiling into a kiss. "All in good time."

19

Aster ripped open a Mars Bar, linking her arm through Grace's. They'd been at the airport for an hour, and now they were waiting to board their flight. All week, she'd anticipated the moment she would be picked up by Grace, grabbing Eden and her belongings on the way. She was definitely ready for the sun blazing down on her skin.

Grace looked at her, smiling. "You seem happy."

"I'm about to have a ten-day holiday in the sun. Why wouldn't I be happy?"

"It's more than that," Grace said. "And I know you've been a bit giddy since last week and your date with Eden, but this is definitely more."

"Keep your voice down. The team don't know, and Eden isn't ready for them to know yet. The last thing I need is for them all to find out and then they take the piss for the next week or so."

"Okay, I see your point." Grace offered an apologetic smile. "So, it's going well?"

"It's just…going." Aster shrugged. She'd met with Eden on Thursday when she got back from her business trip, and they'd both agreed to enjoy their holiday, no pressure involved. Aster had once again offered to take another room, but Eden didn't like the idea of having a huge, five-star suite to herself. Aster wouldn't protest too much. She loved the idea of a decent room… and throw Eden in with the bargain, and she couldn't go wrong. "We're not together, but I'm not planning on having my eye on anyone else either."

"And Eden?"

"Is here for the sun. Nothing more."

Grace frowned. "Not even you? If the chance presents itself…"

"I haven't put it to her. I want her to enjoy her break and then when we get home, we can figure everything else out. She doesn't know which way is up right now."

"Aren't you worried?"

Aster chomped on her Mars Bar. "About what?"

"I mean, I like Eden, I do. But she's not even gay, Aster. Is she bi? Did she have a fling at university?"

"She's…never been attracted to a woman before."

Grace unlinked her arm from Aster's. "I'm sorry, but I'm getting serious alarm bells here. I don't want her to hurt you."

Aster appreciated Grace's concern, but she wasn't worried. She was getting to know Eden. That was all. Why did people have to read too much into things when it wasn't their business? "She's not going to hurt me. I'm not stupid. If I suspect that she's going to run, I'll know to back off."

"And what if you're in too deep by then? What if you've fallen in love with her and the next thing you know, she's marrying a bloke?"

"Can we not do this now?" Dread settled in Aster's belly. She fully expected Grace to have her back, but she didn't like the scenario her best friend had put to her. "I don't want anyone to overhear you, and I don't want you to put a downer on my holiday. I haven't had one for two years."

"Sorry. But I worry about the woman you've chosen. Like I

said, she's lovely, but I'm not convinced. As your friend, I'm entitled to that opinion."

"Of course you are," Aster said, smiling her best fake smile. "Hopefully, I'll prove you wrong."

"Where is she now?"

"Drinking Prosecco with Blair." Aster chanced a glance in Eden's direction, smiling when she found Eden watching her in return. "Isn't she pretty..."

"She is. But that doesn't mean you should expect all of this to fall in your lap. I want that for you, but you have to be realistic here, Aster."

"I am being realistic." Aster scoffed. "But you shitting all over my hopes is bringing my mood down. It's not even midday. Please hold off a bit longer."

Grace held up her hands. "Fine. Sorry. I'll mind my own business." Without another word, Grace walked away, heading towards Mia.

And then Aster felt a hand grip her backside, a laugh erupting from someone's mouth. "You ready for me to chase you, Bennett?"

Aster turned to find Fi standing behind her. "Please, don't waste your time, Fi."

"Come on. Don't you want a holiday romance with yours truly? A little fun between friends? It's all the rage." Fi held her arms open, grinning. "You know I love a one-night stand. But don't expect more after it."

"Yeah. I'm sure I'll manage without a one-night stand." Aster rolled her eyes, taking a step back. She bumped into another body, swiftly turning around again. "Eden."

"Hey." Eden smiled through gritted teeth. "Wondered if you wanted to join me and Blair?"

"I'd love to."

And then Fi spoke. She was a pain in the arse. "So, Eden. What are you looking for during your holiday?"

"Uh, the sun."

"And a lady to keep you warm at night?" Fi wiggled her eyebrows.

"Oh, no. The humidity is all year-round where we're going. I'm sure I'll be plenty warm." Eden spun on her heel, and Aster knew that was her cue to leave, too.

When she reached the table at the airport bar, Blair glared at her. She pushed a chair out with her foot, clearing her throat. "Sit down."

"Um...okay."

"Now, I really like you. I like you a lot, Aster. But if you break my best friend's heart during this holiday, I will hunt you down, and I will hurt you."

Aster's brows rose with surprise. "Is that right?"

"One hundred percent." Blair winked, barking a laugh. "But I doubt I'll be able to get you two out of the hotel room, so I'm not too concerned."

Eden left the table, moving towards the bar.

"Look, I don't know what she's told you, but we're not together. We're sharing a room, yes, but we've agreed to keep our hands to ourselves."

"Come back to me and tell me that again when she's lounging out on the terrace in a bikini."

Aster's insides rolled. How the hell could she keep her hands to herself when Blair said things like that? She knew Eden would look incredible in a bikini, she wasn't blind, but how exactly did she refrain from visibly drooling at every given opportunity? "I'm sure I'll manage."

"Mmhmm. And I'm sure you won't. She's bloody gorgeous, and *you're* only human."

"She's not ready. She told me that herself. And I completely respect the decision she made."

"Oh, boo!" Blair rolled her eyes. "Even I know she won't last the entire holiday. She's called me three times this week to ask if

I think you'll like a particular outfit. Trust me, she's *only* thinking about you. All the time."

Aster's heart swelled. She felt kinda proud hearing that. "Yeah?"

"Absolutely. Now, help your...*friend* at the bar."

Aster glanced over her shoulder; Eden had her back to them. Was she upset about what Fi had done? Eden didn't have to worry. Aster would never go there. "Is she upset?" She turned to face Blair. "Fi was kinda obnoxious then."

"Eden's fine. A little jealousy never hurt no one."

Aster frowned. She wasn't into game playing. "I don't want her to be jealous. And certainly not of Fi. There's not a chance I'd touch that woman."

"Can confirm, it wasn't much."

Aster barked a laugh. She'd momentarily forgotten that Blair had slept with Fi before her and Dom got together. "Shit, I'm sorry. I wasn't having a dig."

"Oh, have a dig. I deserve it for being so stupid." Blair held her Prosecco, a mirror image of how Eden held her own. They were like twin sisters most of the time. "Dom still hasn't let it go."

Aster snorted. "I don't blame her. I mean, Fi?"

"Don't please." Blair winced. "A moment of error. It'll never happen again."

"Damn right it won't."

"Eden is waiting. I think she wants to speak to you without me around."

Aster glanced over her shoulder once again. Eden was, in fact, watching her. She mouthed "I'm coming," and smiled in Blair's direction before she walked over to Eden. "Hi."

"Fi had better keep her hands to herself." Eden stood with her hands clenched into fists against the bar, a look of anger in her eyes. "Seriously."

"Whoa. Don't sweat it. I'm not interested whatsoever." Aster reached out a hand to lay on Eden's shoulder, pulling it back quickly. She had to remember that people were around.

Eden studied Aster, and Aster could see there was a jealousy there. One that was more than unnecessary. "Promise? I can deal with you sleeping with some incredible blonde, but Fi? No. I can't deal with that."

"Huh. You planning to change your hair colour?"

Eden's forehead creased. "What?"

"The only person I have my attention on is you. And you're not blonde, so..."

Eden blushed, lowering her eyes as a smile spread on her mouth. "You know what I mean."

"Actually, I don't." Aster leaned in closer, inhaling Eden's scent. Her mouth brushed Eden's ear inconspicuously. "You know, I'd give anything to kiss you right now. And I'm talking, a kidney...whatever. I'd give it up to kiss your lips."

Eden turned her head away, smiling shyly. "Stop."

"It's not my fault the woman I'm infatuated with is fucking gorgeous." Aster lowered her voice. Painfully low. "Blair seems to think we won't last this holiday keeping our hands to ourselves."

Eden turned suddenly, her bottom lip between her teeth. "My best friend knows me too well."

Oh fuck! Aster was in trouble. Big, big trouble.

Her phone started to ring in her back pocket, Lily's name on the screen as she removed it. "Hey, Lil's."

"Aster, I'm sorry for calling, but it's Dad."

"W-what's Dad?" Aster's heart sank. The look of panic Eden was giving her didn't help either. "Lily?"

"Paramedics are here. His breathing is bad. They're taking him in."

Aster swallowed. "Okay, well I can be there in an hour. I need to get home from the airport."

She hated the thought of Eden being surrounded by hundreds of other women, but Aster would never forgive herself if she got on that plane and something happened to her dad. There would be plenty of holidays in future, but her dad wouldn't always be here.

"No, you don't need to do that. Go and enjoy your holiday. I was calling to let you know."

"No, I'm coming home."

The disappointment in Eden's eyes didn't go unnoticed, but Aster had to do what her heart told her. And that was to go home and meet her sister at the hospital. She…couldn't leave the country.

"Dad's going to go insane if you don't get on that plane with your friends."

"Yeah, well, I can't enjoy myself when I know he's lying in a hospital bed, Lily. And I'd hope you wouldn't expect me to."

"N-no. I know. Maybe you can get a flight out in a day or two. Once we know what's going on…"

Aster ran a hand down her face. "Maybe. I don't know. I'll see you at the hospital as soon as I can get there, okay?"

"Okay. I'm sorry for calling." Lily ended the call, leaving Aster staring down at her phone.

Eden stepped closer, placing a gentle hand on Aster's wrist. "Everything okay?"

"I have to go home. T-to the hospital. It's Dad."

Eden lowered her hand, a sad smile on her mouth. "I'm so sorry."

"I can't get on that flight not knowing, Eden."

"I wouldn't expect you to," Eden said, pulling Aster into a hug. "What can I do to help?"

"Go to Spain and have an amazing time for both of us. And, you know, try not to fall in love with someone while you're there."

Eden cocked her head. "You think I'd do that?"

"Hard to say." Aster blew out a breath. "I can't even get a fucking holiday right so you should at least see what's on offer while you're there. If there's going to be anyone else, *please*…not Fi. Anyone else I can at least try and live with it, but not her, Eden."

Eden leaned in, her lips brushing Aster's ear. "I want you like you couldn't begin to imagine. And this time away is only going to make it all worse for me."

"Well, I hope you still think that when you get back. H-have a lovely time. I'll say bye to the team and find Grace before I figure out how to get out of here."

"Call me?"

"I'll wait to hear from you. I'm sure you'll have much better things to do than sit on the phone to me." Aster quickly took Eden's hand, squeezing it tight. "Be careful."

20

Eden gripped her gym bag in one hand, a hold-all slung over her shoulder. She peered up at the building in front of her. Was this the right idea? She wouldn't know until she went inside. But how exactly did she get inside? She cleared her throat, eyeing the intercom at the side of the door. Flat 7 - Bennett.

She pressed the buzzer, praying Aster wouldn't turn her away. She may need space, time to be alone. Eden didn't know. But she needed to see her. To know that Aster wasn't beside herself with worry. She'd sent Eden a message around an hour ago to say that she'd gone home from the hospital tonight and hoped they'd landed safely abroad, but Eden decided to simply show up instead. The last thing she needed was for Aster to demand she stay away and go back to the airport.

The intercom crackled to life. "Hello?"

"Hi, it's me," Eden said, stepping closer. "Eden."

"Eden?" Aster sniffled. "Y-you're supposed to be in another country."

"Yeah, well, I'm here…for you."

"Come up."

Aster unlocked the door, the sound of the receiver dying out as Eden stepped inside the building. She tugged her hold-all higher up on her shoulder, the lift doors opening as she pressed the call button. Of course she'd love to be lying in the sun, who wouldn't, but Aster was here, and Eden needed to be close by. Okay, Aster may not want that, Eden wouldn't expect her to always be around while her dad was in hospital, but she could still be around for anything Aster needed. Whether that was a friendly face, a shoulder to cry on, or someone to vent to…Eden was here for it all.

As she reached Aster's floor, stepping out of the lift, she found the object of her desire waiting out in the hallway. "Hi."

"You're not coming inside," Aster said, folding her arms across her chest. "You're going to turn around, go back to the airport, and get the next flight out."

"Yeah, that's not going to happen." Eden approached Aster, her shoulder dead from carrying a stupid weight around. "I've taken a coach, a train, and a cab to get back to you. I want a cuppa and maybe a shower if you could stretch to that."

Aster's bottom lip trembled. "Eden, why didn't you get on that flight?"

"I thought about it. I was actually at the boarding gate when I decided to turn around and come back. I just…you can ask me to go home, that's fine, but I'm not going to Spain without you."

"Y-you stayed for me?"

Eden knew deep down that she should have left the airport at the exact moment Aster did. She'd kicked herself once that realisation sank in, but she was here now, and that was what mattered. She smiled. "Came straight here."

Aster held out a hand, taking Eden's hold-all from her shoulder. As she dragged it inside, taking Eden's hand, Aster kicked the door shut, turning the lock. "Eden, I feel awful. You shouldn't be here. You've been looking forward to this holiday for months."

"Because I was going to be with *you*." Eden dropped her gym bag to the floor, taking Aster in her arms. "You probably don't need or want me here, I'm not that important, but I didn't know if you'd need an ear, you know?"

Aster sobbed into Eden's chest, her arms tightening around her waist. It was a hard time for her, but God, Eden couldn't think of anything better than holding Aster. It was all she wanted to be doing. "How is he?"

"He has to stay in until they're happy he's stable enough to be at home." Aster pulled back, smiling weakly when Eden wiped tears from her face. "He's not been taking his medication. He told me he doesn't want to be here anymore because he's holding us all back."

"Oh, Aster."

"But he's not. He's our dad. And we love him. He's never been a burden to us. I don't understand."

"I'm sure he knows how much you love him."

"I told him before I left the hospital that he's not allowed to die on me. That he has to meet you and get to know you and…I need him to stay alive, Eden."

Eden rested a hand against Aster's cheek, remaining when she leaned into Eden's touch. "I don't think he's going anywhere. He wouldn't want to leave you behind."

And then the realisation that Aster had told her dad about them hit her. Aster clearly had no plans to walk away from Eden if she'd told someone so important in her life. Eden didn't know how to feel about that; her own parents had no idea she was even embracing another woman right now.

"He can come home once he's back on his meds and stable. They don't know if stopping them has caused any more damage. He's on IV antibiotics at the minute."

"He's in the best place." Eden pressed a kiss to Aster's forehead. "I'm glad he's okay. I saw how upset you were when you rushed from the airport."

"When Mum died, I didn't think he would cope. Not only did he have two teenage girls to raise, but a toddler, too. He stepped up, and I'm so proud of everything he did for us. If I lose him, Eden…"

"Hey, now." Eden enveloped Aster, running her hands through her hair. As her nails gently grazed the back of Aster's neck, she sighed lightly. "One day at a time, okay?"

"Okay."

"I don't know about you, but I could eat. Should I go out and get some things in? I don't suppose either of us have anything in the fridge since we were supposed to be on a sunny island right now."

"Please, you should get another flight out. There's no use in us both being here and miserable."

Eden shrugged. "I'm not miserable. I'm with you, and that's good enough for me."

Aster stepped back, chewing her lip. "Did you maybe want to stay over?"

Eden's palms turned clammy. Yes, they would have been sharing a room in Spain, but this was Aster's home…and as she looked around, she only found two doors off the main space. One had to be a bathroom, the other a bedroom. So, where exactly would she be sleeping? The couch? The bed? *Jesus*. Eden's throat dried at that prospect.

"You don't have to. I thought since you were here, we could snuggle down on the couch and then fall into bed whenever we want to."

Eden loved that idea. She loved everything about Aster. "Yes. I'd like to stay over."

"My place isn't much. And it's tiny. But it's cosy and warm."

Eden reached out a hand, lacing their fingers together. "I love your home. And I can't wait to spend the evening with you."

Aster nodded. "I mean, it's not a fancy hotel in the heat, but you're welcome to do anything you need. Make yourself at home. I'll nip out and grab some things for dinner."

"We could order in…"

"I'd rather make dinner for you, if that's okay?" Aster's eyes held Eden in place, their bodies gently pressing against one another. "It's the least I can do after you turned down a holiday to be with me."

"I wasn't sure if you'd appreciate it or not. I'm sure you have a lot to do with your dad and your family, but I'll be in the background if you need me, okay?"

Aster cupped Eden's cheek, leaning in for a kiss. When she did, Eden's body fired up like never before. It could have been the fact that she was spending the night, or it could have been her body's response to such a genuine, kind soul, but Eden itched to take this further. She shouldn't, though. Aster wasn't in the right frame of mind to give her the attention she would expect in such an intimate moment.

"I don't want you to be in the background. I want you by my side. You being here means so much to me, Eden. I never for one second thought you would ditch the girls and show up here."

"I want to be here."

Aster dipped her head, creating a slight space between them. "So, I'm going to leave." She cleared her throat. "Because if I don't, I'm going to show you my gratitude in other ways, and well…"

Eden's blood travelled south, her skin flushed.

"Anything in mind you want?"

"Surprise me." Her voice hoarse, Eden grabbed her bags and dropped them on the couch. "I'll get some things out while you're gone. Maybe take a shower if that's okay?"

"Do whatever you need to do. Fresh towels are in the cupboard in the bathroom. Put whatever you need in my bedroom, take over my space." Something changed in Aster's facial expression, and then she shook her head.

"What is it?"

"Nothing. It's stupid." Aster blushed.

Eden took a step forward, gripping Aster's waist. Her hands

had never been so busy before, that desperate need to be touching Aster becoming more noticeable each day. "Tell me." She dipped her head, capturing Aster's lips. "I want to know what you're thinking."

"Oh, you don't." Aster reddened further. "Nothing good can come from you knowing."

Eden's insides burst into flames as Aster met her eyes. Dark and filled with want, she'd never noticed anyone looking at her that way before. "I should know. Because we could well be thinking the same thing."

"I…doubt it."

Eden quirked an eyebrow. "Try me."

"I was thinking about how amazing it already feels having you here. I've never shared my place with anyone, and…I don't know. It feels nice. You know, a positive step."

"I like being here. Because you're here."

Aster swallowed, her hands settling on the bare skin beneath Eden's blouse. "I *really* like you being here."

"Yeah? You're sure?"

Aster gripped the back of Eden's head, leaning in for a heated kiss. They'd danced around one another since the bar at the airport, and Aster had clearly had enough of that. Eden moaned when Aster slipped her tongue past her lips, hot wet heat pooling between her legs. And then her hands found either side of Eden's body, her nails grazing Eden's ribs. A light gasp escaped Eden's lips. "Oh, God." She pulled back, breathless. "You shouldn't do that."

With their foreheads pressed together, Eden felt consumed by Aster's eyes. "No?"

Aster repeated the movement, gaining another low moan for her efforts as Eden's body tingled.

"N-no."

And then her right hand moving higher, her thumb smoothing across the underside of Eden's breast. If Aster continued with her incredible hands, Eden was going to strip bare before her. Fuck the uncertainty. "Then you should stop kissing me like that."

"A-Aster," Eden whimpered.

"Mm?" Their lips met again, this time fervently. The passion in each swipe of Aster's touch almost had Eden on the floor. She couldn't contain herself any longer. She needed Aster to show her what she'd been missing. Aster's hand grazed higher, gripping the back of Eden's neck. "I don't think you realise how much I want you right now."

Eden took a step back, Aster's lips so full and inviting. She pulled Aster with her, almost stumbling back as her foot caught the corner of the couch.

And then Aster grazed her fingertips across Eden's lace covered nipple, bold but confident. Eden bit down on Aster's lip as she swiped her fingertips across once more, her eyes fluttering shut with each graze. "O-oh," Eden murmured. "That…"

Aster pulled back, grinning as her hands fell away from Eden. "Is only the beginning." Eden's legs shook, her body quickly following, but Aster was backing off. She threw her thumb over her shoulder. "I'm going to go out and get that stuff for dinner."

"W-what?" Eden's eyes narrowed. "You're seriously going to walk away after that?"

Aster shrugged. "It's too soon for you. But at least we know when the time comes, it'll certainly be worth it."

Eden took a deep breath as the hot water cascaded over her body. She should have been taking a cold shower with how she was feeling, but she was pushing Aster to the back of her mind. She had to. If she thought about earlier for one more second, she was going to step out of the shower and demand Aster fix the problem she'd created. Aster was back from the supermarket;

Eden had heard her rummaging around the kitchen before, her hands probably working their magic.

But those soft hands kept creeping back to the forefront of her every thought. How Aster's lips reassured her while her fingers were...*elsewhere*. How the room faded away around them, that touch, the light gasps from Aster as Eden reciprocated every kiss. Nobody had ever caused such an intense arousal throughout her body.

And then it ended. Eden was left standing alone, wet between her legs. The cause...a woman.

She inhaled a shaky breath, lathering the soap over her body. This shower was supposed to calm her racing thoughts, it was meant to quell the throbbing between her legs, but it was only making everything worse. When she was alone, it gave her all the time in the world to imagine rolling around in bed with Aster. Something, for the first time as of today, Eden was *really* thinking about.

Her hand skimmed her lower stomach, another shudder rippling through her. If she closed her eyes, it was Aster touching her. If she focused on the kiss they'd shared in the living room, her body ached for more. As much as she wished this wasn't happening, Eden *did* have to release that pent-up tension she felt. Aster would never take this further tonight—she had too much on her mind—and that was perfectly okay.

One hand dipped lower, the other pressed against the black tiled wall of the shower. A low moan rumbled in her throat when her fingertips touched her clit, the urge to come now overpowering her every sense. All she could smell was Aster, her perfume. As she licked her lips, Aster remained there. And those deep brown eyes...God, they were everywhere.

Eden dug her nails into the wall, widening her stance ever so slightly. She rubbed vigorously at her swollen clit, slipping her fingers inside her. Deep, hard, fast. Eden's chest heaved as thoughts of Aster flashed through her mind. And then she trembled, overcome with the intense orgasm thrashing her body. "Oh, fuck." Eden's fingers slowed, her breath coming in short and sharp. "A-Aster," she whispered, shockwaves jolting her body as her fingers slowed to a stop. *God, I need more than that.* Eden's body was hypersensitive. Her own hands hadn't doused the flames deep within. It hadn't even touched the surface.

A sudden knock on the door had Eden's heart rate rocketing through the roof. "Did you shout me?" Aster asked through the door.

Had she been louder than she first thought? *Shit!*

Eden cleared the lust from her tone. She knew it would be there. "N-no."

"Sorry. I must be hearing things."

Eden stepped fully under the shower, turning the temperature to cold momentarily as she washed the soap from her body. "I'll be out now. Just finishing up in here."

"Yeah, no rush." Aster's soft voice had Eden smiling as she shut the shower off.

Grabbing a towel, she wrapped herself up in it and pulled the bathroom door open. She needed to see Aster's face, the sweetness in her smile. That would make everything else feel more… normal. "Hi."

"Hi." Eden's first thought was how she could drag Aster inside the bathroom. *Stop! Not now.*

"I wasn't rushing you. I thought I heard you call my name."

Oh, if only you knew… "I'm done."

"Right."

Aster's eyes trailed Eden's body. The towel she was wearing wasn't the ideal length, but it was the first thing she'd grabbed. Aster didn't appear to be concerned, her eyes dark and intense.

"I'm making dinner. Can I get you anything?" Aster leant against the doorframe, her sweet smile making Eden weak at the knees. "I can whack the heating up so it feels like we're abroad…"

Eden took Aster's hand, pulling Aster towards her. "Stop trying to make up for it. It's not the end of the world."

"Feels like it. I was looking forward to seeing you in a bikini."

Eden took her lip between her teeth, blushing. Could she tell Aster what had happened in the shower? How she couldn't hold back from touching herself, making herself come, with only Aster in her mind? *God, no.* Eden had *never* done that before. She'd never felt so overcome, so desperate for release. "There are going to be plenty of times when we can go on holiday."

"And I'm looking forward to every last one."

"Let me dress, and I'll be out to help with dinner." Eden pressed a kiss to Aster's cheek, stepping back. "If you trust me to help."

"I'd love your help. Standing around watching would be *very* helpful."

"It…would?" Eden's forehead creased.

"Oh, yeah. A bit of eye candy never hurts while I sweat it out over a stove."

Aster had never felt so content. Eden was lying between her legs, her fingertips were settled on her calf, and a romantic film played out in front of them. Aster had no idea what was going on in said film, but this all felt lovely. Different for her, but lovely. In all honesty, Aster couldn't quite believe Eden was here.

She'd expected lots of calls during her time away, maybe a FaceTime or two, but she never expected Eden to show up at her flat. Blair, Dom, the rest of the team…that's where she expected Eden to be. Not here, settled on her couch, her hands on her. The intensity was off the scale if she thought about it too much.

"Can I tell you something?" Eden's voice pierced the silence, her eyes finding Aster's as she glanced up at her. "I mean, I know we're watching a film…"

"You can tell me anything you want, any time." Aster leaned down and pressed a kiss to Eden's forehead.

Eden's eyes closed, her lips parting slightly. "First of all, I love it when you do that."

"Do what?"

"Kiss my forehead." Eden looked away, but Aster knew she was blushing. "But that's not what I wanted to say."

"Hey," Aster whispered, lowering her lips to Eden's head once again. "I love that you love that. And honestly, I love all of this. You and me, wine, films…it's perfect."

"Dinner," Eden started. "That casserole, it was amazing."

"Thank you. I do try."

"And I know it probably doesn't seem like much to you, but I've never had someone cook me dinner before. That sounds pathetic, I'm *very* aware of that, but I wanted to say thank you. For doing that for me. It was…special."

Aster's heart constricted. Nobody had ever cooked dinner for Eden? Surely not… "Well, whatever company you've been keeping…it's really shitty."

"Not anymore." Eden leant up on her elbow, capturing Aster's lips. "You've been more than anyone I've known before, and it's only been a short time since we got together."

"Got together, huh?" Aster smirked. "I'm totally here for that, by the way."

"Yeah?" Eden caressed her lips again, her tongue slipping into Aster's mouth. They both moaned, deepening the kiss. But then Eden pulled back. "I'm sorry. I'm trying to not get carried away. It's just…hard."

"Don't ever think you can't get carried away. All of this is absolutely what I want. I'm ready for anything with you."

"But why?" The lines in Eden's forehead creased. "I mean, I could be terrible at this."

"The way you kiss me," Aster said. "Nobody has ever kissed

me like that. My body has never responded the way it does around you. I'd say you're doing pretty damn good at this."

"I'll remember that when I'm having a meltdown at home."

"No reason for a meltdown, baby. I'm not here to put any pressure on you at all. If you want to hide away at my place, I'm fine with that."

"Y-you are?"

"Only if I'm allowed to touch you in the process."

Eden's lips curled. "I'm sure we can figure that out between us."

"Fancy getting into bed? I'd like to snuggle you if you're okay with that."

Eden's hands ghosted up Aster's sides, settling on her stomach. Honestly, it was the most incredible touch Aster had ever been subjected to.

"Come on. Let's snuggle."

21

Eden woke to an arm wrapped around her waist. Aster's light breathing was calming, but Eden's mind *and* body raced. Her thoughts...well, they weren't appropriate for this morning. While she had enjoyed falling asleep beside Aster last night, both of them talking complete rubbish until they couldn't hold their eyes open anymore, she needed to move. Slowly. Quietly. Without waking Aster.

As she shifted slightly, Aster's arm tightened around her waist. *No, not now.* Eden couldn't lie here while her body craved more. She couldn't pretend nothing was wrong when she ached to feel Aster's hands beneath the oversized night shirt she was wearing. Eden never wore clothes to bed, she preferred to sleep naked, but she couldn't exactly climb into bed with Aster last night wearing nothing but her birthday suit. *God, I wish I had.*

Eden took Aster's wrist gently, lifting her arm from her body. And then she slid out of the bed, the chill in the room doing little to help the heat of her body. She fixed her hair, tugging her shirt down her thighs. Then she turned around, watching Aster as she slept peacefully.

Aster lay on her stomach, her legs splayed out across the

bottom of the bed. The white sheet that they'd shared as they drifted off last night was crumpled in a ball next to her, her blonde hair dragged up high on her head. She looked adorable as she slept, her tank top riding up her back to expose dimples at the base of her spine. But it was the shorts Aster wore that caught Eden's attention, tight to her thighs and only just covering her backside. And what a beautiful backside it was.

Eden desperately wanted to reach out and touch Aster. She needed to feel how soft her skin was. But she couldn't bring herself to do it. Because if Aster backed away, Eden wouldn't last another moment in this room. Something definitely could have happened last night when they held one another, but both had been a little drunk after sharing almost two bottles of wine, and Eden never wanted her first time with not only a woman but *Aster* to be that way. She wanted to remember every second of it. She needed to memorise everything Aster liked and everything her own body responded to. Drink could never be involved during a moment like that.

The sound of buzzing broke Eden from her desire, her phone lighting up on the nightstand. She rushed towards it, hesitating when she saw her mum's name on the screen. Now wasn't the best time to talk to her; Eden feared she'd blurt out everything that had happened recently. But if she didn't answer, her mum would only continue calling.

"Hello?" Eden whispered as she slowly crept out of the bedroom, closing the door behind her as she stepped into the kitchen.

"Hi, love. How's the holiday?"

"I, um...change of plans. I didn't go." Eden rested back against the counter, flicking the kettle on.

"Oh. Well, why?"

"It wasn't a concrete plan, to be honest," Eden lied. "And I had to be around for a friend who is having a hard time at the minute?"

"What friend?" Angela asked. "Blair?"

"No. Not Blair. It's a friend I work with." *She's not your friend. She's close to being the love of your life.* "But we can rearrange. I'm sure another holiday will pop up soon."

"Of course."

"So, how are you? Anything going on?"

"Oh, you know me. Just plodding along."

Eden stared down at the floor. She hated the guilt her mother made her feel for not always being on hand. "Well, you could go out to lunch with Dad or call some of the ladies from the social club."

"The weather isn't great. But I bet it would have been abroad. How hot is it?"

Eden shrugged. "I've no idea, but it has to be high twenties over there."

"Ooh, I could just enjoy some sun."

"I've told you to book a holiday with Dad. You've been retired for almost three years, and you've only gone away once since." Eden didn't understand why her mum constantly warred with herself regarding holidays. She loved the sun, she loved to sit with a book and a glass of wine, so it made sense for them to book a month-long trip to Spain or the likes of and enjoy their retirement. "Did you want me to have a look at some deals for you?"

"Oh, no. Don't worry. I'm sure I'll find something to do. Now tell me, how's that second daughter of mine?" Angela was referring to Blair.

"Blair and Dom are both fine, Mum." Eden swallowed, wishing she could just come out and say what she wanted to say. But maybe she *could* just say it. What was the worst that could happen? "Actually, I had something I wanted to discuss with you."

"I'm sure it can wait. You're probably busy."

"Mum, it's fine. I've only just climbed out of bed." Eden

wouldn't usually do something like this over the phone, she hated that kind of thing, but she couldn't deal with the uncertainty in her mum's eyes. "You know how Blair is ridiculously in love with Dom…"

"I do. I'm so happy she found the love of her life. But don't get me started. You know how I feel about that…*thing*, she used to be married to. Don't start me off because I won't stop. And I'll swear. That's never a good look."

Eden grinned. She loved this side of Angela. "Mum, calm yourself down. We all know how you feel about Barrett."

"Don't say his name, love. He doesn't deserve to be spoken about."

Eden lowered herself onto the couch, running a hand through her hair. Maybe she should have done this last night when she felt brave and confident as she sat comfortably between Aster's legs.

"Anyway, do you have a few minutes to stay on the phone? I need at least three coffees before I even think about getting ready."

"Okay, if you're sure it's not eating into your day."

"I have plenty of time. Don't worry. You know I'm only on the end of the phone whenever you want to talk. Don't forget that."

She got to her feet and prepared a coffee. Once she had some caffeine in her, she would feel better.

Eden chewed her lip, tugging at the hem of the shirt she was wearing. She'd felt so positive and confident as she lay in bed this morning, enjoying Aster's warmth. Now, she just needed to build up the courage to be honest with her mother. That was easier said than done.

Eden cleared her throat. "So, about Blair and Dom."

"Like I said, I'm thrilled for them both. And Dom, she's wonderful. She has lovely manners, and she certainly takes good care of Blair. You know I love her like a daughter of my own."

"I know, Mum." Eden and Blair had been inseparable as kids,

teens too, but recently, not so much. "So, you know Dom plays football?"

"I do."

"Well, one of the players on the team, Grace…her best friend comes to watch. Turns out she's a photographer, and I hired her a few months ago. Her name is Aster. She's lovely."

"Aster…" Angela tried the name out. "Does her mother like to garden?"

"She did actually, yes. But that doesn't matter right now." Eden sipped her coffee, sighing lightly as the intense aroma overpowered her senses. "She was supposed to go on holiday with us, but her dad took ill while we were at the airport."

"Oh, poor love. I know you'll be there for her, especially if she's your employee. You take wonderful care of your staff."

"I'm dating her." Eden spoke with an excitement in her voice. Now that she'd said those words, she realised just how much she wanted this to work out for her. "You there, Mum?"

"I'm sorry, the line went funny. I thought you said you were dating her."

"I did say that. I'm dating Aster."

"But…she's a woman." Angela grew confused, that much was clear in her voice and how it wavered. "You don't like women."

"I've recently discovered that I do. Well, not women, just this one woman."

"Oh, love. Don't be so ridiculous." Angela barked a laugh. "You're 42. Try acting like it. You've never dated a woman before, so I find it hard to believe that you want to now." Angela sighed. Every word she had just spoken broke Eden's heart a little bit more. "Is this because you feel left out? Jealous, perhaps?"

"Jealous?" *What did she have to be jealous about?*

"Blair. She's happy. You see it and you want some of it, too? Because life and love doesn't work like that."

Eden stared down at the coffee table, tears in her eyes. Her bottom lip trembled, devastated that her mum could say that. "No, it's not like that."

"I beg to differ. Get these daft thoughts out of your head. When you visit, we'll discuss this silly idea of you turning gay."

"I'm not turning gay, I—" Eden looked at her screen. Her mum had ended their call. "Wow."

Every thought she'd had about her future had just been obliterated in a matter of seconds. She knew her mum would be surprised and shocked, but Eden never for one second thought that she would have reacted the way she did. It didn't make sense; Angela had always wanted Eden to be happy. She didn't force her into dating, expecting her to conform by a particular age. And while she didn't imagine her mum would jump for joy, she didn't expect her to find the idea of Eden dating a woman so ridiculous. This was a blow. One that felt like a punch directly in her gut.

Blair could do no wrong in her mother's eyes, but Eden? She was absurd.

22

Aster stared out the window of her dad's hospital room, the air humid and sticky. She hated hospitals, they'd always made her feel a little uneasy, but her dad was here so Aster was, too. And Lily was due back in the next ten minutes, so Aster didn't need to hang around much longer.

"You seem to be in your own head, my love."

Aster turned, smiling at her dad. "You know I told you about the woman I'm dating?"

Ted nodded, no longer wearing his oxygen mask. Seeing the lack of mask instantly calmed Aster when she arrived. Her dad looked brighter today, and he definitely had more life in him.

"Well, she turned up last night at my door. She decided not to get on the plane and came back to be with me instead."

Ted smiled, his eyes bright. "I'm glad you told me about her. I'd love to meet her someday."

"I'm sure I can arrange that." Aster eased into the seat beside her dad's bed. "But I need you to promise me you'll keep taking your medication. Because what you've been doing isn't good, Dad. What if we'd lost you?"

"I'm sorry, Aster. I was having a bad time. I promise to take whatever I'm prescribed."

"But I mean, really promise me? Pinky and all?" Aster held up her little finger.

Ted lifted his hand, holding out his own. "Only if you promise me that you'll fall in love with this woman who seems to be *very* fond of you."

Aster blew out a shaky breath. Ted may already have his wish. But…something felt off. "I think it's already happened."

"Well, only you'll know when it has. And if you feel this strongly about her, I want to meet her sooner rather than later. Because I have to be sure she's good enough for you. What would your mother say if I didn't do my research?"

Tears welled in Aster's eyes. "Mum would have loved her. I know she would. They'd probably go to lunch together and stuff. And have their hair done afterwards."

"I don't doubt that, sweetheart."

"It's just…she left suddenly this morning. She stayed over last night, and we watched films together. But when I woke up this morning, she'd gone."

"Maybe she had something to take care of…"

Aster wrung her hands. "I thought so, but it feels like more than that. Like…she's backing away maybe. I've tried to think of anything I did wrong last night, but I can't recall a single thing."

"Have you called? Sent her a message?" Ted clasped his hands in his lap, his face not as pale as it had been when Aster arrived here yesterday afternoon. He definitely had more colour in his cheeks.

"I called her this morning, but she wasn't available to answer. She texted me back to say she'd speak to me this evening."

"Don't panic. I'm sure it's nothing. She could have been called into work or had a family emergency."

Ted didn't need this. If he knew Aster was worried, he'd stress himself out. "You're right." She turned her watch towards herself.

"I spoke to Lily a few minutes ago. She's trying to find a space to park."

"What time does your ticket end?"

"I've got fifteen minutes before I'll have to put another tenner in. Greedy buggers in these hospitals."

Ted laughed, coughing as he did so. "You sound like your mum more and more lately. You go, love. You'll probably bump into Lily on the way down."

"You're sure? I'll be back tomorrow to see you."

"Do me a favour?" Ted asked, sitting up better in the bed.

Aster nodded. She'd do anything for him.

"Go home and have a look for a last-minute break. Take your girlfriend away and treat her. That was a big thing she did by cancelling her holiday for you. I'm sure you'd both enjoy some time together."

"I can't. I need to be here for you."

Ted took Aster's hand. "You've always been there for me. And I know you always will be. Just for a few days. I'm not going anywhere."

Aster chewed her lip. She'd love to disappear for a few days with Eden, but she needed to hear from her first. If Eden didn't contact her, there was nothing Aster could do. Realistically, Eden's head was probably up her ass.

"I'll have a look when I get home." She got to her feet and bent down to kiss her dad's cheek. "But if you feel unwell at all, you call me, okay?"

"I'm okay."

Satisfied that her dad was on the mend, Aster took her jacket from the back of the chair and draped it over her arm. She'd text Eden on the way down to the car and hope for the best. If it came to nothing, she'd give her some time. Aster had to remember that this was all still a big deal for Eden.

Once she'd said her goodbyes, Aster slipped out of her dad's room, strolling along the hallway as she took her phone from her pocket.

A: Hey! Need some company?

E: I'm busy right now. Sorry.

A: Right, okay. Did you decide to sneak off and get a flight to join the team?

E: No. I'm at home.

A: Well I can totally be invisible while I sit and watch you just being beautiful.

E: Can we do this another time? Today isn't great.

Aster frowned. Eden was speaking to her as though she was a colleague. How had they fallen asleep in one another's arms last night, but Eden was giving her the cold shoulder today? None of this made sense.

A: Is everything okay? Did I do something last night to make you feel uncomfortable?

E: No. You're perfect. Always.

A: Then I will go home and just see you when I see you. Sorry again for ruining your holiday plans.

Three dots appeared…until they faded out. And then her phone vibrated in her hand.

E: You didn't. And I had an amazing time last night. Thank you.

A: It can't have been that amazing if you left before I woke up. But you know what, it's fine. You have a life of your own and stuff to work through. I'll…see you soon, hopefully.

Aster locked her phone and held her head high. Something was going on with Eden, and she was going to find out what before this day was over. If she had to stand outside her door until she opened it, Aster would do that. Because this, whatever was happening between them, was far too good to lose.

Aster clenched her hands at her sides, exhaling a slow, steady breath. Eden had been silent since they spoke earlier in the day, and now Aster was done with waiting. She may not look like she'd demand answers, Aster was generally laidback, but she couldn't sit at home wondering if Eden would ever bother to call her again.

She rasped on Eden's apartment door, steadying herself and remaining calm.

The door opened. Tired, weary eyes stared back at her.

"You promised me you would always be honest. You stood in front of me and agreed to always speak to me." Aster's voice, hoarse from lack of conversation all day, filtered through the silence. "If you don't want to go any further with me, that's perfectly fine, but please don't disappear and then give me nothing. I deserve more than that. You know I do."

Eden came out into the light, her eyes more bloodshot and swollen than Aster had first thought. "I'm sorry."

Aster immediately stepped closer to Eden. She held her face in her hands, concern pulsing through her. "What's wrong? Why are you upset?"

"This morning I woke up feeling on top of the world. I couldn't wait to spend the day with you, and God, you've no idea how hard it was to keep my hands to myself when I felt your arms around me…"

Aster wanted to love everything Eden was saying, but she couldn't. There had to be a 'but' coming. It was inevitable.

"My mum called me. I had it in my head that I could tell her about us. I was terrified, but I was excited, too. I couldn't hold it in any longer."

"O…kay." Aster frowned.

"She basically shit all over it and told me I was being ridiculous. That I was jealous of Blair and Dom so now I want to be with a woman. And it's not like that for me, Aster. I *need* you to believe me when I tell you that."

"I-I do believe you. That's not what I think is happening here."

Eden lowered her eyes, wrapping her arms around herself. "I thought she would be at least a little bit happy for me. Or that she'd be shocked but not completely against the idea."

Aster dropped her head, blowing out a deep breath. "But she was. She was very against it, wasn't she?"

"She put the phone down on me," Eden spoke barely above a whisper. "She's never done that before."

"What does this mean for us, Eden?" Aster completely understood that Eden had her family to think about. But didn't she deserve to be happy? "I mean, I want to work through this with you, but are you ending this before it's started?"

Eden looked up at her, her long lashes glistening, tears falling down her face. "I thought about it."

"Right." Aster took a step back, rubbing her forearm. She didn't know what to say or how to change Eden's mind. Because Aster was just Aster. She was nothing special. If Eden's mum had reservations about them, she'd be even more disappointed on meeting Aster. She probably wasn't worthy in Eden's parents' eyes. "Well, uh…"

"But I can't walk away from you, Aster. Not now. I feel like I'm in too deep, and I'm not prepared to see you years down the line and realise you were the one that got away." Eden reached out a hand, taking Aster's. It felt safe…wanted. "I have things to discuss with her when I visit, but I can't end this with you. I don't *want* to do that."

"Y-you mean…you choose me?" Aster was taken aback. She wasn't sure she'd ever be worth that much to another woman. "If it comes down to it…"

"I think I'd choose you time and time again," Eden said, pulling Aster against her. "I needed a moment today. I needed to understand what the hell was going on in my life, because everything feels so intense that I don't know if I'm coming or going."

"I get that." Aster lifted a hand, brushing her knuckles against Eden's damp cheek. "I hate seeing you cry."

"I'm okay. I was more worried about how much I'd hurt you today. I don't ever want to hurt you."

"I'm glad I came here tonight. I needed to see you. To do this. Just hold you."

"I was coming to you." Eden said. "I just needed to get things straight in my head."

"And…have you done that?" Aster narrowed her eyes as she stepped forward. This woman…she wasn't sure how much longer she could keep her hands to herself. "And like, are you inviting me in?"

"Y-you want to come in? After today?" Eden seemed surprised by that, but right now, Aster just wanted to lock the door and slip beneath the sheets. "I mean, I'd love you to…but you don't have anywhere else to be? Out with friends?"

Aster curled her fingers under Eden's chin, tilting her head and meeting her eyes. "If I want to stay in with a gorgeous woman, I will do that. And if I want to kiss you slowly, while I undress you, I will *also* do that." Eden's eyes fluttered closed, her mouth falling open as Aster pressed her lips to one eyelid, then the other. "So, why don't we take this inside and get to know one another?"

Eden's hands trembled as she held Aster's waist. "Y-yes."

"You're sure?" Aster smiled against Eden's ear, her body begging to get naked with this woman. "No pressure, remember…"

Eden lowered her hands to the button on Aster's jeans, her breathing laboured. "I'm not sure I can wait any longer. I *need* to feel you."

That was all Aster needed to hear. She reached around Eden, pushed the front door open, and guided her inside. Their lips met as they fumbled through the apartment, finally reaching the bedroom door with a thud. But a door wouldn't stand in Aster's way. She kicked it open, stumbling her way inside.

As the backs of Eden's knees hit the edge of the bed, Aster lowered her down, falling on top of her. She stared down at Eden, her eyes black with desire, and whispered, "*You* are all I've ever dreamed of."

23

Eden's heart was ready to burst from her chest as Aster rested against her between her legs. Though Eden was fully prepared to experience a woman for the first time, Aster's languid kisses didn't quite quell the dread she couldn't kick from her mind. Eden didn't want it to be this way. What she wanted was to know *exactly* what she was doing.

As if sensing Eden's concerns, Aster pulled back, staring down at her. Those chocolate eyes pierced Eden, her fear overtaken by the most intense tingling throughout her body. "It's just you and me here."

Eden smiled, hoping it would satisfy Aster. "I know."

"And all I want is to touch you. To show you what you mean to me."

Eden wanted that too, but could her own hands reciprocate? Would Aster be unimpressed when this was all over? "I'm afraid I don't know what I'm doing…"

Aster sat back on her knees, lifting her T-shirt over her head. Her white bra contrasted beautifully with the gentle tan on her skin, her stomach muscles contracting as Eden lifted a hand, feathering her fingertips above the waistband of her jeans. "Trust me, you're doing amazing." Aster shuddered when Eden repeated the movement. "Fuck. Really good."

Okay, that praise helped a little.

"I never thought I'd feel your fingers against my skin."

"It's all I've thought about," Eden said, her voice low. "This moment…with you."

"Then I hope I live up to your imagination." Aster unhooked her bra, allowing it to slowly fall away from her body. Yes, she was absolutely living up to every fantasy Eden had allowed herself.

She wrapped her legs around Aster's waist, satisfied when Aster braced herself above Eden. Her exquisite breasts hung freely, but Eden's instant reaction was to trail her tongue up Aster's neck, finally capturing those full lips.

Aster's hand wandered, palming Eden's thigh before moving further back and over her knee, then down the back of her calf. Just that simple touch had wetness slipping between Eden's cheeks. God, it was intense.

Emboldened by just how calm Aster appeared, Eden lifted her hand, squeezing one breast, her thumb grazing Aster's hard nipple.

Aster pulled away from the kiss, her mouth falling open as she gasped lightly. "Yes. That feels…"

Eden tweaked a nipple, lifting her head and covering it with her mouth. If Eden focused on what she, herself, enjoyed, she surely couldn't go wrong.

"O-oh, shit," Aster whispered, staring directly into Eden's eyes. "Your mouth is everything I knew it would be. And more."

Eden sucked, rolling her tongue as she watched Aster's reaction change. Okay, she was doing something right. But then Aster sat up, taking Eden with her.

"May I?" She gripped the hem of Eden's T-shirt.

Eden nodded, lifting her arms as Aster undressed her. As her T-shirt hit the floor, Aster's eyes never leaving her chest, Eden felt the intensity of her stare. Nobody had ever looked at her that way, and no look had ever felt so…all-consuming.

"Beautiful," Aster whispered, lowering Eden down to the bed again. Her hips pushed Eden's legs up, her knees bent mid-air. But it was the press of nipples that had Eden instantly soaked through her shorts. Aster settled her hand against the side of Eden's neck, her lips parting as she took Eden's bottom lip between her teeth. "So fucking beautiful."

"Aster…"

Aster pressed her forehead to Eden's, her eyes soft. "Talk to me. Tell me what you need."

"I need to be naked. With you."

Aster didn't hesitate, climbing from the bed and tugging her shorts down her legs. She kicked them away, her boy shorts following. But then her eyes landed on Eden's shorts, her lip between her teeth.

Eden lifted her hips, urging Aster to take control.

And she did. Aster got to her knees in front of Eden, her palms smoothing up her thighs, teasing with each stroke. And then her fingers held the waistband, Aster's eyes finding Eden's.

She lifted an eyebrow. Eden simply nodded.

With the steadiest hand, Aster lowered Eden's shorts, her eyes lighting up when she discovered Eden wasn't wearing underwear.

Lay naked, Eden felt exposed, but she felt safe first and foremost. It was hard to feel anything else in Aster's company. This woman hadn't once given her a reason to worry.

As Aster placed her hands on Eden's skin, she gently nudged her legs open, desire written all over her pretty face. Her hands moved higher, massaging as they reached the junction of Eden's thighs. The intensity that roared through Eden had fresh arousal spilling from her.

Aster shifted forward, dipping her head and pressing lazy kisses to Eden's inner thighs. "God, I need to taste you."

Eden wasn't shy when it came to sex, but Aster's voice, that look in her eyes…nobody had ever wanted Eden quite like this. But Eden's biggest fear now was that Aster would touch her, and she'd explode.

The longing, the teasing in each kiss, the want spanning months…it all came down to this moment. It *couldn't* be premature.

"What do you want, Eden?" Aster watched her with a hunger.

"I want your mouth on me."

"Yeah?" Aster grinned, swiping her thumb down between Eden's wet folds, garnering a low, throaty moan.

"O-oh."

Aster swiped her thumb again and then dipped her head and replaced her thumb with one long drag of her tongue.

Eden's hips lifted, her hands grabbing at her breasts, pinching her nipples. It was the simplest action, but God, it meant everything. The trust she felt when Aster had her hands *and* mouth on her…it was indescribable.

"Fuck," Aster breathed, her hooded eyes looking up at Eden, desire staring back at her.

She dove back in, expertly lashing her tongue against Eden's clit. And when she held Eden's hips down, separating her lips to expose her engorged clit, Eden lost her mind. Gripping the bedsheet with one hand, the other pressed against the back of Aster's head.

Eden's thighs quaked, but she wouldn't give in. She'd waited this long; she could wait some more.

Aster teasingly dipped a finger inside, slowly but surely building her orgasm again. And then she placed a gentle kiss to Eden's mound, climbing up her body. When Aster's body pressed her into the bed, the weight providing a comfort, Eden dug her nails into her shoulder, their mouths crashing together.

"I want to touch you," she murmured against Aster's lips. "I *need* to touch you."

Aster repositioned herself, guiding Eden's hand between her legs. "I want you to know just how wet you make me."

Eden's eyes fluttered closed when her fingertips found hot, wet heat. Aster was more than ready. But was Eden?

Aster placed a slow kiss to her lips, her own fingers drifting to where Eden desperately needed them to be. "Ever fucked yourself?" she asked, smirking as her tongue swiped Eden's sensitive earlobe.

Fuck! That's hot.

Eden nodded, blushing. "Y-yes."

"Then I want you to touch me how you know *you* like it."

Eden's body thrummed. Aster was certainly vocal.

She pressed her fingers to Aster's clit, rewarded with a guttural moan as she dipped lower. She eased two fingers into Aster, capturing her lips as she sunk deeper. And then Aster followed suit, entering Eden in one swift move.

Eden clenched her jaw, breathing through the climax she felt building. But it wasn't to be; she couldn't hold on any longer. Aster scooped her up in one arm, pushing in and out while her thumb landed on her clit. Her lips caressed Eden's neck, her throat, and her hand…God, her hand was doing unimaginable things to every nerve ending in Eden's body.

"Aster, I-I…" Eden trailed off, her head falling back as her mouth gaped. Aster only lavished her neck even more, sucking on a spot below her ear. "Oh, shit…" Eden's breath hitched, her fingers moving inside Aster matching her rhythm.

Aster shook when Eden pressed her thumb to her clit. A deep moan rumbled in her throat. "I'm gonna come, babe."

Those words tipped them both over the edge, a strangled cry erupting in Eden's throat. But Aster continued to work her magic between her thighs, curling her fingers as they convulsed against one another.

So this is what it feels like when the person in bed with you knows what they're doing?

Incredible.

Eden shook, her thighs closing around Aster's hand. She didn't want this to end, but she *did* need a moment to breathe. To gather her thoughts and her emotions. As Aster slowed, placing soft kisses to her collarbone, a tear slipped from Eden's eye. She couldn't help it. That had to have been the most intense orgasm she'd ever had.

"Hey," Aster whispered, noting how Eden's eyes were squeezed shut. "Look at me, beautiful."

Oh, when she calls me that... Eden's emotions were close to exploding.

"Eden?"

Eden's eyes opened, an overwhelming sense of love sitting in her chest.

"Checking in with you." Aster smiled, stroking her skin. "You good?"

Eden lifted her head, craving Aster's lips. "Oh, you've no idea."

24

Eden leant against the window frame, looking down onto the city. Considering she should have been soaking up the sun in Spain this morning, she couldn't think of anywhere else she'd rather be. Because she'd woken up in Aster's arms, enveloped by her scent, their legs tangled. If she had to rate this on a scale of her greatest experiences, it was up there at number one.

She sipped her coffee, smiling as Aster turned on the shower. Not only was this morning entirely different to *anything* she'd ever known, but Eden couldn't quite believe that it was a woman she'd curled up against last night. Over the years, she'd wondered if her life would ever feel complete without someone by her side. She knew in her heart that she longed for something more, a love so intense that it left her breathless, but as the years passed, it didn't seem possible. As she aged, she considered whether she'd always be alone. But this morning, here and now, her chest swelled.

Eden settled on the window seat, pulling her knees up to her chest. As she closed her eyes, her mind cast back to last night. How Aster had been patient as they explored one another. The way in which she made Eden feel at ease with every stroke of her fingertips. One moment, her heart was almost beating out of her chest, but the next, calmness washed over her. It was incredible how things could feel so different with another woman.

And then the thought of sneaking into the shower with Aster suddenly flashed in Eden's mind. Was it possible to be at such a place yet? Eden smirked. She was about to find out. She got to her feet, rolling her head on her shoulders as a little courage built in her chest. From last night, Eden knew Aster wasn't shy. And as luck would have it, Eden didn't appear to be either.

As she placed her cup on the kitchen island, Eden curled her fingers beneath the hem of her T-shirt.

And then a knock on the door had her frozen in place. Who the hell had bypassed the buzzer on the main entrance? She snuck towards the door, peering through the peephole. *Fuck!* It was her mother.

Eden didn't need this right now. Of course the time would come to have a conversation with her mum about her newfound sexuality, but did it have to be this morning? Aster was here, and Eden really needed her to not be. Angela would frighten her away within a second.

There was another knock.

"Eden, I know you're home. Your car is parked in its spot."

Eden clenched her jaw, fisting her hands. If she didn't answer, Angela would let herself in with the spare key. It hadn't occurred to Eden that giving her mum a key would ever be a problem, but now the realisation was beginning to dawn on her.

"Eden!"

"Alright! I'm coming!" Eden unlocked the door and swung it open, gritting her teeth as she stared back at her mother. "What?"

"We need to talk."

"No, Mum. Not right now."

Angela frowned as she disregarded Eden's wishes, her heels

clicking on the floor when she slipped inside. "Yes. Now. I've been going out of my mind all night."

Eden snorted as she slammed her front door shut. "Why? Because you're *so* distraught by the fact your daughter is dating a woman?"

Angela spun on her heel; her eyes narrowed. "You're not alone, are you?"

"This is my place, Mum. Who I have here is none of your business. It's 8 a.m. for God's sake!"

"So, she's keeping you from work? Because you'd usually be at the office by now. This is already a mistake!" Angela threw up her hands. And then she started to pace. Pacing was never good. It usually involved a lot of ranting. "I mean, how can you possibly be dating a woman?"

"Quite easily," Eden said. "And no, she's not keeping me from work. In case you forgot, I'm supposed to be in Spain."

"None of this makes any sense, Eden. I just…I don't understand."

Eden exhaled a breath. There was no use arguing with her mother. They could be civil. She moved towards Angela and guided her to the couch. "What exactly don't you understand?"

"You've never dated a woman."

"How do you know?"

"Because you would have told me."

Okay, Angela had a point. Eden *would* have told her. But that didn't mean that this had to be difficult to understand. It was straightforward as far as Eden was concerned.

"And I don't know. It just seems…off."

"Off or *wrong*?" Eden quirked an eyebrow. She'd never thought for one second that her mum would be so against this. "Because you were perfectly happy when Blair met Dom."

"It's different."

"How so?"

"Blair isn't my child. I may love her as though she is, but she's not. *You are.* And that is where my priorities lie. With you and wanting what's best for you."

Eden opened her mouth to speak, but she wasn't sure she had any comeback. Did it really matter who gave Eden what was best? Did gender really matter? It hadn't felt that way last night when Aster treated her with respect in the bedroom.

"In my opinion," Aster said, her voice filtering through the air, "what's best for Eden is whatever she decides, and what I have between my legs shouldn't play a part in that." Eden and Angela turned at the same time. Aster stood towel drying her hair in the doorway of the bathroom. "And I completely understand your uncertainty, any parent would probably feel the same way, but Eden makes me incredibly happy. I'd hope she felt the same way about me."

Eden smiled, tears pricking her eyes. "I do."

"When I met your daughter, I didn't realise I was even looking for a relationship. I had no idea the impact she would have on me from working with her."

Angela cleared her throat. "She's a successful businesswoman."

"I know. And I love watching her around the office. Her confidence is pretty astounding. She knows what she wants, and I think her success is proof of that."

"What exactly can *you* offer her?"

Eden's heart sank. The tone in Angela's voice didn't go unnoticed by either of them. That was clear in the way Aster's eyebrow rose.

"Support. Someone to come home to and talk about her day with. A shoulder if she's having a bad day. Trust, understanding, compassion, space when Eden needs it...and one day, love. The same things any couple would or *should* offer one another."

Eden glanced in her mum's direction. Angela simply stared Aster down.

"I'm not sure what you think the point of me being here is,

but I know it's nothing you could be thinking. I don't want Eden because of who she is in business. I want her because of how she makes me feel when we're together."

"And what does your mother think of this? You must be what...in your early twenties?"

"I'm flattered, but I'm 32. And my mother would be thrilled I'd found someone like Eden. I know she would. But since she's no longer around, I don't have the pleasure of introducing them to one another." Aster cleared her throat, eyeing Eden momentarily. A tear fell down her cheek as she smiled. "I should probably head off. Leave you two to discuss everything." Aster dragged her hair up into a wet ponytail, turning her back. Eden's heart broke for her. But then Aster turned back suddenly, another tear gathering at her jawline. "I know what I want, but Eden, if this is too much for you...if it's going to turn your family against you, I completely get it, okay?"

Eden got to her feet, frowning. "N-no."

"Babe, just give it some time," Aster said. "I don't want you to come to any rash decisions. Talk things through with your mum, and when you know, you know."

Eden lowered her head, her eyes closing as she fought back the urge to cry. Why did her mum have to come here this morning and ruin everything?

"Well, that was quite the speech." Angela sat back, crossing her legs. "Almost rehearsed."

"Can you leave please?" Eden pinched the bridge of her nose.

"I'm not finished talking to you."

Eden laughed. "Oh, you are. I'm not listening to another word you have to say."

"Excuse me?"

"Leave, Mum. I can't deal with this right now. And change the attitude; it's appalling."

Angela got to her feet, facing Eden. "You heard her. Give it some time."

"Do you want me to be alone? Do you want me to just exist between here and the office?"

"Don't be ridiculous."

"Then what *do* you want? Because considering you've always told me you want me to be happy, you're making it very hard to do so this morning."

"I'm just not convinced this is what you want. You *think* it is because you see how happy Dom makes Blair, but she had a terrible time with Barrett."

"So?"

"So, you're not a beaten housewife, my love. You don't need to find love in the first person who shows an interest."

Eden nodded. Not only was Angela insulting her, but she was insulting Blair, too. "You can leave now."

"Eden—"

"I'll make sure I let Blair know how you feel about her. And Dom. Which is a shame because they're both very fond of you. As was I. But standing here this morning, I can't fathom why."

Angela's forehead creased, the realisation of what she'd said now sinking in. "That wasn't what I meant."

"Sure sounded that way to me." Eden moved towards the front door and opened it. She may have been unsure about her mother's reaction, but this was just sad. "You know, it was Blair who told me you'd be okay with this. She was the one who encouraged me to go after what I wanted. After watching how her mum treated her, disowning Blair, I thought I would have a totally different experience. Seems I was wrong."

"I-I don't know what you want from me, Eden."

"Your love and support would have been nice, but it looks like I only receive that when it suits you." Eden tilted her head towards the outside corridor. "Leave. I'm done."

Angela opened her mouth to speak, but Eden held up a hand.

"Leave. I won't ask you again."

"As you wish. But we're not done with this conversation."

Angela stepped out into the corridor, fixing her cerise pink jacket. Eden couldn't put her finger on the look in her mother's eyes, but it left her feeling cold.

Eden barked a laugh. "Oh, we are. Don't bother calling unless you change your attitude *and* your opinion. Because this, what I have here, isn't ending. Like it or don't. I'm not interested."

Before Angela could respond, Eden closed the door. She needed a moment to breathe before she tackled everything Aster had said. While she loved most of it, she hated the idea of Aster thinking she was uncertain. This morning, Eden was more certain than she had ever been in her life.

Go in there and kiss her like there's no tomorrow.

Aster sat perched on the edge of Eden's bed, holding the hoodie she'd borrowed last night. She lifted it up to her nose, smiling against the material as she inhaled. Eden's perfume wasn't overbearing, it was just right. A slight fragrance that didn't blow your head off. It was just there—calming and delicate—kinda like Eden herself. But that calmness was likely to be out of the window now after her little speech in the living room. Aster knew Eden wouldn't have appreciated anything she said; it wasn't her business after all. It was between Eden and her mother.

She cleared her throat and got to her feet, folding Eden's hoodie and placing it neatly on the bed. Aster would love to take it with her, a memento of sorts, but it would only remind her of the one woman she knew had been off the table from day one. Last night may have been everything to Aster, but she feared the memories of touching something so precious, someone who meant far more than Aster thought, would keep her awake at night. This wasn't supposed to be their first morning together. It was supposed to be all encompassing. They should have been lounging around, kissing one another and making plans.

The bedroom door opened slowly, Eden's dark eyes coming into focus as Aster lifted her head. She smiled weakly, lifting her phone from the bed. "Sorry, I didn't really want to leave while your mum was in the living room. I already feel shit enough."

Eden frowned. "Why?"

"I shouldn't have said what I did out there. I should have kept my mouth shut and minded my own business. I'm sorry."

Eden closed the bedroom door and approached Aster. When she took her hand, Aster's body tingled. "I'm glad you said what you did."

"You are?"

"If Mum was unsure before, she's certainly not now." Eden pressed her body to Aster, smiling into a kiss. "You stood your ground, and I admire you for that."

"I needed her to know that she has a wonderful daughter. But I'm not sure she'll go for it."

"That's a problem my mum will have to deal with herself. And I told her that."

"Eden, are you sure you're willing to potentially fall out with her over this? Over me? I'd like to think I'm absolutely worth it, but what if I'm not? What if in a week or a month you regret choosing me in all of this, and then it's ruined everything with your family?"

"I very much doubt that's going to happen, Aster."

Eden had a sparkle in her eyes that Aster couldn't imagine seeing from anyone else. Bright, yet so dark. Inviting, yet a little apprehensive. Eden's eyes always told a story, but this morning, Aster was struggling to read her completely. "Whatever you want to do, okay?"

"What I want is to keep doing this with you," Eden whispered, her arms wrapping around Aster' waist. "This morning... my God!"

"Did you feel okay?" Aster asked. It wasn't the kind of conversation she wanted to be having, but Eden and how she was feeling meant a lot to her. "I mean, after last night. Did you wake up wishing it hadn't happened?"

"Quite the opposite actually."

"Oh yeah?" Aster couldn't fight back the smirk she was wearing. Knowing Eden had enjoyed last night as much as she had herself...well, it helped a lot.

"I sat with my coffee this morning wondering what the hell took me so long."

"It's a big change in your life."

Eden's hands slid up the back of Aster's T-shirt as she grinned. "Still, I feel like I've missed out on too much. And to be perfectly honest, I don't plan to dwell on it for too long. That time could be spent doing much more *exciting* things."

"Now that I could get on board with."

"Good. Because I was hoping we could spend the day together. And the night..."

Aster winced. She would love to spend every moment with Eden, but she had to visit her dad first. "The night I can definitely do, and I can't wait, but I have to head to my dad's. Lily called a few minutes ago. He's just been discharged, and I want to make sure he's okay."

"That's great. I'm glad they've discharged him."

"Me too...I think." Aster pulled Eden down into a seated position on the bed. Was her dad in the right frame of mind to be home? "I hope he hasn't convinced them to discharge him."

"They wouldn't do that if he wasn't ready."

"You don't know my dad. He's very persistent."

Eden nodded, squeezing Aster's hand. "Well, you'll know when you get there. Maybe you should stay for a few days."

"Lily will be there. She lives with him."

"Right. Yes."

"He can't wait to meet you, by the way. I told him all about how gorgeous you are yesterday when I visited the hospital."

Eden blushed, shaking her head. "I think he's going to be

disappointed when he meets me then. I'm really nothing special, Aster."

Aster lifted Eden's hand, kissing her knuckles. "Well, you are to me. And if I think you are, my dad will think so too. I can't remember a time when I introduced him to anyone as important as you. Actually, I never have. Nobody seemed worth it in the past."

"I'd love to meet him. But I don't know when the right time for that will be. He's your priority, and I've never done the whole meeting the parents thing before."

"I'm happy to introduce you to him whenever you're comfortable with that. There's no rush, so don't stress about it."

"Okay. Maybe once he's feeling up to visitors?"

Aster leaned in, her lips lingering against Eden's when she kissed her slowly. "I can't wait for him to meet you."

"If he's like you, I don't think I have anything to worry about."

"No, you really don't need to worry. He's great." Aster pulled back, aware that her hands were itching to roam Eden's thighs. "Do you think things will be okay with your family?"

Eden shrugged. "Right now, I don't care. I have much more interesting people on my mind. Meaning you. *You're* people."

"Good to know." Aster sat for a moment, enjoying the intimacy of Eden's bedroom. When she arrived yesterday, she hadn't for one second imagined she would wake up here. But she had, and it felt incredible. "Now, should we have breakfast before I head off?"

"Yes. I'll cook dinner tonight. Just give me an idea of what time you'll be back, and I'll have it in the oven ready for us."

"That sounds like the perfect night to me."

"Me too."

25

Eden moved around her office, clearing away the paperwork she'd left sitting around since before she took time off work. The thought of getting back into the swing of things had been hurting her head for the last couple of nights. It didn't matter how truly wonderful life had been recently; she wanted to lock herself in her apartment while Aster waited in the bedroom for her.

The idea of a no-pressure relationship had grown on her overnight. Actually, that was a lie. In the last couple of weeks, Eden wanted to *only* be with Aster. She couldn't care any less about pressure…because there was none.

Aster wasn't one to call incessantly even though Eden missed having her around when she wasn't at her place. She wasn't the kind of partner who demanded to know Eden's every move. Aster Bennett was the breath of fresh air Eden had been subconsciously praying for. Everything they did, it worked. Dinner together, walking around the city, waking up with one another…there wasn't a single thing Eden could think of that irked her about Aster, but she hadn't imagined she would anyway. From the moment they'd met, Eden felt at ease and in good company. That wasn't going to change now that sex and a relationship had been thrown into the mix—it was quite the opposite, really.

A gentle knock on her door brought Eden from all thoughts of Aster. She had work to do; she needed to concentrate. "Come in."

A flash of blonde hair greeted Eden. "Well, it's good to finally see you."

Eden grinned as Blair stepped into her office and closed the door. "Look at the tan on you. I'm not jealous."

"Oh, you are. And you should be. Pride was…intense."

Was Eden jealous? No, she couldn't be. While Spain would have been lovely, Aster was where she wanted to be. And she would choose Aster time and time again. "It's been intense here, too."

"I thought you were taking time off work?"

"I did."

"So, why was it intense? You're supposed to relax when you're not at the office."

Eden chewed her lip, wringing her hands where she stood. Blair eyed her, but Eden didn't know where to begin with explaining the whirlwind she'd faced lately.

"Edes?"

"Aster…is amazing."

Blair splayed a hand across her chest, blowing out a deep breath. "Don't do that to me. I thought something was wrong."

Eden dragged her best friend to the couch, both landing with a thud as they sunk into the soft leather. "You've no idea just what I've been up to since you left for Spain."

Blair quirked an eyebrow.

"I can't pull myself away from her. She's like a friggin' drug."

Blair grinned. "Uh-huh."

"And I don't know," Eden said, shrugging. "It's *everything* I want, Blair. Aster is one hundred percent the woman I could fall in love with." That wasn't quite the truth, but Blair didn't need to know that she was in love already. She'd only try to talk Eden out of those feelings, citing that it was far too soon. "We cook dinner together almost every night. We've spent one night apart since I showed up at her apartment two weeks ago. And I know you'll probably tell me I'm moving too fast, but I don't know how to slow down."

"Do you want to slow down?"

"No. Never."

Blair twisted in her seat, facing Eden. "Then why are you worrying if I think it's too fast?"

"Because I know you. You'll tell me what I *don't* need to hear, and then I'll slowly start to panic that Aster will run."

"Hey," Blair whispered, holding Eden's face in her hands. "I want you to be happy. I don't care how fast or slow you go, so long as you embrace these new feelings and enjoy every second of it."

"Oh, I'm more than enjoying it." Eden's voice betrayed her, dropping low.

"You've slept with her!" Blair shrieked. "You, Eden Kline, have been banging a woman for two weeks, and you didn't call me!"

"Uh, you may want to shout that a little louder next time. The staff on the third floor didn't hear you."

Blair winced, placing a hand over her mouth. "Sorry."

Eden's skin flushed when she reminded herself of last night. Aster may have appeared quiet on the surface, but my God, that woman could really take Eden to another existence. And she had, three times within the hour. That morning, Aster's soft roaming hands had only continued to pleasure Eden. Right up until it was time to leave for work. How they'd managed to not interfere with one another's projects today was anyone's guess.

"If you could stop thinking about fucking your girlfriend while your best friend is sitting next to you, that would be fab."

"You've changed your tune. I'm usually the one interrupting your thoughts."

Blair offered a sheepish smile before lowering her chin to her chest.

"What?"

"I…we…Dom isn't speaking to me at the minute."

Eden frowned. That wasn't possible. Dom worshipped Blair. So much so that Eden had often wondered what either of them would do with themselves if they were without each other. "I don't understand. Why wouldn't she be speaking to you?"

"I kinda flew off the handle because she was a bit friendly with Zoe in Spain."

"Zoe?" Eden cast her mind back. "Ah, the new manager."

"Yeah. Her."

"So, you've not been speaking to one another while you were away?"

"No. Spain was *amazing*." Blair paused, twisting her engagement ring on her finger. "It all happened when we landed back here. Zoe was making plans with the team. Dom seemed too eager to put some of her own ideas forward, and I lost it once we got into the cab."

"Blair."

"I know, I know. I'm a fucking idiot. But now she's not speaking to me because I accused her."

"Whoa." Eden threw up her hands, shaking her head. Had Blair lost her mind? "You accused her?"

Blair swallowed, tears welling in her eyes. Eden hated seeing her best friend upset, but Blair had brought this on herself. Dom would never do anything to hurt her. *Everyone* knew that.

"I don't know what's wrong with me. I'm terrified of losing her, Eden."

"You're going to if you do something stupid like accuse her."

Her best friend nodded slowly, wiping a tear from her jaw. But then Blair started to sob, and Eden could only take her in her arms. "I think I've ruined everything."

"I'm sure you haven't. Dom just needs some time."

"She always worried that I wouldn't trust her. That I'd be waiting for her to mess up. And now I've proved that to her even though I know I'm talking complete rubbish. She just…she's never going to forgive me for this."

Eden's heart ached for Blair, it really did, but Blair would have to bite the bullet on this one and grovel until Dom forgave her. "You have some serious making up to do."

"How? Should I buy her a gift? A car…a holiday?"

Eden wasn't sure she was qualified to give advice about such a serious relationship, but she knew Blair's money wasn't going to fix this. "Maybe you should stick to some flowers and a bottle of wine. Dom doesn't want your money, sweetheart. She wants your love, undivided attention, and trust."

"I do trust her. I trust her with my life, Edes."

"And she knows that. Deep down, at least."

As Eden wiped fresh tears from Blair's face, her office door opened. Aster stared back at them, frowning. "I…can come back."

"No, it's okay," Blair spoke, clearing her throat as she did so. "I have to leave soon. I need to call into work and check on one of my cases."

"Is everything okay?" The concern in Aster's eyes warmed Eden to the core. "Did something happen? I got a text from Dom about twenty minutes ago."

"S-saying what?" Blair turned her attention to Aster.

"She asked if I'd meet her this evening for a beer before she heads to her mum's or something. I'm assuming she needs a friend right now if her fiancée is sitting in my girlfriend's office crying."

Blair slumped back against the couch, hiding her face in her hands as her shoulders shook. Eden got to her feet, approaching Aster. "Did you agree to meet her?"

"No, babe. I know we have plans tonight, so I asked if we could do it next weekend instead."

Eden admired Aster for wanting to keep to their plans, but

Dom and Blair needed them tonight. "Text her back. Tell her you're free. I'll take Blair home with me for a few hours."

Aster frowned. "B-but we had plans." Then she lowered her voice. "Very sexy plans."

"And those plans will happen. But maybe not tonight. If Dom has been in touch with you, it means she trusts you. Please, for me?"

Aster leaned in, her lips lingering as she kissed Eden softly. It took everything within Eden to suppress a moan. "Anything for you."

Eden needed another moment with Aster, gripping the front of her shirt and pulling her closer. "Call me when you're leaving the bar. If you still wanted to stay the night…"

"Oh, I'm staying."

Eden released Aster, offering her a thankful smile as her girlfriend backed out of the office. She glanced at Blair, her smile now faint as she disappeared from sight. Eden wanted a night with Aster, one that replicated every other night they'd spent together lately, but she had to be there for Blair. It was her duty.

"Right. Let me get my stuff together and then we're out of here."

"Eden, it's fine. I'll head home. You have plans with Aster; this is my own fault."

"Nope. Wrong answer."

Aster didn't know Dom on a level that some of the team did, but she knew when something was seriously wrong. Today was one of those times. Dom's eyes were dull and lifeless as she mindlessly picked at the label on her beer bottle, her jaw clenched. Aster would like to think she could help here, but she wasn't sure she was cut out for such a serious conversation.

"You know, picking at labels is a sign of sexual frustration."

Dom scoffed. "Well, if things don't change, I'll have major sexual frustration going on. I'll never sleep with another fucking woman again!"

Okay, something had definitely gone down. "Wanna talk?"

Dom's eyes found Asters. "If Eden accused you of sleeping with another woman, how would you feel about it?"

Wow. That was a question. "I, uh…I'd be devastated in all honesty."

Dom nodded, her eyes focusing back on her beer bottle.

"Is that what's happened? One of you has accused the other?" This really wasn't Aster's territory.

"Blair thinks I'm shagging Zoe."

Ouch, that had to hurt. Zoe was gorgeous, the entire team agreed, but Dom wasn't that kind of person. At least, Aster didn't get that impression. "And she thinks that because…"

Dom lifted a shoulder. "Because she doesn't trust me. But why would she? I used to sleep around before I met her."

"Sleeping around and cheating are two entirely different things, mate."

"Tell that to my *supposed* fiancée." Dom exhaled, sitting forward in her seat. She looked like she had a lot to say, so Aster swigged her beer, giving her whatever time she needed to process. "You know, I've never met anyone like Blair before. She's so confident but complicated. And I get that, she had a terrible marriage, but we've always just clicked. I think we've had an argument once since we got together, and it was over something stupid that I don't even remember. But this? God, this hurt."

"I bet it did."

"And now I don't know how to go home and just pretend nothing happened. She's apologised, she's been grovelling since she realised what she'd said, but I can't even look at her. Because when I do, will she be trying to figure me out? Will she be watching me for any sign that I'm lying?"

"I think she realises the mistake she's made, Dom."

"You don't mistakenly accuse someone of cheating, Aster. That kinda thing comes from somewhere."

Dom had a point. Something must have caused Blair to accuse Dom. "No, I suppose you're right."

"So, I have some stuff in my car, and I'm leaving for my mum's tomorrow."

Aster wasn't sure that was wise. If she left, would they ever figure it out? Blair and Dom were the perfect couple until now. Aster couldn't imagine them not being together. "You're leaving?"

"For now." Dom nodded.

"Blair was in Eden's office earlier. She was really upset."

"Poor Blair." Dom rolled her eyes. "I know she's had a really shit time, but why is she the one everyone is concerned about? What about me?"

"I am concerned about you. And so is Eden. That's why I'm here, because Eden knew you needed a friend." Aster reached a hand across the table, squeezing Dom's. "Look, why don't you stay at my place? I'm at Eden's most of the time, and if you need somewhere to gather your thoughts, nobody will bother you there."

Dom didn't respond. She just sat staring at the table, chewing her lip.

"Think about it, at least. You can stay there until you and Blair have figured this out."

"I only had a drink with Zoe," Dom explained. "While we were away, she wanted to know about the team and who was who. You know, asking around to get a better idea of what she was dealing with. So, we planned to meet at the pool bar one afternoon for coffee. She's great, professional, and I think she's going to take the team further than Mark ever could."

"That sounds like something the team needs."

"Maybe…I don't know." Dom blew out a long, slow breath. "I called the wedding venue this morning."

"Oh, yeah? Have you two decided on more plans?"

"No. I called to ask how much notice we have to give if we want to cancel."

Aster's heart dropped into her stomach. She couldn't imagine making a decision like that. Thank God her and Eden had only just met. It meant Aster could make sure she learned from everyone else's mistakes.

"We'll lose the deposit, but I have some savings that I was going to buy Blair's dress with. So, I'll just give that to her for what she'll lose. I know she doesn't need the money for a dress, but I wanted to be the one who bought it for her. Just to make it that bit more special, you know?"

"I do." Aster eyed her phone sitting on the leather booth beside her. Should she send Eden a quick message to let her know what was going on? She didn't want to betray Dom's trust, but Aster was torn. Blair needed to know if this was something her fiancée was considering, didn't she? "I'd hate to see you two end things."

"Yeah, well…" Dom visibly swallowed. "I mean, have I not shown her how much I love her? Do I not do enough?" Dom laughed. "You know, that was always one of my biggest worries. Not being able to give Blair everything she deserves. Because she's fucking amazing for what she's been through, and I'm just…me. And to be honest, I'm exhausted with trying to make everything perfect."

"Has Blair ever expected you to make everything perfect?"

"That's not the point. If she didn't trust me deep down, which she clearly doesn't, why has she spent the last two years with me? Why did she ask me to live with her, agree to be my wife, if she doesn't fully trust me the moment someone comes along and smiles in my direction?"

Aster sat forward, resting her elbows on the table. "Imagine a world where Blair doesn't exist. For one minute, just put yourself in a place where you live alone, play football, and go to work.

Blair isn't in your life, she doesn't call or hang out with you, and you see one another occasionally in passing."

Dom's bottom lip trembled, her eyes squeezed shut.

"I know she's really hurt you, mate. And I can't imagine how it feels to be accused of cheating on your fiancée, but you and Blair are made for one another. If you can find it inside you to forgive her, I think you should at least try. Because I can't visualise you two apart."

"Can I take you up on that offer of your place? Just for a couple of nights?" Dom wiped the back of her hand across her cheek.

"You know you can." Aster took her keys from her jacket pocket, sliding them across the table. "Make yourself at home, and when you're ready, call her."

"I...I will."

"You two will get through this. If you don't, there's no hope for any of us."

"How's Eden?" Dom asked, relaxing her shoulders ever so slightly. "Are you two getting on?"

"Really well. Amazing, actually." Aster was certain Dom didn't need to hear how fantastic her relationship was, but Dom wouldn't have asked if she wasn't interested. "Except for her mum. They're not speaking."

"What? Why?"

"Because Eden is with me. A woman." Aster felt her own issues surface, but she didn't want to think too hard about them. Whether Angela was on board or not, it didn't change their relationship. "I don't think she likes me very much."

"But Angela was great when I met her with Blair."

Aster shrugged. "I guess it's different when it's your own flesh and blood. I don't know."

"Nah. Blair won't have that. They're like sisters, and she thinks a lot of Angela. Leave it with her, and she'll fix it."

"You two have enough to deal with. It really doesn't matter."

Dom shook her head, reaching forward for Aster's hand. "You've sat here with me when you didn't have to. Give me a few days to figure my own shit out, and then I'll deal with yours. Eden deserves to be happy, and Angela will have to come to terms with that."

Aster cleared her throat. This evening wasn't about her and Eden. "Drink up, and I'll drop you off at my place."

"Hey," Dom said, dipping her head and finding Aster's eyes. "Thanks for coming here. I really appreciate it."

"Wouldn't see you struggling, mate. Remember that."

"I know." Dom lifted a beer mat from the table, fidgeting with it. "I...always say goodnight to Blair. Feels kinda weird knowing I won't even see her tonight."

Aster smiled. There wasn't a single world where Dom *wouldn't* forgive Blair. Yes, she was angry, and that was completely understandable, but Aster knew they'd be back on form soon. "She's with Eden. At the apartment."

"R-right."

"Maybe you could come back with me? Test the water...maybe try talking to one another on neutral ground?"

Dom narrowed her eyes as she ripped the beer mat, shredding it and watching it fall against the wood. "I don't know. I'm really pissed off with her."

"Tell you what, I'll get us another beer and then we'll go from there. We can cab it back."

Dom simply nodded, tears in her eyes. "Yeah. I just need a bit more time. I don't want to see her and be angry. I *never* want to be angry with her."

"I'll go the bar. This can all be solved, don't worry."

26

Eden placed a gentle hand on Blair's knee, stopping her from repeatedly bouncing it up and down. Blair was a nervous wreck, but Eden needed her to remain calm. Worrying wouldn't solve anything, but that was easy for Eden to think; she wasn't the one potentially about to lose the love of her life. And that's exactly what Dom was to Blair. The way they looked at one another, how they fit together so effortlessly...Eden couldn't have wished for a better partner for Blair than Dom. All the years of worry disintegrated once she saw the smile on Blair's face.

"Love, it's all going to be okay."

Blair shook her head, biting her nails. "It's not. I can feel myself losing her, Eden. And you know what? I wouldn't blame her for running away. I'd deserve it."

"No, you wouldn't."

"The same way I deserved the twenty years I had with Barrett."

Anger flared in the pit of Eden's stomach, rising through her body in milliseconds. "Don't you fucking dare!"

"Oh, come on. We both know I'm a piss-poor wife. It wouldn't be any different with Dom. She'd see right through me eventually. When that phase of a happy life wears off, when she discovers I'm nothing more than a waste of space, Dom would be disgusted with the decision she'd made in marrying me."

That saddened Eden more than she'd thought it possibly could. Blair had done so well to work through the issues Barrett left her with. Eden couldn't bear to see her revert back to the vulnerability and low self-esteem. It was too painful the first time around.

"I think I should leave. Head home." Blair got to her feet and moved towards the floor-to-ceiling window. She leant against the frame, staring out at the city. "I always knew I'd fuck up, Edes. I've told myself time and time again that it would be different with Dom, but I've hurt her, and I know she'll never look at me the same way again."

A key in the door had Eden's head turned. She'd never been so happy to see Aster. And then she spotted Dom walking in behind her. God only knew what was about to happen.

But then Blair spoke again, unaware they now had company.

"She should be with someone who doesn't still live with the past. And she should be with someone who can give her everything she needs. The idea of being her wife was a dream come true, but I've been fooling myself all along."

Eden swallowed as Dom stood in the middle of her apartment, frowning. Aster rounded the couch, taking a seat beside her, their hands finding their way to one another. Aster squeezed, offering a small smile.

"I'm so happy you found Aster. Just don't make the same mistake I did and fuck it all up. Losing the best thing to ever happen to me is more painful and devastating than every last punch Barrett landed on me."

"Blair..." Eden said, her best friend breaking her heart with every word she spoke.

"I could deal with that, I always knew when it was coming, but this...I can't deal with this," Blair paused, pushing off the frame, her eyes focused on the busy roads outside. "So, I'm going to go home and pack some things. Dom loves our place, so I'll leave for a while. She can stay there. Just…make sure she's okay for me. Check in on her." Blair turned, her face pale as she focused on Dom. "Y-you're here."

"And I always will be," Dom said, her voice hoarse and filled with emotion as she crossed the room and took Blair's face in her hands. "Kissing away every reminder you have of him. Replacing every memory of his fists with *my* hands instead."

Eden wiped a tear from her cheek, side-glancing in Aster's direction when she heard her girlfriend sniffling. They were a right pair when it came to emotions.

"And things aren't okay, but I can't walk away from you. I'm angry and disappointed, but I can't imagine a life without you, Blair."

"If I've destroyed everything, if you need to walk away because it's the best thing for you, I'll be okay. But if that day does come, I need you to know that I never meant to hurt you. And that I *do* trust you."

"It's something we need to talk about."

Blair lowered her eyes. "I can live with talking."

"Now, did you want to head back and give Eden and Aster some space?"

Eden stood and crossed the room. "You can stay as long as you want. Both of you."

Blair smiled, pulling Eden into a strong hug. "I don't know what I'd do without you."

"I think it works both ways," Eden said as she took a step back. And she meant it. Without Blair, Eden wouldn't have found herself falling in love recently. "Should I order in for the four of us?"

"No. I think it's time we went home and sat down to talk." Blair took Dom's hand.

Eden knew things were different at the moment, but in time,

everything would be back to normal. She had no idea what Aster had said to Dom, but it had worked. "Well, call me when you've both spent a few days alone, okay?"

Dom moved back into the living room, crouching down in front of Aster as she took her hands. "Thanks for being there, mate. I owe you big time."

"You don't. I just want us all to be happy."

Dom got to her feet, placing a hand on Aster's shoulder and squeezing. "Drinks are on me next time we head out into the city." And then she turned to Blair, holding out a hand and cocking her head towards the door. "Come on. Let's fix this mess at home."

Eden watched Dom and Blair retreat out of the front door, arms wrapping around her from behind as the door closed. Aster's lips found her neck, soft and wet, and just the idea of her mouth reaching other places had Eden's body on alert.

Eden turned in Aster's arms. "What did you say to Dom?"

"Just what she needed to hear." Aster leaned in, a languid kiss dragging a moan from Eden's throat. "She needed to remember what was important. How different things could be."

Eden's forehead creased.

"I asked her to imagine a world, a life, without Blair," Aster said, her head cocked as she pulled back and focused on Eden. "The one thing that terrifies me lately is imagining my life without you in it, so I told her to imagine the same thing. I'm not very good when it comes to figuring out people's relationships, so I went with what I thought was best."

"I don't think anyone has ever been afraid to lose me…"

"I don't want to scare you off, we haven't been dating for that long, but you mean so much to me, Eden. The night you showed up at my place because my dad was ill…it was that night when I realised just how much I wanted you in my life. By my side. And I know we weren't even together at that point, but it was the concern you had for me and my family that did it. Nobody has ever done something like that before."

"I didn't want you to be alone."

"It meant so much."

Eden nuzzled into Aster's neck, resting her head on Aster's shoulder. She felt safe, warmth spreading throughout her. "My life has had a major change, but I wouldn't want to be anywhere else or *with* anyone else."

"Good, because I'm not going anywhere."

"Mm. Dinner was lovely. As always." Aster pressed a kiss to the base of Eden's neck, one hand falling to her thigh. They'd had another evening together, and every night seemed better than the last. Aster couldn't complain. Spending time with Eden outside the office was all she could have dreamed of when she first laid eyes on this woman. "But you know what's really lovely?"

"W-what?" She felt Eden shudder, her palms flat against the dining table.

"You...in this skirt." Aster smiled against Eden's skin, her hands slipping around the front of her blouse. As she popped the buttons slowly, Eden released an audible moan. "Very, *very* lovely."

"Aster..." Eden stood upright, gripping the edge of the dining table.

"Yes, beautiful?"

"I-I need to clear the table away." Eden trembled against her, but it only spurred Aster on. When she had a woman trembling, she was never going to step away. Not in this lifetime.

"Yeah, that's not really what I had planned." She glanced over Eden's shoulder as she got to her tiptoes and frowned. There was barely a thing on the dining table. "And I don't think it really requires much tidying up, do you?"

"Well, no."

Aster slipped Eden's blouse from her body, her lips pressing softly against one shoulder, then the other. Eden's subtle perfume —intoxicating as ever—reached Aster's nose, a smile instantly settling on her face. "You're gorgeous," Aster whispered against Eden's skin, lowering her hand to Eden's thigh and dragging her nails up and under her skirt. "Turn around. I want to kiss you."

Eden turned, her legs shaking. She rested back against the dining table, wrapping her legs around Aster's waist as she dragged her into a heated kiss. Eden's fingers tugged at the button on Aster's jeans, and then they lowered her zipper, sending Aster's body wild with want.

She leaned in, taking Aster's earlobe between her teeth. "And *I* want to fuck *you*."

Aster suddenly found their positions reversed, Eden's hands pushing her further back on the table. But it was the urgency from Eden as she curled her fingers around the waistband of Aster's jeans that had her lifting her hips and willing to do anything Eden required. "Eden, shit."

Eden quirked an eyebrow. "What?"

"You. Like this. It's so fucking hot." Aster wrapped her legs around Eden and pulled her closer, claiming her lips with the very same urgency Eden's hands had. She nipped at Eden's bottom lip, moaning into her mouth as she massaged Aster through her underwear. Right now, tonight, she'd never been so wet. Or so desperate to be taken.

"Babe, you're killing me."

"Lift," Eden demanded as she hooked her fingers around the crotch of Aster's underwear. "You may be desperate for more, but so am I."

Once her underwear was discarded, Aster studied Eden's eyes. This was the first time since they'd met that Eden had taken control during those intimate moments. But Aster wasn't worried. This woman knew *exactly* what she was doing and *exactly* what she wanted. Aster sat back on her elbows, her bare legs dangling over the edge of the table. "Where do you want me?"

Aster's arms gave out when Eden palmed her thighs, those soft fingertips dipping between her legs and spreading them. "Knees up, beautiful."

Aster complied, lifting her head slightly only to catch Eden staring, her lip between her teeth. If she was going to do what Aster imagined, this was entirely new territory for Eden. But the mere thought had fresh arousal gathering between Aster's legs. Eden had an incredible mouth; she was more than welcome to use it wherever she pleased.

And then Eden dipped her head, smoothing her palms over Aster's thighs as she kissed along her lower belly. Aster's stomach tightened, her fingers hopelessly gripping at the table, but when Eden's lips enveloped her clit, she lost her mind completely. "O-oh!"

"Mm." Eden released her clit slowly, licking her lips before she dove back in. Aster could only watch in delight, her knees trembling with every swipe of Eden's tongue. "You taste so good."

"Oh, fuck!" One hand held the back of Eden's head, the other flying up to Aster's forehead. This…was heaven. "Shit, yes. Right there." She bucked against Eden's mouth, quivering as her orgasm drew closer, throaty moans the only sound in the apartment. "Y-yes."

Eden sucked Aster's clit between her lips, filling her with two fingers. It was in that moment that Aster knew her world would turn black any second now. This woman, her hands, that delicious mouth…life couldn't possibly be the same again. And then Aster's walls tightened when Eden released a throaty moan of her own, the vibration plunging Aster over the edge.

She arched up from the table, her thighs closing around Eden's head as she cried out into the open space. But Eden didn't slow, she didn't stop, she just drank Aster in as though her life depended on it. "Shit, babe." Aster's entire body trembled. She'd *never* had an orgasm quite like that. Eden...yeah, she knew how to work a woman up. No doubt about it.

"God." Eden lifted her head, her fingers still buried inside Aster, and leaned into a kiss as she slowly coaxed whatever she could from Aster. Tasting herself on this woman would always produce the expected results for Aster. She wanted more. No, she *needed* more. And then Eden pulled back, a shy smile on her mouth. "H-how was it?"

"Oh, you've no idea." Aster sat up, pressing her upper body to Eden. "But I'm about to show you. Bedroom, now!"

27

Eden put her car into park, puffing out her cheeks as she cut the engine. She'd opted for a simple black pantsuit this morning when she was rummaging through her wardrobe for work, but now it felt a little too formal. She wasn't meeting a client; she was meeting Aster's dad. Formal wasn't what she wanted this evening. But it was too late to go home and change; she already should have been here almost an hour ago.

All day, the anticipation had been slowly eating away at her. What if Aster's dad didn't take to her? She knew she was overthinking this meeting, but Eden had never been in this position before. She'd called Blair multiple times, spent the day clock watching, and then she'd moved onto the idea that it didn't matter. It was a lie, all of this mattered, but the more pressure Eden put on herself, the more her heart pounded.

Meeting Aster's dad shouldn't feel this way. Eden had to get a grip.

"Okay, get out of the car." Eden swallowed, climbing from her Mercedes as coolly as she possibly could. With her nerves on edge, she had the potential to fall over her own feet. *And that wouldn't be cool.* "Right, this is going to be fine," she muttered as she rounded her car and opened the boot. She had no idea why she'd done so; she didn't need to collect anything from it. Just one more second, and she'd be good to go. "You have absolutely *nothing* to worry about."

"Eden?"

Eden froze. Aster was calling her name, which meant that she'd been watching her mild panic from the window. "Yeah?" Eden closed the boot of her car, plastering on her best smile. "Sorry I'm late. I got caught on a call and then I hit the rush hour traffic."

"Don't worry. I just…noticed you'd been sitting in your car."

Eden couldn't lie to Aster. No chance. "I'm a little nervous. I'm sorry."

"Nervous?" Aster opened the garden gate, a gentle smile playing on her mouth. "You've nothing to be nervous about. Dad already loves you, and he's never met you."

"All the more reason to be nervous. The last thing I need is to disappoint your dad, Aster."

Aster reached out a hand, beckoning Eden closer. Once their skin touched, Eden's hand securely in Aster's, she immediately settled. Perhaps if they'd travelled here together, this wouldn't have felt so daunting for Eden.

"I don't want you to worry about a single thing. Dad is excited to meet you, and I can't wait to show you off."

Eden blushed. She wasn't sure she'd ever get used to Aster and her fondness. Really, she was the breath of fresh air Eden urgently needed. "I…didn't bring anything. I didn't know what to pick up, and then I was running late, so I just headed straight here."

"You didn't need to bring anything," Aster said, leaning in and kissing Eden. "So long as you're here, that's good enough."

"Still, it's rude to show up empty handed, isn't it?"

"I don't know. Is it?" Aster frowned.

"I suppose it doesn't matter anymore. I'm here now."

Aster grinned, slipping her arm around Eden's waist as she led her up the path. Aster always made Eden feel comfortable, today was no different. "Lily couldn't get out of work early. She's on the late shift tonight. She asked me to apologise."

"Honestly, that's okay. I don't want to overwhelm myself on the first visit. Perhaps it's best if it's just the three of us."

"You're right. I never thought of it like that."

Aster pushed the front door open, the warmth of the house relaxing Eden further. She followed her girlfriend down the hallway, glancing to her left at the framed photographs running up the wall to the side of the staircase. When her eyes landed on a particular one, Eden smiled. Aster, as a child, was being held by a woman who looked *a lot* like her. She assumed it to be her mother, the resemblance striking. Eden made a mental note to bring Aster's mother up in conversation when they were alone. Aster had never really given much information regarding her death.

"Dad?"

"Yes, love?" Eden's stomach lurched as Aster's dad called out from the living room.

"Eden's here." Aster squeezed Eden's hip, releasing her as they stepped into the living room. "Dad, this is Eden, my girlfriend. Eden, my dad, Ted."

"Oh, lovely." Ted braced his hands against his chair, attempting to stand.

"Please, don't stand for me," Eden said, stepping closer as she held out her hand. "Lovely to meet you."

"Our Aster has been pacing for the last hour. I think she thought you'd done a runner." Ted laughed, winking in Aster's direction as he shook Eden's hand. "I told her you were probably stuck in traffic coming out of the city, but I don't think she settled until she heard your car pull up."

"It was a nightmare getting onto the motorway…"

"Have a seat, love." Ted motioned to the couch, his eyes

bright considering he'd been under the weather. "I told Aster she should have picked you up. It would have saved the long drive after working all day."

"I didn't mind." Eden settled on the couch, placing her handbag to the side of the couch. "It's just nice to be invited here."

"Oh, any time." Ted waved a hand. "Fancy a cuppa?"

Eden breathed a sigh of relief. Ted was wonderful and very calming. "I'd love one."

"Go on," he said, glancing at Aster. "Make your old dad a cuppa. Eden's parched sitting here."

Aster chanced a look in Eden's direction, silently asking if she was okay. When Eden smiled, her attention turning back to Ted, Aster left the room. "Lovely house."

"Oh, I can't take the credit. The girls have always looked after it. One of them is forever bringing colour scheme ideas for me to look at, but I let them get on with it. I won't be here one day so they should do what they like with it."

Eden's heart constricted when Ted said that. She couldn't imagine losing one parent, let alone both.

"And Heather was the one who picked this house when we met. I didn't get a say so. But I'm happy about that; she picked well."

"She certainly did." Eden's eyes took in the layout of the room. The patio doors at the back of the house let in a tonne of light, the evening sun bouncing off the glass as it started to descend behind the trees. Then Eden noticed the oxygen canister to the side of Ted's chair. "How are you feeling?"

"Much better now that I'm home. I like my own things around me, you know."

Eden nodded. "Familiarity."

"I'm sure Aster called me fit to burn when I ruined her holiday. But I told Lily not to call her."

"Aster was glad Lily called her. And holidays aren't important. Family is."

"You're close with your family too?"

Eden would like to believe she was, and most of the time everything was okay, but her mother still played on her mind. Her dad hadn't been in touch either, which meant that Angela probably hadn't updated him on Eden's love life, but everything had to come good in the end. Eden needed it to. "Sure. I'm an only child, so I was very close to my parents growing up."

"And now?" Ted asked, fixing the oxygen tube under his nose.

"I don't see them as often as I once did because I moved into the city, but I go home to visit whenever I have the chance. We talk often, too."

"Good. That's good."

"Brews are up." Aster carried three cups into the living room, setting a coffee down in front of Eden and a tea for Ted. "Did you want a biscuit with yours, Dad?"

"Who doesn't have a biscuit with their brew?" Ted looked between Aster and Eden, that sparkle in his eye making Eden smile. "Eden?"

"Sure. I'd take a plate of them." She shrugged, praying her stomach didn't yell just how hungry she was.

And then Aster turned to face her. "You didn't have lunch again, did you?"

"I...didn't have time. I had back-to-back meetings until two."

"You should have said. I would have brought you something in." Aster shook her head and then offered Eden an admonishing look. "You should always make time for lunch, babe."

"It was your day off. And it won't happen again." Eden reached for her coffee, sipping slowly as Aster sighed. She eyed her girlfriend once more. "I promise."

When Eden glanced in Ted's direction, he was wearing a gentle smile. "I like that. You look out for one another."

"Aster is..." Eden paused, suppressing the huge grin she felt working its way to her mouth. *The love of my life...* "Yeah, we do. She's great."

Ted offered a single nod. "She is. I don't know what I'd do without her. All of them, actually, but Aster is... I'm sure you know what I mean."

And Eden did know exactly what Ted meant. He didn't have favourites, but Aster was the one he could rely on time and time again. Knowing that only made Eden even more proud to call Aster hers. Because when all was said and done, someone who was caring and had a heart of gold was the most important thing Eden could ever look for in another person. "I do."

Ted winked as he watched the cogs turn in Eden's mind. She knew the look in her eyes gave away just what she felt for Aster, but Ted was a gentleman, and Eden knew her secret was safe with him.

"Now." He cleared his throat. "Tell me all about you."

Great! The boring life of Eden.

Eden placed the empty cups and plates into the dishwasher, smiling as she watched Aster and Ted through the kitchen window. He wanted her to check on some of Heather's plants, but Eden had decided she would remain indoors and tidy around from their dinner. Plants and Eden didn't go very well together; she'd never forgive herself if she killed Aster's mum's rose bush.

Eden had learned more about Heather's death during dinner —a brain haemorrhage when Lily was just two years old. And now, knowing what Aster had contended with at just seventeen... Eden had a newfound admiration for her girlfriend. Aster was strong, there was no doubt in Eden's mind about that. This family were a rock to one another, and the love in Ted's eyes for Aster was heartwarming.

She smiled as her gaze fell to Aster, laughing with her dad as they slowly walked around the edge of the garden. This home was lovely, a real family home. Warm, inviting, a thousand and one memories adorning the walls and shelves. It was the kind of home Eden always imagined she would own someday. Now that she had Aster in her life, there was no reason why that couldn't one day come to fruition. Aster loved her family; anyone who paid attention could see that.

Her phone started to ring in her pants pocket, but the last thing Eden needed right now was to deal with a client or someone from her staff. She took it from her pocket, prepared to send the call to voicemail, when she noticed her mum was calling her. Okay, this was a surprise. Eden hesitated, but then she accepted the call. She didn't want to avoid her mum, even if she was a little mad with her. "Hello?"

"Does she make you happy?" Angela asked quietly.

"I'm sorry?"

Angela cleared her throat. "Your girlfriend. Does she make you happy?"

Eden's eyes strayed to Aster again, complete bliss settling in her chest. "Incredibly."

"Then that's what matters," Angela said. "That she makes you happy. Because you've never been happy, Eden. Not really."

Eden rested against the counter, crossing her legs at the ankles. "You're right. I haven't. But I'm still angry with you for how you spoke to Aster, Mum."

"I'm sorry. You have to understand that I wasn't expecting this. And I know I could have handled it better, but I am happy for you, sweetheart."

Eden narrowed her eyes. "But are you? Really? I don't want you to tell me what I want to hear if you have any issues with this. I know it was probably a shock, but I didn't deserve the way you spoke to me. *Or* how you showed up at my apartment."

"I am happy. And she seems…nice." Angela didn't sound overly convincing, but Eden wasn't particularly bothered. In an ideal world, she'd have her parents' blessing, but it was neither here nor there if they chose to support her or not. Aster wasn't going anywhere, and Eden would do everything she could to ensure that. "She certainly stood her ground when it came to you. I admire that."

Eden grinned. Nobody usually stood their ground where her mother was concerned. "She did. She's got my back, and I've got hers. I'm actually at her parents' home right now meeting her dad. He's lovely. He's a hugger; I like that."

"Oh. That's nice."

"We've just had a cuppa and a light dinner."

"Maybe you could join me and your father one day for lunch. With Aster too, of course."

Eden's brows rose with surprise. She'd love to reintroduce Aster to her mum. It couldn't possibly be any worse than last time. "I'm sure we can arrange something in the next few weeks."

"I'd like that."

"Right, well, let me speak to Aster tonight when we get home. I'll have a look in my diary and see what events we have coming up. Can I let you know?"

"Home?" Angela quizzed.

Eden winced. If only it was home for them. "Slip of the tongue. Aster doesn't live with me."

"Right. Well."

"But she will…one day." *I hope.* "We haven't been together long, so it's not something we've talked about. But I'm sure when the time is right, it'll happen."

"Well, if she loves you, I'm sure that day will arrive, my love."

"Okay, well, I'll call you tomorrow with some dates." Eden loved that her mum appeared to be on board, but she wasn't getting ahead of herself.

"Fantastic."

Eden relaxed her shoulders, sighing. "And Mum?"

"Yes?"

"Thanks." Eden paused. "For giving me the opportunity to be happy with who I choose to be happy with. She really is great. You're going to love her."

"Do *you* love her?" Angela's question caught Eden off guard, silence settling between them. "Eden?"

"Honestly? Yeah, I'm pretty sure I do."

"Then I'm sure I'll love her too. Call me tomorrow. I'll let your father know we'll have company soon."

"Okay. Bye, Mum."

Eden stared down at her phone, unable to comprehend what had just happened. Okay, her mum shouldn't have reacted how she did in the first place, but she also hadn't expected her to come to terms with it so soon either.

"Everything okay, babe?" Aster shocked Eden as she appeared in the doorway. "Did you have a work call?"

"N-no. It was my mother. She…wants to meet you again."

Aster shrugged. "Sure. Free whenever you need me to be."

"Really? I mean, I wouldn't blame you if you weren't keen on the idea. She wasn't exactly pleasant to you the last time around."

"Babe, I understand that it was a surprise for her. But I'm not worried about how she feels about me. I only care that you're happy with me. Everyone else is…not really my concern."

"You're amazing." Eden held out a hand, pulling Aster towards her when she took it. "Are you coming home with me tonight, or do I have to let you go after such a lovely evening with your dad?"

"You like him?" Aster's eyes brightened. Why she thought Eden *wouldn't* like him was a mystery.

"Of course. He's lovely."

Aster relaxed beside Eden, mirroring her position as she leant against the counter. "I knew you'd love him. Well, I hoped. He's just always so down to earth. But I've never brought anyone home to meet him. Not like this, anyway. It was always just an in passing kinda thing, you know?"

"Then I'm glad I'm the one you did this first with."

Aster nudged Eden's shoulder, grinning. "He really likes you. He didn't stop talking about you once we got outside. And that means everything to me."

"Me too. Now, should we have another cuppa with him before we head off?"

"If you needed to get back, that's okay."

"Um, Ted and I have things to talk about. You do your own thing, but I'm having another cuppa with him."

"Incredible," Aster whispered, squeezing Eden's hand. "You really are."

28

"Okay," Eden paused, pencilling Blair's wedding date into her business planner *and* personal planner. "I'm so happy you and Dom figured everything out."

"I was a fool to think she could hurt me. I know better than that."

"You do, but you've had some massive changes in your life over the last few years, Blair. And I think maybe that's why Dom kinda understands."

Blair cleared her throat. "Still. I could have handled things better. Dom has never done a single thing to break my trust in her."

"Well, it's over now. And I'm excited to get to work on your wedding plans. As your maid of honour, of course."

"I trust you to only send in the very best when it comes to planning. I know you want to take the reins, but I'll need you to stop me from turning hysterical on the day."

Eden would love to handle all of this, but Blair had been adamant from day one that she didn't want Eden to plan the day. And that was perfectly fine. "They know I'm here if they have any issues. That doesn't mean I have to work your wedding rather than be a part of it. My team knows what they're doing."

"They do. You wouldn't have them on your team if they didn't." Blair was right. Eden didn't hire just anyone when it came to event planning. "But I have to go now. I'm meeting Dom and her mum for dinner. If I don't leave work now, I'll hit the rush hour traffic."

"Call me next week if you have a day off. I'll clear my afternoon, and we'll have lunch."

"I'd love that. Now, I'm leaving work and *you* should do the same, Edes. Go and spend the night with Aster."

Oh, if only. Aster had too much on, and Eden wouldn't likely see her this evening. That knowledge sat low in her belly; she hated going home alone lately. One taste of Aster and nothing had been the same. Six weeks since meeting Ted, Eden couldn't deny she was head over heels in love with Aster Bennett. "Maybe I'll get an hour with her later. If I can prise her away from that bloody suite."

"Go in there with a little extra cleavage on show. She'll be crawling out the door on her hands and knees to be with you."

"Goodnight, Blair," Eden laughed, shaking her head. "Say hi to Dom."

"Bye, love. I'll see you soon."

Eden locked her phone and shoved it into the side of her bag. It was Friday, there were no events booked in for tomorrow, but Eden found herself feeling a little more miserable than she should. Aster's talent had only grown since she joined *The Garden of Eden*, and now everyone who booked in with them wanted Aster to capture the day. That meant more work for her and less time with Eden. Honestly, it wasn't what either of them wanted. But that was the life when you were in demand. Eden only knew it all too well.

She powered down her computer and grabbed her belongings. Eden would love nothing more than to sit around the office all night so she could be with Aster, but she was dead on her feet today. The sooner she got her heels off, the sooner Eden could spend the *entire* weekend relaxing. In an ideal world, she would spend her time in pyjamas until Monday morning.

Yawning as she turned out the office light, Eden stepped out into the reception area and locked up for the weekend. Her secretary had left an hour ago, the only sound the ticking of the clock on the wall above the entrance. Six on a Friday night…and she was still working. *I didn't create this business so I could work stupid hours week in, week out.* Dragging a hand through her hair, she spied the suite door Aster was behind. They hadn't even had lunch together today.

She knocked gently, turning the handle when Aster called out for her to come in. She sounded tired, worn out, but Eden knew better than to ask Aster to leave work at the office. Her girlfriend prided herself on finishing tasks when they were handed to her.

"Hi," Eden said as she leant against the doorframe. Aster had dragged her hair up into a bun, discarded her blazer and pumps, and sat with her knees pulled to her chest in her huge office chair. "How goes the work?"

Aster's tired eyes found Eden's. "Mm?"

"Work. How is it going?"

"Oh, yeah. Fine." Aster yawned and Eden immediately followed. "You headed home now?"

It saddened Eden to know she was going home alone. All week, she'd prayed that they could spend the weekend together, but as with last weekend, it didn't look as though it was going to be.

"Yeah. Thought I'd just order in. No use cooking if it's just me."

Aster frowned. "Am I…not invited?"

"What? Of course. But we both know you have no intentions of leaving that chair until you've finished. And I'd ask you to bring it back to mine with you, but I've asked you that several times over the last month, and I'm yet to see it happen. So, I thought I'd head home and just see you when you were finished. I know you hate it when I nag."

Aster climbed from her chair, almost slipping on the tiled flooring in her socks. "Whoa."

Eden instinctively reached out her arms to save Aster, smiling when they collided. "I really don't want any broken bones in here. Maybe you should wear nonslip socks if you're going to be here until late in the evening. At least then I can go home with the knowledge that you're safe."

"Babe, have I been neglecting you?"

Eden almost burst out laughing, but Aster had a deadly serious look in her eyes. Did she honestly believe that? Wow.

"No, you haven't. Work is important to you. Getting it right the first time around is what you thrive on. And I understand that." Eden lifted her hand, settling it against Aster's cheek. "I'm so proud of you, you know."

"Proud?"

Eden smiled. Aster still had issues with taking praise. "You've become invaluable here. Clients love you, my team thinks you're Jesus, and I know how hard it is for you to accept that, but I am. I'm so proud of you."

"Thank you." Aster blushed, pulling away from Eden.

"Uh, where are you going? I wasn't done looking at your gorgeous face."

Aster held up a hand as she bent towards her computer screen. A few clicks of the mouse and the screen turned black. "I'm done." She slipped her pumps on and grabbed her camera bag from the desk in the window, turning back to Eden and smiling fully. "So, how about we head out of here and make dinner together?"

"You're...done?" Eden's heart jumped at the prospect of walking out of here with Aster. But that happened more often than not lately. Just the thought of climbing into bed alone was enough to ruin her entire day.

"I wanted to spend the weekend with you. Unless you had plans?"

"Oh, no. I *want* you to spend the weekend with me. Get your crap and let's go."

Aster stalked towards Eden with a smirk plastered on her mouth.

For the first time in weeks, Eden knew exactly the weekend she would have. Alone with Aster was a different kind of special. Just being in the same room as Aster had Eden's blood pumping harder through her veins. Really, she could barely remember a time when Aster wasn't making her feel that way.

"Let's go, pretty lady. I'm going to lie on the couch and snuggle the shit out of you for the next two days."

Eden's fingers laced with Aster's, a content sigh slipping from her mouth. In an ideal world, Aster would never leave Eden's place. She was beginning to understand Blair's reasons for lack of social interaction since she met Dom. Eden would happily lock the world outside and spend forever with this woman.

But for now, the weekend would do just fine.

Aster watched Eden as she perched herself on the kitchen island. Dinner was cooking, and Eden was sipping wine while she went through a recipe they would try together tomorrow, her gorgeous dark hair dragged over one shoulder to expose her delectable jawline. *You're one lucky bastard, Aster Bennett.*

In the three months or so that they'd been together, Aster felt pure bliss coursing through her veins from the moment she woke up. Now that Angela seemed more enthusiastic about their relationship, Eden had no qualms when it came to telling people she had a girlfriend. Some friends had looked at her funny, others had rolled their eyes and laughed, but Eden didn't appear to have a single care in the world when it came to those people. A couple of family members seemed pretty vocal about it, a lack of contact from them ever since, but Aster struggled to care. If Eden was happy, so was she.

It would be easy to give into the pressure Eden likely felt when it came to suddenly dating a woman at the age of 42, but Aster believed that Eden knew exactly what she wanted, and this was anything but a phase. With the way she felt about Eden and the way Eden looked at her, it couldn't possibly be anything of the kind. No, it was love. Without a doubt.

Now Aster just had to pluck up the courage to tell Eden that. But fear of her running still sat at the back of her mind more often than she would like. *She's not going to run.* But she could. And then Aster would find herself in a position she'd never been in before. Heartbroken.

"Okay," Eden paused as she spun around. "Did you want to make this with beef or chicken?"

"I don't mind." And Aster really didn't. So long as she was cooking with Eden, she'd eat whatever was put on a plate in front of her. "What do you think?"

"Well, we're having chicken tonight, so…beef?"

Aster nodded, smiling as she studied every inch of Eden's face. She itched to reach out and touch her skin, to tell her just how in love she was, but Eden was looking at her funny. "What?"

"Beef? Yay or nay?"

"Beef is fine. Looking forward to it."

Eden set her wine glass down and came to rest between Aster's legs. "You seem in your own head. Is everything okay?"

"Why wouldn't everything be okay? I'm spending the weekend with you." Aster wrapped her arms around Eden's shoulders, cocking her head.

"I don't know. You seem a little distant tonight." Eden leaned up and kissed her softly. That continuous thrum of love in her chest heightened, but Aster still couldn't say the words. "If you have something on your mind, I'd like to hear it."

"Oh, I have a lot on my mind. But some things are better left unsaid."

Eden took a step back, her forehead creased. "O...kay."

"Wait, that's not what I meant. It's nothing for you to worry about." Aster dragged Eden back in, their lips crushing into one another's. *Just say it.* She pulled back and gazed into Eden's eyes. Right now, they were filled with apprehension and confusion. Aster never wanted Eden to feel that way around her. "Babe..."

Eden swallowed and lowered her eyes between them. "Look, if this isn't working for you, all this time we spend together, just say. I just thought that being together was what you wanted."

Oh, no. Eden really did have the wrong end of the stick. "Eden—"

"I just thought you were busy the last few weekends. But if this is too much, if *I'm* too much, I can handle you telling me so. It's...I hate being apart from you, Aster. When you're here, life is so good that I don't even know what day it is, but when you're not, I've never felt so miserable."

Aster grinned. Hearing Eden speak so honestly was something beautiful.

"Is that what this is? You worrying about telling me that we're together too much?"

"God, no." Aster slid down from the island and took Eden in her arms. "I don't think it's possible to spend too much time with you. It's *all* I want to do."

"But?" Eden quirked an eyebrow.

"But nothing."

"Aster..." Eden paused as she blew out a deep breath. "I need to say something to you, but I need it to not change anything between us. And I know you'll be a sweetheart and let me down gently, but I'm prepared for that."

"Let you down gently?" Okay, Aster was officially lost.

"I love you." Eden didn't miss a beat, her eyes focused fully on Aster. And the way in which she spoke those words, so sure, Aster felt them deep in her belly. "I've known it for some time now, but I didn't know when the right moment was to say it. I've…never been in this position before."

"Hey," Aster said, tilting Eden's chin and leaning into a kiss. Eden's lips mirrored how she was feeling, but Aster knew her girlfriend was still panicking, so she pulled back and whispered, "I love you, too."

"Yeah?" Those luscious eyes brightened and softened all at the same time.

"Aren't we a right pair?" Aster laughed, lightening the mood. "I can't believe it."

Eden frowned. "I-I don't…"

"I've been going out of my mind panicking about when I should tell you. But that was ridiculous on my part. I had no reason to worry."

Eden rested her head on Aster's shoulder, sighing as her arms tightened around her waist. It was a simple action, but one that had Aster swooning for this woman all over again. Aster got the impression that Eden was a little overwhelmed, so she simply pressed a kiss to the top of her head and waited until Eden was ready to allow their conversation to sink in.

"I feel so lucky to have you in my life."

Aster ran her fingers through Eden's hair, smiling. "I feel lucky too."

Eden lifted her head, those full lips curling as the realisation hit her. Aster understood, though. She couldn't quite get her head around what this year had involved either.

"Y-you really love me?" Eden asked barely above a whisper.

"I do. I *really* love you."

"Wow." Eden dragged a hand through her hair and grinned hard. "I mean, *wow*."

"Give yourself a little credit, babe. These last few months have been unbelievably good. That wouldn't have happened if it weren't for you."

"God, I'm so happy."

Aster turned off the stove and pulled Eden out of the kitchen, almost tripping over the back of the couch. It didn't matter what plans they had this evening. It had all gone out of the window the moment they spoke those three little words that meant everything. "Then I suggest you get your delicious ass into the bedroom. Dinner can wait."

EPILOGUE

God, Eden looked stunning.

In her ivory floor-length gown, the split finishing at the top of her thigh, those silky-smooth legs teasing Aster with every moment that passed…this was a dream. One Aster never wanted to wake from. But then Aster always knew Eden would look remarkable on Blair and Dom's wedding day. Was it possible for the bridesmaid to look better than the bride? Aster wouldn't say that out loud, but Eden really had turned heads. Aster's more so.

Still can't believe she's mine…

"You know, I think it's time I settled down and found myself a wife."

Aster frowned, turning to find Fi standing behind her. She couldn't fathom why Dom or Blair had invited Fi today; she caused nothing but trouble. But it wasn't Aster's wedding…or business.

"Don't you think, Bennett?"

Aster's brows rose. "I mean, sure. If you're ready to settle down."

"What about you?"

Whoa. Was Fi asking Aster what she thought she was? Surely not.

"I don't mean with me, stupid ass." Fi punched Aster's upper arm, laughing as she shook her head. Aster didn't know whether to laugh or be offended that Fi found the idea so hilarious. "I mean with your woman. She's gorgeous."

"Uh, yeah. And *taken*. So if you could stop drooling over my girlfriend while you're standing next to me, that would be great."

"What? I'm allowed to admire a beautiful woman."

Aster groaned internally. Fi made it a habit to rile the team up; why did Aster think she could get away with it? "You are... just not mine."

Fi winked as she wrapped an arm around Aster's shoulders. "Even if I wanted to, I couldn't take her off your hands. Eden *only* sees you. It's kinda sweet at times."

"Are you drunk?"

"Nope. Perfectly sober. I haven't even finished my first glass of champagne."

Aster was impressed by Fi's attitude today. Maybe she really was considering settling down. Aster believed she had more chance of seeing a chair walk, but if Fi was contemplating it, Aster would refrain from offering her opinion.

"Seriously, Bennett. That woman loves you."

"She does," Aster agreed, her eyes settling back on Eden as she spoke with Angela. "And you know what? She's perfect for me."

"This could be you next." Fi winked as she turned and walked away.

Aster would admit to allowing the idea to float through her mind once or twice, but she wasn't sure at what point it was acceptable to seriously think about such an event in her life. She'd marry Eden tomorrow if Eden asked her, but marriage hadn't been something they'd discussed with one another since they finally got together. Perhaps Eden was all out of wedding days. She spent so much time planning everyone else's, maybe she no longer wanted one of her own.

But it didn't matter today. This was Dom and Blair's day, and it had been truly beautiful so far. Even though Blair didn't have her parents or much family here, Aster knew she had everyone she needed. Family wasn't always everything; Aster understood that even though her own family were her world. But it was nice to see Eden's mum here and enjoying herself. They were on better terms, but Aster felt Angela watch her every move. If she was waiting for her to mess up, she'd better take a seat and get comfortable, because Aster wasn't going anywhere.

Eden walked towards Aster, weaving through the tables in the marquee. Aster's breath quickened. Just the mere thought of Eden in her space sent her head spinning. "There she is," Aster said, smirking. "The most beautiful woman in the room."

"Don't let Blair catch you saying that." Eden grinned as she leaned in and gently pressed her lips to Aster's. "But thank you. You're always really good for my ego."

"Seriously, babe. You look incredible." Aster slid a hand around Eden's waist, bringing her lips to Eden's ear. "You've no idea the kind of thoughts I have running through my head."

"If they're anything like mine…I know exactly what you're thinking. You look *excruciatingly* good today."

Aster shivered with those words. Knowing Eden wanted her out of her suit only meant the rest of this day was going to be painful. "Yeah?" Aster smiled against Eden's ear. "We could slip off somewhere…"

"Oh, the anticipation is so much more fun."

"Ugh. Speak for yourself." Aster swigged her beer from the bottle, the idea of standing around with a glass of champagne not really up there with her top priorities. She couldn't stand the stuff. "How's Blair?"

"God, she looks so happy." Eden pulled Aster towards the edge of the marquee, stepping out onto the decking. "This is all I ever wanted for her. To be happy and smiling because she was in love with someone who couldn't bear to be apart from her. And now that she has it, I feel like my own heart can fully settle for the first time in so long."

"Are *you* happy?" Aster touched Eden's cheek lightly, guiding her fingertip down to Eden's jawline. "With me?"

"You know I am." Eden's eyes closed, her lips parting as she leaned into Aster's touch. "Happier than I've ever been."

"Good."

"Are you?" Eden countered, her deep brown eyes soft and inviting. Gentle.

Aster had so much she had to thank Eden for, but right now wasn't the time. Or maybe it was. "When I walked into your office fifteen months ago, the last thing I expected was *you*. I didn't even expect a full-time job, let alone a girlfriend, so it feels kinda weird knowing that we're here now at a wedding together. You know?"

"Neither of us were looking, Aster."

"And maybe that's why this all worked out so perfectly. Because that's exactly what you are to me, Eden. The very definition of perfect. We didn't pressure ourselves or one another, it just happened as it happened."

"I wouldn't change a single thing."

"No. I wouldn't either." Aster leaned in, pressing a kiss below Eden's ear. She'd wanted to kiss the face off her girlfriend all day, but she wouldn't be responsible for ruining Eden's makeup. "Come on. Let's go and mingle. I've never mingled at a wedding as one half of a couple before."

"No, me neither." That realisation seemed to hit Eden, a slight frown gracing her beautiful face. "But that changes right now. Because I'll always have you by my side, right?"

"Always, beautiful."

Eden relaxed back in her chair, crossing her legs as Blair flopped down in front of her. Considering Eden hadn't been allowed to touch or plan a single thing today, she was impressed by her staff. She'd found herself trying to take over once or twice, but Aster gave her a look, and Eden immediately took a step back. It wasn't that she wanted to interfere, it was just in her blood to change the position of a flower arrangement or a seating plan.

"My God!" Blair placed her hand to her chest as she flung herself into a seat. "I've never been so shattered. Is it bedtime yet?"

"Oh, we all know why *you're* looking forward to bedtime." Eden wore a smirk as she studied her best friend. She couldn't recall a time she'd looked more beautiful. "How has your day been?"

"Amazing," Blair said, scanning the room. "Everything I could have wanted. Magical."

Eden sat forward, taking Blair's hand. "I'm so happy you got your *happily ever after*."

Blair reached out a hand, tucking Eden's hair behind her ear. She smiled fully, tears in her eyes. "It's time for you to have your *happily ever after* now, honey."

Eden blushed, lowering her eyes. She'd never felt so loved and well looked after, and she'd never felt so compelled to return those very same feelings. But Aster…God, she made it easy for Eden to love with every fibre of her being. They got one another, they shone when they were together, and Eden couldn't imagine a world where Aster didn't exist. "I am happy. I'm so happy, Blair."

"I know. And I love that."

"I want so much more with her," Eden said, spying Aster as

she threw her head back laughing, her suit jacket discarded to show strong biceps in her short-sleeved shirt. "So much."

"You and I both know Aster is the one for you. So, whatever you want, grab it with both hands."

"Is it that simple? Can I really have the life I've always wanted…with a woman?"

Blair's brow rose. "Forgive me if I'm wrong, but that's *exactly* what you're doing right now. You lost a few friends and family along the way, but you're happy. You're thriving. You work with the woman you love, and I'd say that's more than most people have."

Eden *had* lost some friends and family along the way, but it wasn't anything she missed. Those friends had been the very same friends who'd talked behind her back for the best part of twenty years. And the family, well, they didn't matter. Her mother had come around to the idea, and that was the most important thing. Blair was right. Eden *could* have the life she wanted.

"I have you."

"Sweetie, you'll always have me. Forever. You and I have been through too much together."

Eden cleared her throat, shifting her seat closer to Blair. Aster smiled as she caught her eye, winking in Eden's direction. But then Eden blew out a deep breath as she leaned in towards Blair. "Do you…think I'm too old for kids?"

Blair rested a hand on Eden's. "Not at all."

"Are you sure? It's just that I've been thinking about it lately. I'm not sure how Aster feels about it, and it's not something I desperately crave, but I think it could be something to consider bringing up. She's never mentioned it, but I know how much family means to her. I'd…like to be a family with her."

Blair smiled, a tear slipping down her cheek. "I think that's the most beautiful thing I've ever heard."

"I won't get my hopes up, but I wanted to run it by you first. See what you thought."

"I think…" Blair paused as she turned in her seat and took Eden's face in her hands. "That you would be a wonderful mum. You've got the biggest heart of anyone I know, Eden. Use it. Fill it with as much love as you possibly can. Tomorrow is never promised…be happy."

Eden closed her eyes when tears threatened to fall. The last thing she needed was to ruin her makeup; she'd managed to keep it together all day. "Thank you," Eden whispered, her hand settling against Blair's. "For cheering me on. For encouraging me. I know it didn't quite go to plan in the beginning, but without you, I wouldn't have told Aster how I felt."

"Sometimes we just need a little push in the right direction." Blair replaced the hand on Eden's cheek with her lips, and then she wrapped Eden up in a strong embrace. "Now, the first dance is about to begin, so I should go and find my wife. While you go and find the one who will be yours one day…"

Eden watched Blair climb to her feet, squaring her shoulders as she did so. And then she caught Aster's eyes again as her girlfriend rested against a pillar across the room from her. The love Aster's dark eyes held took Eden's breath away, the sheer thought of spending her life with this woman turning her entire body to jelly. Aster Bennett…the love of her life.

Aster was ready to head for their room. It was after eleven, everything was winding down, and Eden looked dead on her feet. Right now, they needed to relax. And by relax, Aster meant that Eden needed to lie on the bed while she undressed her slowly. Grinning at that thought, she left the table she'd been sitting at for the last twenty minutes and approached her girlfriend.

"Hi." Eden's eyes lit up. "You look tired."

"I am. You ready to head back to our cabin?"

"Absolutely. Let me find Blair and say goodnight." Eden took Aster's hand. "Come with me?"

Oh, Aster would follow Eden to the ends of the earth.

Blair spun around when Eden called her name, smiling as her eyes landed on their entwined hands. "You know, I'll never get tired of seeing you two looking so fucking gorgeous together."

Aster lowered her eyes, heat creeping up her neck. This hadn't been in her future, the idea of her settled down and happy, but here she was…ready to fall to her knees for anything Eden wanted.

"We're heading back to our cabin. We'll see you in the morning for breakfast, okay?"

Blair's face fell. "Um, excuse me?"

"As much as I've loved this day, your wedding is over, Blair."

"It's not over until you do the one thing you promised me you'd do." Blair paused, frowning. "Seventeen years ago."

"I…don't remember what I promised you seventeen years ago. I've slept since then, Blair."

Aster was suddenly intrigued. "What did she promise you?"

"Dina Carroll?" Blair arched an eyebrow, and then she stared Eden down. "You told me, when I came out to you during my marriage to Barrett, that when I found my one true love, you'd sing it at my wedding."

Aster's world lit up. She would never tire of hearing Eden's voice, and tonight, after so much love throughout the day, it would be the perfect ending to this gorgeous occasion. "Oh, she did now?"

"I don't remember that." Eden held up her hands. "And if I did say it, this is the first time you've brought it up since then."

"Please…"

"No can do. I'm not a wedding singer. I'm just…me."

"No, you're not a wedding singer," Aster said as she wrapped an arm around Eden's waist. "But you have one hell of a voice, and I'd love to hear it again."

Eden shook her head and lowered her eyes.

"Oh, come on. This is the greatest gift you could *ever* give me, Edes. For me, please." Blair stuck out her bottom lip. "And Aster."

"Fine." Eden puffed out her cheeks as she wrung her hands. "The things I have to do for the pair of you."

"I'll ask him to get the track ready."

The giddiness in Blair had Aster laughing, a soothing hand placed on the small of Eden's back. "You don't remember saying that to Blair?"

"Of course I do. I just hoped she wouldn't bring it up."

Aster frowned. "Why?"

"Because I hate singing in public," Eden explained, running a hand through her hair. Aster noted just how pristine she still looked, twelve hours on from getting ready this morning. An absolute beauty. "But I said it, and now I have to come good on my promise."

"Did you know..." Aster pressed her body to Eden, wrapping her arms around her shoulders. "That the moment I fell in love with you was the night you got up in the bar and I heard your voice for the first time?"

"You don't have to encourage me. I'm doing it anyway."

"Oh, I'm not. That's the truth." Aster ghosted her lips over Eden's. "That voice. How you looked into my eyes. I fell in love with you, Eden."

The sudden clearing of Blair's throat through the microphone pulled them apart, Eden's body tensing as Aster loosened her grip. "I love you."

Aster brushed a thumb across her cheek. "I love you too. Everything about you."

Aster reluctantly released Eden, taking a seat at an empty table along the edge of the white marble dance floor. As the backing track floated through the marquee, Aster swallowed. Was Eden Kline really hers? It was hard to believe most days.

Eden's soft voice reached her ears. Just that one opening line —the look in Eden's eyes—Aster felt as though she would slip from her chair and fall to her knees at any moment. This was what heaven felt like, surely. Blair and Dom slow danced, the room silent except for Eden's serenade, and Aster...well, she was falling more and more in love every minute of the day.

As Eden reached the chorus of *Don't Be a Stranger*, a shiver worked its way through Aster, every nerve ending tingling. Right now, tonight, Aster had never felt so whole. So...accomplished. With Eden Kline in her life, it was hard to feel any other way. Everything just worked. Better than it ever had. And as Aster gazed into Eden's soulful eyes, she knew life would always be something special with Eden around.

Eden was hers, and she was Eden's. *Wow...*

Aster sighed as the song came to an end. This day was officially over, but she wished it wasn't. Eden was always charming and looking drop dead gorgeous, but today it all felt different. Like, Eden had fully accepted who she was and the path her life was taking once and for all. Radiant and certain, that's the impression Aster got. And she loved it.

Blair and Dom pulled Eden into a hug, but it was Aster who really wanted to have her arms around her girlfriend. Preferably in bed and naked.

After Eden kissed Blair on the cheek and gave Dom one of her beaming smiles, she turned her attention to Aster. She had that look in her eyes that told Aster they should be alone, and as beautiful as this day and night had been, Aster had to agree. They may have spent most of the wedding together, but it didn't feel as though they'd *actually* spent time together. It was time to do exactly that.

"You ready to go, beautiful?" Aster lifted her suit jacket from the back of a chair and slung it over her shoulder.

Eden sidled up beside her, that smile spreading further. "Absolutely."

Eden threw the cabin key onto the coffee table, rolling her head on her shoulders as she relaxed for the first time since last night. The day had been unbelievably beautiful, but she hadn't felt as though she could truly switch off for a single moment. Call it the event planner in her, but she'd spent so many years doing this that the thought of taking a day off terrified her. Especially when it was her best friend's wedding.

"You looked beautiful today," Aster whispered as she stepped up behind Eden, arms wrapping around her waist. "Really amazing."

Eden smiled as her eyelids fluttered closed, tilting her neck as Aster worked her skin with her lips. "Thank you."

"And I kinda want you out of this dress, but then I want you to leave it on all at the same time."

Eden settled her hands on Aster's against her stomach. "Well, if you knew what I was wearing underneath, I think you'd want me out of it."

"Is that so?" She felt Aster smirk against her neck, those safe arms tightening around Eden's body. "Maybe I should do the honours and get you out of it then…"

Eden turned, swallowing as she stared into Aster's soft brown eyes. All day her mind had swam with what the future held, and as much as she wanted to lie on the bed while Aster worked her up, Eden wasn't sure she could hold it in any longer. She needed to gauge what Aster wanted in the months and even years to come.

"What's wrong?" Aster pulled back, but her arms remained.

"Nothing. I just…today has been so lovely."

"It has, babe. I don't think I've ever felt so loved and *in love* as I have today."

Okay, that was helping Eden with her whirring thoughts. "Yeah?"

"Honestly, I just wanted to whisk you off somewhere quiet and kiss you. I wanted you all to myself so I could show you, tell you, exactly what you mean to me."

Eden lifted a hand, feathering her fingertips across Aster's cheek. When she said things like that, Eden wondered why she hadn't found Aster sooner. There would never be enough years left to make up for wanting this woman. "I know what I mean to you."

"I-I don't think you do," Aster said quietly.

All Eden could do was focus on Aster's beautiful face. That little button nose always warmed her heart, but it was Aster's gentle lips that had Eden wild with love and want over the last year. Aster's lips…she had no words.

"I mean, I know I tell you I love you every day, but I fear it's not enough. And I don't know how to show you, how to guarantee that you'll always be mine. But I do, Eden. I love you so much."

Eden leaned in, smiling into a kiss. Aster didn't often get flustered, but when she did, it was Eden's favourite kind of Aster. "You don't need to guarantee anything. I'm not going anywhere."

"I'm sorry. I don't want you to think I doubt how you feel or that you worry I don't feel the same way, but today has only shown me how much I love you. How much I want to still be at weddings with you in ten, even twenty or thirty years down the line."

Aster pulled Eden towards the bed and took a seat, frowning when Eden didn't join her but instead stood between her legs. "I want to be doing the same things with you."

"You seem…like you have something on your mind, babe. Is everything okay?"

Eden smiled as she cocked her head. "For the first time in my life, everything is so okay that I'm waiting for it to fall to pieces."

"Yeah, that's not going to happen. Not with us, anyway."

"And I don't know, Aster," Eden paused, caressing her girlfriend's cheek. "I have so many things I want to say to you, but I don't want to scare you off."

"Babe, it's been a year. And in that year, my love for you has grown so much that my heart probably can't take much more. There is *nothing* you could say to me that would scare me off. Trust me. I love you."

Could Eden be brutally honest with Aster? She felt as though she could, Aster had never shown any discomfort in anything they'd done or shared over the last year, but this was still all very new to Eden. Aster had always been so sure of who she was, but Eden...sometimes she got the impression that she was still coming to terms with the fact that she was in love, and living, with a woman. "I want something different..."

"Different?" Aster visibly swallowed, her grip slowly loosening on Eden's waist. "W-with someone else?" She scrubbed a hand over her face, blowing out a deep breath. "I mean, am I not giving you enough?"

"N-no. That's not what I meant."

"O...kay."

Eden sat beside Aster, taking her hand and squeezing it. "I said that wrong. I'm sorry."

"You had me worried for a moment then." Aster offered a hesitant smile, but Eden could put her mind to rest. At least, she hoped she could.

"I know things work really well how we are, and I know I'm happy with where we're at, but do you ever wonder what the future holds for us, Aster? Do you ever lie in bed at night and think about what the next step for us is?"

"Honestly?" Aster quirked an eyebrow, and Eden nodded. "Yes. I do."

"And..."

"And in an ideal world, we'd be married with kids down the line. But it's not something we've ever talked about, and if I'm being truthful, I didn't have the courage to bring it up with you."

"Why?" Eden turned fully, taking Aster's other hand into her lap.

"Fear of you rejecting the idea. That sheer panic of losing you because we may want different things."

Oh, Aster.

"But as this year has gone on, I stopped thinking about it too much. Because when all is said and done, you make me happier than I've ever been, and that's enough for me. If this, how we are, stays the same...that's okay."

"I don't ever want you to disregard what you want in your future to make me happy." Eden trailed her thumb over Aster's knuckles, a hint of sadness sitting in her eyes. She hadn't witnessed that look from Aster since they'd gotten together. "Please, don't ever feel like you can't talk to me."

"Babe, can we do this another time?" A tear slid down Aster's cheek as she lowered her eyes to their hands. "Today has been so gorgeous, and I just...I want that feeling to last a little longer."

"If that's what you want, yes."

"It seems like we have stuff to talk about, stuff I didn't know you'd had on your mind, but for tonight...can we just be together?"

Eden's forehead creased when she realised what Aster was saying. Did she...think they were breaking up? Oh, God. Not in a million years. "Hey, I'm not ending this with you."

"Really? Because it feels that way," Aster said quietly, picking at an invisible spot on her pants.

Eden got to her feet, lowering the hidden zip to the side of her dress. When Aster looked up, confusion in her eyes, Eden simply smiled. "What I'm saying," Eden paused as her dress gathered at her feet, "is that I want more in our future." She curled her fingers under Aster's chin, bringing her gaze back to her. "I want it all, Aster."

Aster's eyes widened when she caught the white lace lingerie Eden was wearing. Sitting back on her hands, a grin spread wide on her mouth, those dreamy eyes pricked Eden's skin as they travelled the expanse of her body. "Y-yeah?"

"Mmhmm." Eden straddled Aster, surprised when Aster suddenly flipped them and settled on top of her.

"Do you have any idea what you do to me when you wear lingerie like this?" Aster's fingertips brushed Eden's cheekbone, the gentlest of touches caressing her skin. "I mean, you've got my head up my arse with everything you're saying, but you're definitely not breaking up with me, right?"

"Never." Eden curled her hand around Aster's neck, pulling her into a kiss. "Aster…" Eden said, whimpering as Aster pressed her thigh between her legs. Eden lifted her head and took a swipe up Aster's ear with her tongue. And then she whispered, "They're crotchless."

Aster lowered her head to Eden's shoulder. "Sweet. Fucking. Jesus."

"And I'm so wet for you."

Aster lowered her hand down Eden's stomach, her eyes fluttering closed as she was, in fact, met with hot, wet heat. "Shit, babe. You're too much."

Eden braced herself for what she knew was coming. Aster seemed to have a thing for her in sexy underwear. The issue was, Aster was still fully clothed, and that wouldn't do. "I need you naked with me."

"Oh, you'll get me naked. Right after I've fucked you good." Aster grinned, holding herself up on one elbow. When she pressed a finger to Eden's clit, Eden cried out, arching into Aster. "I can't wait another second to have you. And this…tonight… isn't ending anytime soon."

"No?" Eden smirked, her eyes holding Aster's.

"Oh, no." Their lips met, gentle but so demanding. "Where do you want me?"

"I-inside." As Aster lowered her hand and teased Eden's entrance, Eden gripped her wrist, her heart bursting with unimaginable joy. "Marry me."

"W-what?"

"Marry me." Eden's heart leapt up into her throat. Perhaps right now wasn't the time to propose. She didn't even have a ring to offer. *Shit!*

Aster's confusion turned into a heart stopping grin, her soft fingers gathering Eden's wetness. God, that look, the intensity of Aster's eyes as she stared down at Eden…incredible. "Yes."

"Y-yes?"

Aster eased two fingers inside Eden, moaning when Eden's walls contracted. "Fuck, I'd marry you right now."

Satisfied that they would have the perfect ending to a perfect day, Eden relaxed and gave herself over to Aster entirely. But as Aster buried her face in Eden's neck, smiling against her skin, Eden's heart swelled. This woman…was her world.

Aster pressed her thumb to Eden's clit, moving slowly inside her. The love, the care, was mirrored in her every move, and it only encouraged Eden's first of many orgasms. "Aster, I-I…"

"You feel so fucking good," Aster whispered as she curled her fingers. "And you'll feel even better as my wife."

Aster's voice, her words, tipped Eden over the edge, her orgasm crashing through her as she cried out Aster's name. Those incredible fingers slowed, and then Aster eased out, wrapping Eden up in her arms.

"I can't believe you've just asked me to marry you." Her voice broke as she buried her face deeper into Eden's hair. "I can't believe just how lucky I feel this evening to have someone like you in my life…wanting to spend forever with me."

"I want a life with you," Eden paused, her own arms wrapping around Aster. "I want a life *and* a family with you."

"Yeah?" Aster lifted her head, tears slipping down her face.

"Together." Eden searched Aster's face, the love shining from her eyes stealing her breath.

And then Aster leaned in, kissing her slowly, their foreheads pressed together. "Forever…"

SIGN UP TO WIN

Sign up to my mailing list to be the first to hear about new releases, and to be in with a chance of winning books!

www.melissaterezeauthor.com

DID YOU ENJOY IT?

Thank you for purchasing Holding Her Heart.

I hope you enjoyed it. Please consider leaving a review on your preferred site. As an independent author, reviews help to promote our work. One line or two really does make the difference.

Thank you, truly.

Love,
Melissa x

ABOUT THE AUTHOR

Oh, hi! It's nice to see you!

I'm Melissa Tereze, author of The Arrangement, and other bestsellers. Born, raised, and living in Liverpool, UK, I spend my time writing angsty romance about complex, real-life, women who love women. My heart lies within the age-gap trope, but you'll also find a wide range of different characters and stories to sink your teeth into.

SOCIAL MEDIA

You can contact me through my social media or my website. I'm mostly active on Twitter.

Twitter: @MelissaTereze
Facebook: www.facebook.com/Author.MelissaTereze
Instagram: @melissatereze_author
Find out more at: www.melissatherezeauthor.com
Contact: info@melissatherezeauthor.com

ALSO BY MELISSA TEREZE

ANOTHER LOVE SERIES
THE ARRANGEMENT (BOOK ONE)
THE CALL (BOOK TWO)

THE ASHFORTH SERIES
PLAYING FOR HER HEART (BOOK ONE)

OTHER NOVELS
MRS MIDDLETON
BREAKING ROUTINE
IN HER ARMS
BEFORE YOU GO
FOREVER YOURS
THE HEAT OF SUMMER
FORGET ME NOT
MORE THAN A FEELING
WHERE WE BELONG: LOVE RETURNS
NAKED

TITLES UNDER L.M CROFT (EROTICA)
PIECES OF ME